STAR TREK
THE NEXT GENERATION

D1323048

STAR TREK:
THE NEXT GENERATION NOVELS

STAR TREK:
THE NEXT GENERATION GIANT NOVELS

STAR TREK
THE NEXT GENERATION

GULLIVER'S FUGITIVES

KEITH SHAREE

TITAN BOOKS
LONDON

STAR TREK **THE NEXT GENERATION 11:**
GULLIVER'S FUGITIVES
ISBN 1 85286 286 6

Published by
Titan Books Ltd
58 St Giles High St
London WC2H 8LH

First Titan Edition May 1990
10 9 8 7 6 5 4 3 2

British edition by arrangement with Pocket Books, a division of
Simon and Schuster, Inc., Under Exclusive Licens e from
Paramount Pictures Corporation, The Trademark Owner.

Printed and bound in Great Britain by Cox and Wyman Ltd,
Reading, Berkshire.

For Jane and Shelly

With thanks to Paul Fontana
for designing the artificial intelligence
that helped create Data's poetry,
and for lifting with extreme precaution
the cuticle of a grand piano

Chapter One

THE END OF EVERYTHING heralded itself as a metallic hum near Montoya's left ear.

He kept his eyes on the stairs under his feet and marched upward—one short, brown-skinned, gray-haired, slightly overweight man in a crowd of workers at the end of their munitions factory shift.

No need to turn around and look. The hum had to come from a one-eye: a lead-colored object, about the size of a human torso, with a single staring camera eye and a bristling, spiky penumbra of antennae. It was gliding behind Montoya's head, intercepting and reading his thoughts.

Montoya knew his only chance for survival was to keep from thinking about . . .

The small case rested lightly in his hand. He ignored it, shut his eyes to it, hummed a tuneless tune to forget about it.

What the case held was of no monetary worth yet was valuable beyond reckoning. To possess it here, on the planet of Rampart, was a crime punishable by death.

Montoya's anxiety made him short of breath. His

1

legs felt rubbery as he trudged. The one-eye hummed behind him like a giant chrome mosquito.

He was near the top of the stairs. He could see cold light from the sun, rho Ophiuchi, slanting through the dusty panes of the factory's outer wall, silhouetting the vacant-eyed men and women who waited in line at the timeclock.

Montoya took sanctuary in the thought of his wife by enfolding himself in her smooth brown arms, replaying the last time they had made love. He sought the most vivid, tactile moments. He involved his entire mind and body, trying to confuse the one-eye hovering behind him.

In spite of his efforts, fugitive thoughts that lurked in the shadows of his mind tried to interrupt the imagined scene.

He heard the one-eye come closer.

He switched his thoughts to the sound and movement around him, the clang and hum of the machines, the tired clunk-steps of the workers above and below him on the stairs, industrious but lost little people like . . .

In the right temporal lobe of Montoya's brain, an evanescent web of electrochemical impulses danced for a scant second, expending only a millionth of a volt, as a certain image formed in his mind.

It was an image of the very thing in his case. An entire society of tiny humans, scuttling around in there, waiting for a very large revelation.

The thought died away, but Montoya knew the one-eye must have picked it up. It swung from behind his head, hummed to a position in front of his face, and stopped. Montoya was forced to halt his steps at the top of the stairs to avoid collision. The workers below him had to halt as well. A pool of silence widened around him as he looked directly into the camera lens and antennae of the one-eye.

2

Two broad-shouldered figures, their white uniforms bearing the blue Cephalic Security logo, walked with smartly clicking steps as they threaded their way along the upper floor to the top of the stairs, where they confronted Montoya.

Montoya would not look at them. He didn't want to indulge himself in contempt now. There had to be something better to do as one's last act.

They were saying something to him about arrest, clamping handcuffs on him.

One of the CS men pulled at the case in Montoya's hand. Montoya let it slip out. They guided him along the wall to a cage-like elevator. Their one-eye floated along behind Montoya's head. He saw the service-issue radiation guns the CS men carried on their belts. That might be a better way to go, he supposed, than what they had planned for him.

As the lift ascended toward the helipad on the roof, Montoya stared at the grating under his feet. He allowed himself to be overcome with sadness by thinking about the tragic course of his life, and rubbing salt on it. He smote himself for the momentary lapse—just one stray thought!—that would mean the arrest of friends and family. He started to weep.

The lift emerged onto the roof. A strong hand gripped him and pushed him out onto the tarmac. The white tilt-rotor hovercraft ahead of them started its engines and chopped at the air.

Montoya let the sobs shudder through him, tears streaming down his face. The CS men led him within a few meters of the roof's edge as they approached the door of the hovercraft.

Suddenly Montoya flailed out with his cuffed hands, causing the surprised CS man to lose his grip. With all his strength Montoya grabbed at his case, ripping it out of the other CS man's hands. He whirled

3

toward the edge of the roof and flicked the catch on the case. Both CS men scrambled to hold on to him and the case, but Montoya was too fast. With a triumphant yell he flung the case outward; it opened as it fell toward the ground far below. Yellowed old pages fluttered free and scattered in widening gyres on the wind.

The CS men regained control of Montoya. The small man let them push him into the hovercraft. As it took off he leaned toward the window and saw the pages being borne in all directions.

He smiled to himself. His trick, his sadness, had worked, a sop for the one-eye so the device wouldn't guess at his spontaneous last act and kill him to prevent it. He kept his eyes on the pages as they grew smaller and smaller.

For several minutes after the hovercraft took Montoya away, the pages from his case floated and drifted down, coming to rest on the streets of the metropolis called Verity.

A hundred CS officers and special agents converged on the area where the pages had fallen. They all wore protective helmets with electronic visors that turned printed words into gibberish for their eyes.

They quickly set up roadblocks and evacuated residents, then set to work finding the scattered pages and burning them in portable mini-incinerators.

When the clean-up was complete, the streets were reopened. But one-eyes remained; they floated among the pedestrians and traffic, their antennae hunting for the mind-echoes of the pages that were now ash.

One page had floated far; it alone had escaped the CS and their incinerators. It lay nakedly on a small patch of grass behind an elementary school.

At noon recess, a red-haired girl from the third-grade class chased a ball and came upon the page. She had never seen such an old and discolored piece of paper. She picked it up, and with big green inquisitive eyes, looked at an illustration on the page.

It appeared to be of a man tied onto a kind of sled and surrounded by a busy swarm of people no bigger than his finger.

She read the words on the page.

About four Hours after we began our Journey, I awaked by a very ridiculous Accident; for the Carriage being stopt awhile to adjust something that was out of Order, two or three of the young Natives had the Curiosity to see how I looked when I was asleep; they climbed up into the Engine, and advancing very softly to my Face, one of them, an Officer in the Guards, put the sharp End of His Half-Pike a good way up into my left Nostril, which tickled my Nose like a Straw, and made me sneeze violently . . .

The green-eyed girl laughed.

She looked at the top of the page and saw a title line: "GULLIVER'S TRAVELS—A VOYAGE TO LILLIPUT."

She sensed that the page was something forbidden, something the grown-ups told you to never ever touch or look at, or you'd get a disease. But looking at it now she found that she didn't believe all that. They always told you not to do the things that were fun. Besides, how could you catch a disease from a piece of paper?

Her fascination with the page overcame her caution. She hid the page in her dress, hoping to take it home that day.

Chapter Two

COUNSELOR DEANNA TROI sat in her cabin on the *Enterprise,* her fathomless, dark Betazoid eyes gazing at her computer, her black hair cascading over her shoulders. She was about to fulfill, in her own way, the primary mission of the starship U.S.S. *Enterprise*— exploration of new worlds and discovery of alien life.

She was about to peer into a boundless new universe, a separate realm, teeming with infinite life-forms.

To open the "door," all she had to do was utter a single word to the computer. She wouldn't even have to leave her comfortable private cabin. The new universe could be observed via the small screen before her.

But, as though she were going on a long journey, she found herself wondering if there was anything left undone on her agenda. She punched up her schedule.

It was a testament to the complexity of her day-to-day job as Ship's Counselor, engineer of emotions, maintenance mechanic to a thousand minds.

But today's appointments had all been fulfilled. There remained only a note that she wanted to talk with the captain about his habit of suppressing too many feelings.

Hardly an urgent problem. He'd been like that as long as she'd known him. It could wait. She cleared the list from the screen.

Now it was time for her to begin her observations. "Computer . . ."

Troi found herself hesitating. She felt unaccountably jittery about saying the word out loud.

She sounded it in her mind. Tukurpa. Tu-kur-pa.

Then, before she spoke the word, she began to feel vertigo, as though something were wrong with her inner ears, her balance center. The feeling intensified. It was as if she were spinning, as if the cabin were at the axis of a centrifuge, going faster and faster.

She tried to bring her hand up to touch her communicator, to call for help, but the vertigo made it impossible.

Now the spinning feeling was so overwhelming, the revolutions so rapid and violent, Troi couldn't focus her eyes. The walls of the cabin were disintegrating. She felt herself thrown out of her chair, tumbling through air or space.

Then she hit the ground facedown.

It was definitely the ground—sand or dirt, not a ship or a man-made surface. For several moments she lay still, getting her equilibrium back. Then she realized that the sand was hot enough to burn her skin, and she got to her feet in a hurry.

What Troi saw gave her a devastating shock. She was in the middle of a wasteland, a desert—an endless expanse of white and tan sands and tortured cracked outcroppings of rock under a blinding sun.

She instinctively felt for her communicator pin. It wasn't there. She had no way to contact the *Enterprise*.

Before Troi had time to consider how she had

gotten here, the heat demanded her undivided attention. It came up through the soles of her thin shoes and in through her nostrils, stinging her rhinal cavities. It penetrated right through her one-piece jumpsuit. She was already sweating like a marathon runner.

The nearest shade appeared to be a distant blue mountain ridge. How far was hard to judge, but she thought it might be fifty kilometers. Maybe too far. She doubted she would make it without collapsing.

Troi was no athlete, but she had been trained at Starfleet Academy and knew how to avoid panic no matter what the situation.

She started to walk, and think about her predicament. How had this happened? It had been a normal day, she had been in her cabin . . . but for some unknown reason she couldn't remember what she had been doing there. Only that she had suddenly been transported away to this desert by means unknown. . . . Some kind of amnesia was blocking the rest.

The heat took its inexorable toll. Troi was dehydrating fast, and her body temperature was getting too high. Still she kept walking. To stop on the burning sand was unthinkable. She had to get to the mountains.

After two hours of walking, she became dizzy and disoriented. She had stopped sweating and her lips were puffing up. Her tongue was stuck to the roof of her mouth.

She looked around and saw she had entered a shallow dry wash. She collapsed to her knees and stared, forlorn, at the yellow dust.

She knew she wasn't going to make it; she wasn't going to get out of this trap. Her body wouldn't carry her much further. She was going to die of dehydration.

"Why, *why* can't I remember how I got here?" she croaked at the sand.

"How you got here?" said a voice in reply. "I don't know. You wanted to come, so you came. 'How' doesn't matter. 'Why' matters."

"Great," Troi told herself. "I'm hearing voices. I guess that means I'm starting to die."

But when she concentrated with her empathic sense, her ability to sense others' emotions which came from the Betazoid half of her heritage, she picked up a living presence. Not in the sand exactly, but in the ground, deeper. It felt big; it had a majestic old personality to fit its colossal size. It could have been as big as the whole planet.

Troi felt some of her strength come back. She wasn't alone here after all. Whatever this being was, it could only improve matters.

"What is this place? Who are you?" she asked evenly.

"You know all that already, if you're here."

"But I don't. I can't remember."

"Before I'll tell you who I am, you'll have to at least remember your purpose in coming here."

"Why?"

"Because I'm old, I've seen a great deal, and I know what's best."

"Can you tell me how I can get back to my ship?"

"No. That I can never do. I might help you accomplish whatever it is you came here for, if you can remember what that was, but how you come and go is your own affair."

Troi concentrated on the voice. She suspected that it belonged to a female. It was an unyielding voice, but not unkind—the voice of a matriarch.

Troi felt something wet on her knees. Liquid had started to well up through the sand in the arroyo. It looked like water. She hoped it was water and not something poisonous like trichloroethylene, because her body was going to make her drink it no matter what it was.

She leaned over and tasted it. Water. She drank greedily.

"Slowly, slowly," said the voice.

Troi sipped the water until she felt sated.

"Oh," she breathed afterward, "that was lovely. Thank you."

"I'm going to help you get to the mountains," said the voice. "I'll give you the water you'll need. If you make it to the mountains I'll give you shade there."

"I guess that means you aren't going to tell me anything else."

"Not now. And you're welcome, for the water."

Troi nodded to herself. She guessed she'd just have to play by the rules of this strange world, at least until an alternative plan came along.

The Matriarch did live up to her promise. She provided Troi with water, making it well up from the dry sand, but only at those times when Troi was too thirsty to go on, and then she provided it silently, without comment.

When the mountains were closer, Troi became aware of another presence besides the Matriarch. It was the unmistakable vigilance of a predatory animal. She could sometimes hear the predator's feet crumbling the sand-crusts behind her, and catch fleeting impressions of it in her peripheral vision. Troi finally saw it when she stopped near a small mesa to request water from the Matriarch.

At first she looked right at the predator without being aware of it, because though it was only a few meters away and very large, it blended in with the stone and stood absolutely still. Then she saw through the camouflage. She felt her whole body stiffen in fright.

The creature moved. It opened its mouth and let out a long coarse howl.

It was perhaps ten feet tall. There was a carcass of some kind at its feet, and other carcasses, bones, and its own droppings nearby.

It had the head of a lioness and a body shaped like a baboon's. From its mind Troi received an impression of predatory blood lust so powerful she was transfixed, like a rabbit before a snake. But within the impression was a clear, cogent message. I am a First Cause, it said to her. I determine the life and death of all in this desert. Your will means nothing here.

It seemed to be true, as Troi couldn't even move her feet.

But something in her rebelled, broke the inertia, and she found herself running. The sand seemed to suck at her feet as she heard the cat-exhalations of the Lioness close behind her. She tried to dodge to the side, but the Lioness' paw swatted at her legs and she tripped, landing on her back on the sand. Troi could smell the beast's carrion-stink breath on her face as its head leaned close and eclipsed the sun, and its awesome dripping jaws opened. In the last instant, she managed to roll away, and was back up and running again. She realized the Lioness was merely playing with her. A feline with its prey.

But as Troi ran she sensed the Lioness dropping far behind. When exhaustion made her stop running, she looked around and couldn't see the Lioness anywhere on the shimmering sands. In front, the ground sloped sharply up. She'd reached the foothills of the mountains.

The scene was cool and inviting. She walked wearily up the center of a wooded valley until the sun went down and then stopped by a creek to rest.

Troi looked up at a sky full of unfamiliar stars, then down at the mossy ground.

"Are you still here?" she asked the Matriarch.

The Matriarch laughed.

"Where would I go?"

"Why didn't you tell me about that animal?" Troi asked.

"This place is full of living beings. You must have known that, or you wouldn't have come."

"I still can't remember. Why don't you stop playing games with me? Why are you keeping me alive by giving me little tidbits? Am I here just to amuse you?"

Troi felt something rumbling underneath the ground. More than that, she perceived the Matriarch's anger.

Then she heard cracking and sliding sounds from the mountain slopes nearest her. Rockslide. She took cover behind a tree and watched the rocks and dirt tumble past her.

When it was over the Matriarch spoke in a grim voice.

"That's just a small sample."

"I didn't mean to offend you."

"Your questions are foolish. You should already know all about me. It's not my fault that you cannot remember. Anyway, I know all about you. I know that you're not married. You don't have time for men because you devote yourself to your work. Your mother is also single and very much in need of a man. You could end up permanently single like her. Do you want to hear more?"

Troi was too stunned to speak. How could the Matriarch know so much about her private life? She felt mushrooming anger at the intrusion, but put it aside.

The Matriarch went on.

"Look for the road that begins up the valley a ways.

Follow it to its source, and there you might find some answers about why you came here. It'll be up to you. Start now; don't wait for dawn. And be careful, there is a danger on that road."

Troi was about to ask more questions but decided not to risk offending the Matriarch again.

"Before you go I want you to see my mate," said the Matriarch.

Troi sensed an unspoken admonition: "Everyone should have a mate."

"Look up," said the Matriarch.

Troi looked at the trees.

"No, all the way up."

Troi looked at the stars. The night was magnificently clear and beautiful.

"I don't see anyone," she said.

Then something slowly rippled the night sky the way a breeze stirs the undulant surface of a pond. Troi felt another vast old intelligence. The Matriarch's husband.

"Now go find the road," said the Matriarch.

The road was a dirt causeway, wide and flat, winding up the valley. The trees around it were dense, and getting denser as the road climbed.

At one point she heard a sound like someone chopping wood. She stopped to listen, then remembered the Matriarch's warning, and hurried onwards in the darkness.

The chopping noise continued, following her, turning into something that sounded more like breaking branches.

Then a shape leapt in front of her. She yelled reflexively.

He had the shape of a man, but larger. Larger even than the Lioness. He was covered with a hard, mirror-like surface on which foreboding crimson, purple, and black reflections danced like flames. His left foot was missing; he balanced on his right.

His eyes were maddening: two shifting mirrors, flashing hot fission-fire, dark smoke, and reflections of herself back at her.

The Mirror Man advanced toward her. She could sense a cold evil, different than the Lioness' predatory urge—more insidious and calculated, more intellectually cunning.

Troi tried to back away but found she was rooted to the spot; her whole body had become cold, numb, and heavy. It felt as though it were being transmuted into another substance, like ice or iron.

She wanted to cry out—for the Matriarch, for anybody, but she was immobilized. The huge Mirror Man stopped and stood still right in front of her, his burnished surfaces reflecting her own paralyzed form back at her.

Then she became empathically aware of many other beings around her, the Matriarch and her sky-dwelling mate and countless others in the darkness. They were watching to see what happened to her, as though this were some kind of test.

But there were friends present, too. Much further away. Their minds were like a distant cluster of candles, glowing and familiar. The *Enterprise.*

As she became aware of her distant crewmates, they seemed to draw nearer in response. Their distance was connected to her will.

She suddenly realized she could go back. Some part of her had never even left the ship.

She concentrated on the *Enterprise,* focused all her will on it and her friends within it. After a desperate, agonizing effort, her surroundings seemed to fade. For a moment she was in two places at once—frozen before the Mirror Man on the dark causeway and sitting in her cabin on the *Enterprise*.

It took all the strength she could muster to bring herself all the way back into her familiar universe.

When it was over, she was exhausted, bedraggled, and covered with a film of sweat. And she was back in her chair in front of her computer.

Chapter Three

CAPTAIN JEAN-LUC PICARD listened to the counselor conclude her account.

Her dark eyes seemed to stare right past him. A rebellious lock of black hair snaked away from its companions. Her skin, normally a light tan, seemed translucently pale. To Picard, her appearance increased the phantasmal effect of her story.

"They're real," she said. "I still feel their presence close to the ship—but it's as if they're in a universe or dimension different than ours. It's hard to describe the feeling."

"There has been no further contact?"

"No. But I can feel them waiting. They want something of me. They want to put me through that transformation they started, that sort of . . . death or petrification."

"Have you seen Dr. Crusher yet?"

"Captain, I didn't hallucinate them. They aren't a delusion."

"I don't say they're delusory. You would know what they are as well as anyone on this ship. Or better. I just want to make sure you're not injured."

"I haven't seen her, but I will as soon as I leave here."

"Good," said Picard. He ran his hand over the smooth top of his head and down through the short gray hair that ringed it.

"Have you any ideas about why you were singled out for contact by these beings?"

He noticed that she relaxed a notch. Good, he thought, she sees I'm accepting her account on her own terms.

"Actually, one of them—I call them the Other-worlders—implied I initiated the contact. And I sense that they are waiting for me to do it again, but I don't know what it was I did! I can't remember anything about it, so how can I keep from repeating it? My amnesia seems to obscure everything I did today, leading up to the moment of contact. There may be some special connection between us, though. They already know a lot about my personal life."

"Have you checked for any records of your activities just before the contact?"

"I'm planning to check the computer."

"Excellent place to start. You have a question?"

"Well, I don't think I can do much counseling until I feel safe from these beings, these Other-worlders. I'm sorry to ask to be excused like this."

"Counselor, you have nothing to apologize for. Contacting new forms of life is our mission. It is why you and I are here on the *Enterprise*. We are stopping the ship right here, and we aren't going to budge until I know who and what these beings are. I'll be with you whenever you need me. And I'll have the ship's computer keep track of your vital signs. If you're under stress or feel threatened, the computer will tell us and we'll find you, even if you can't call for help yourself."

17

Some of the warmth returned to Troi's eyes. "Thank you, Captain," she said softly.

"I'll tell the doctor you're coming," he said, looking away. His hazel eyes found the window and the starfield beyond it.

Troi got up and left, and Picard was alone in his ready room. He realized he could have been a bit less distant at the end. Maybe he really did need to work with Troi on learning to feel more emotion, or show it more often, or whatever it was she wanted.

But he wasn't about to change his overall command style. He'd gotten this far with it, and doubted he would ever be capable of showing his feelings as easily as Troi.

Ensign Wesley Crusher and Lieutenant Commander Data sat at their consoles on the *Enterprise* bridge, waiting while the ship's sensors scanned its surrounding space. Though Data, an android legally defined as "alive," was third in command of the ship, and Wesley, a teenager, was just beginning his career with Starfleet, the two were close friends. Wesley had always accepted Data as a person, not a sentient machine. And Data himself was in the midst of a kind of adolescence, still trying to understand the mysterious humanoid species which had accepted him as an equal.

The main viewscreen showed them a stationary starfield. So far, they'd found none of the anomalies the captain was looking for.

"They might be inside the ship," said Wesley.

"Worf is conducting a thorough search," replied Data.

"Maybe they're hiding right here on the bridge," Wesley said. He twitched at the thought. He'd heard that Troi's encounter with the aliens, the "Other-worlders," had been harrowing. He looked over at Data and for an instant envied the android his imperturbability and patience—as much as Data envied the human capacity for emotion, even fear.

Data touched his keypad, resetting the external sensors for a new arpeggio of frequencies.

"There. We must now wait for this sequence to complete. Perhaps this is a good opportunity for me to present you with my gift. You do seem in need of distraction and uplift."

Data stood, looked down at Wesley, then at the infinite view presented by the screen. He assumed a heraldic pose, one hand on his hip, the other in a frozen gesture at the stars on the screen. He spoke.

"The teachings of macaroon erotica doin' a little thing we call three-toed minty-fresh logo tissue.
Quest for the Golden Aphids where they call the wind 'Mr. Conceited-B-Gone.'
I walk down Spanked Mandrill Strasse with gently yielding fun-bladder under warranty.
Prometheus indicator-light blinking through the hydrogen eternity boo-boo."

Data was still for a moment, allowing a silence to round out his verse. He lowered his hand slowly.

Then he looked back at Wesley. The ensign was bowed over his console, face in hands.

"Wesley! What's wrong!"

The ensign's shoulders shook.

"Are you crying? Were you . . . moved?"

The young ensign looked up. He was laughing so hard he had to gasp for air.

A puzzled, almost sad look crossed Data's face.

"That was not the reaction I had anticipated, or

19

hoped for," said Data. "I had thought I had composed my first serious artistic poem."

"Data, I loved it. Don't be upset. You know how long you've been trying to make humans laugh."

"True," said Data. "But it usually seems to happen when I do not intend it."

Suddenly Data looked down at his control panel. The indices were changing rapidly.

"We have found something," said the android.

"The recorder marker from the U.S.S. *Huxley* was not what we were looking for," said Captain Picard, "but it's a major find, nonetheless. That ship has been lost for a decade. I wish I could say I was happy about what the marker is telling us."

The others in the conference room—Data, Troi, and the handsome, bearded, young First Officer Riker —listened raptly to the captain.

The *Huxley*'s Captain Bowles had been one of the fleet's great explorers, as Picard was now. The fate of Bowles and his ship had been one of the major unsolved puzzles in Starfleet's history.

"We've already recovered the marker. It's badly damaged and has yielded few facts. But it seems the *Huxley* was deliberately attacked, and the attack occurred in the rho Ophiuchi system. Quite nearby, but right in the middle of a nebula thick as bouilla-baisse. You can see the nebula out the port, there. Counselor, you have a question?"

"Is there an indication that the Other-worlders were involved in the fate of the *Huxley?*"

"Inconclusive, but I'd guess not," said the captain. "The marker's damage has been caused by a thermo-nuclear device, of the type used hundreds of years ago on Earth. There appears to have been a battle between the *Huxley* and one or more other ships. We may soon find out more. Starfleet has already told us to enter the nebula and check the planet indicated by the marker for survivors. We'll do that tomorrow morning ship's time."

"Captain," said Data, "the nebula is known to reflect subspace frequencies. We will be unable to contact Starfleet while inside it."

"Yes, Mr. Data, Starfleet knows we'll be out of touch for a while. I've had to speak with our two diplomatic passengers, who are most understanding. Starfleet has gotten permission from their government for the delay in their travel schedule. Number One," said the captain to his first officer, "you and I will meet later to plan the particulars of this mission. That's all."

Picard, Data, and Riker left. Deanna Troi rose, but lingered in the room. She looked out the port at the rho Ophiuchi nebula: a dense blue veil with a single star-eye behind it, peering at her.

The prospect of being in there, cut off from Starfleet, was ominous. It made her feel trapped. It made her more aware of the nearby presence of the Other-worlders, hidden in their own universe or state of being but following with the ship, following her, and she began to shiver with a kind of ague.

She tried to stop her shivering. There should be nothing wrong with me physically, she thought.

She had just come from an examination by Dr. Crusher. "Evidence of stress, that's all," Beverly had said. "Nothing a little rest won't cure."

Dear Beverly had made Troi promise to rest for at least two days. But that wouldn't be possible. She had to talk with the ship's computer, find out what she'd been doing during those hours before her experience with the Other-worlders.

The thought of being alone in her cabin and asking the computer anything filled her with dread, though she didn't know why.

21

She considered the calm curiosity with which Captain Picard always faced the unknown, and wished for a moment that she could be like him. But the thought made her feel lonely. He seemed so solitary and self-contained, his feelings and affections streamlined like a tree growing in a wind tunnel.

No, she thought. I couldn't be like that.

His father had sneered that the pace was too slow, and had hiked off on long adult legs and left him there, a nine-year-old boy on a faltering, treacherous mountain trail. He'd never been alone in the wilderness before, and he panicked, and lurched along, crying, feeling lost in the cold landscape and in the world as a whole. Where do you turn for solace or justice when your own father is unfair to you? He looked about but got no reply from the frigid glacier and the foreboding shadows under the rocky cliffs.

First Officer William T. Riker returned from this memory with a familiar aching feeling as he approached the turbolift.

If I ever find the time to get married and have a family, he thought, I won't be like my father. I'll be kind to my kids. I'd probably have to watch out for overcompensation, for being too kind.

He boarded the turbolift and was surprised to see that it already contained two preschool-age children.

"Deck Twelve, gymnasium," Riker told the lift, which began to move.

Riker wondered what the two children were doing unattended on a turbolift. He'd have to ask them. He felt it odd that they seemed to have appeared as if cued by his own reverie.

The toddlers were turned toward each other in a close huddle, and Riker couldn't see their faces. They were whispering and giggling and making soft smacking noises.

Riker was about to speak but suddenly his eyes widened in alarm and his question died in his throat. The toddlers were kissing. This wasn't just child's play. This was Eros. They were really making out.

Riker was baffled. Surely they shouldn't be engaging in such behavior for at least another decade. What was he supposed to do, throw water on them? He wished someone more experienced were here to handle it.

He coughed discreetly.

They kept right at it.

"Um, ahem!" said Riker.

"Oops, we're sorry," replied the little girl, without actually turning toward Riker. Then she spoke to her partner. "Let's tell him that we're married," she said.

"Later," the little boy said with a laugh. He started kissing her again, and still neither of them had bothered to turn and look up at Riker.

Riker couldn't shirk responsibility. He was determined to be firm.

"Uh, well, I'm not the best person to explain to you about marriage," he said as a single drop of sweat slipped down the side of his face and lodged in his beard. "But I don't think you're quite ready for it."

It was as though he'd told the biggest joke in the galaxy. The toddlers sputtered and laughed so hard Riker thought they might hurt themselves. The first officer found himself feeling at a disadvantage, as though, incongruously, these children had played a sophisticated joke on him and were laughing at his expense.

After a moment they contained themselves. For the first time, they turned to face Riker, and the little boy spoke with a steady, measured voice.

"I am Oleph, and this is my wife Una."

They bowed gracefully.

"But I think we've already met, First Officer Riker,"

he continued, "under more formal circumstances, when we first arrived on your ship."

"I realized I had been talking to the two cultural envoys from the First Federation. Grown adults of their species! One hundred years ago, their people had initiated a first contact with us, and now I was condescending to correct their sexual behavior."

Riker chuckled and glanced over at his captain, who walked beside him along the corridor. Picard looked more disquieted than amused.

"I don't think any diplomatic damage was done, sir," said Riker. "They seemed to have found it funny rather than offensive."

"Good," said Picard. "We have more pressing matters to contend with. Counselor Troi dug around in the ship's computer and found out her location on the ship in the hours before the Other-worlders came to her. It turns out she was with Oleph and Una. Her amnesia keeps her from recalling what she did with them, but she's sure that Oleph and Una have some connection with the Other-worlders. I want to ask Oleph and Una about it—before we begin our mission to rho Ophiuchi."

"Here's your chance," said Riker.

Farther down the corridor, a door had opened. Oleph and Una had stepped out. Now they saw Picard and Riker approaching.

"Greetings Captain, First Officer," said Una.

"Greetings to you," said Picard.

Picard and Riker realized they were standing at the door to Worf's cabin. And there was Worf himself. The dark-skinned, herculean Klingon, chief of *Enterprise* security, was standing just inside, in the act of receiving an electronic padd from Oleph's tiny hand. Worf towered over the two diminutive envoys from the First Federation, making them look like porcelain figurines.

Worf shared a private look with Oleph as he took the padd and held it nonchalantly at his side.

"Hello, Lieutenant," said Picard.

"Captain," intoned Worf, in a deep fearless voice that seemed to vibrate the ship's bulkheads.

The awkwardness of an interrupted moment kept all parties silent, until the captain spoke directly to Oleph and Una.

"I'm sorry to trouble you, but I need information. My counselor, Deanna Troi, had contact with alien and possibly dangerous life-forms shortly after she was with you today. Do you recall what you did while with her?"

"We discussed her work, and our work," Oleph said.

"We are ethnographers," Una added. "We study and record aspects of indigenous cultures all over this part of the galaxy. On your planet we might be called cultural anthropologists."

"Nothing unusual happened?" Picard asked.

Oleph and Una looked at each other. Una's child-eyes pleaded a mute question. Oleph gave her a silent nod of confirmation. He looked at the floor for a moment, and when he looked back up at the captain of the *Enterprise,* his face wasn't that of a toddler, but of the formidable adult he in fact was. A firmness in his voice completed the transformation.

"Just a visit, and the exchange of ideas."

For a moment he and Picard held a tense stare.

"I'm grateful for the information," Picard said finally. "And to your government for its cooperation —I'm sure the mission in the nebula will be short, and we'll have you back on your itinerary in no time."

"We don't mind at all, Captain," said Una. "We are

enjoying your ship—and the scintillating company of your security chief."

Worf gave a short, deep grunt of acknowledgment, his eyes looking over everyone's head toward the opposite wall. Una squeezed his huge hand. Actually she was able to squeeze only two fingers.

Picard and Riker looked at Worf, both wondering what this fiercely loyal, taciturn security chief was finding in common with the two tiny ethnographers. This was clearly a friendship of a kind uncommon for Worf. As the only member of his warrior species permanently stationed on the *Enterprise,* he tended to keep to himself.

"Is there any other way we can help you?" asked Oleph with unmistakable impatience.

"No, and I'm sorry we interrupted," said Picard. "Good night."

"Captain, Commander Riker," Worf said to his two superior officers in his resonant bass voice.

Riker added his own good night and he and Picard continued walking down the corridor.

They heard Oleph, Una, and Worf speak in muted tones behind them, then Worf's door hissed shut. Riker glanced rearward. The incongruous trio had gone back into Worf's cabin.

"I've often thought, and still do," said Picard, "that we know little of all there is to Worf. But he's more than proven his trustworthiness, and I'm sure he'd report to me anything he knew of contact with new life-forms. I'm just as sure that Oleph and Una are hiding something. Professional people from their world have a code of confidentiality with colleagues; it's a sanctified relationship. That's got to be why they're holding back about what they did with Counselor Troi. Will, I want you to have a talk with Worf before he retires for the night. Tell him he has to be the one to keep an eye on Oleph and Una. Tell him they may have something to do with the Other-worlders."

"I'll watch them all the captain wants," Worf told himself as he sat in front of his computer terminal later that night, after Riker had spoken with him, "but I'll be one with the dead before I'm forced to tell anyone else about . . ."

He thought of the portentous secret he shared with Oleph and Una. He looked at the keypad of his terminal. Would he make the call now?

He growled like a wolf and took a sip of tranya left him by Oleph and Una before they'd returned to their cabin. Their ceremonial beverage had gotten him quite drunk.

The possibility of glory, of vertiginous triumph undreamt just days before, swirled around his cortex, overwhelmed him with unfamiliar joys and terrors.

After an endless adrenal moment, he managed to order his thoughts.

He entered his personal code into the computer, then he opened up a secured and scrambled channel to a place thousands of light-years across the lonely void.

But the tranya caught up with him and he passed out before he was able to make his call.

Chapter Four

Seated in her spot to the captain's left, Troi watched the planet grow larger on the bridge viewscreen. Behind the planet its mother sun, rho Ophiuchi, illuminated a nebula that surrounded star, planet, and now the *Enterprise* like a candescent blue fog.

Again Troi found herself feeling that this hidden star system was some kind of trap for her. She sensed the Other-worlders around her, sensed their intention to send her through that awful paralyzing transformation they'd attempted once before, and feared that this star system would be the stage for the transformation. She couldn't tell if this was a purely irrational fear on her part or if she had picked up some real intention from the Other-worlders.

Suddenly wary of attracting another contact with them, she shifted her awareness away from the Other-worlders. She focused on the minds of Picard and Riker beside her.

So cool and remote these men were—emotions suppressed, the mien of command. She tried for a moment to alter her mood to match theirs. She imitated them the way a non-empath imitates a facial expression.

She surprised herself, for she found she could achieve that coolness, that absolute restraint, at least for the moment. It was a place of respite and eased her anxiety.

"Five minutes until orbital insert, Captain," said Ensign Crusher, navigating.

"Subspace communications, Mr. Data?" asked Picard.

"Blocked by the nebula, Captain."

"Sensor information on the planet?"

"Coming in range now. I'm picking up electromagnetic transmissions from the surface. Radio band."

"Please put them through the translator."

"That will not be necessary, sir. They are in our own language."

The bridge became very quiet. Picard rose slowly.

"Put them on the speakers, Mr. Data."

Data touched his controls. For several moments, the bridge crew listened to a mix of voices—telephone conversations, weather forecasts, civilian navigational chatter. An entire populated planet going about its business.

Riker, sitting to Picard's right, spoke up.

"There are no Federation colonies on record here, Captain. No Starfleet ship besides the *Huxley* has ever strayed near this nebula."

"That was only ten years ago," said the captain, "not time enough to seed an entire society. I'd say we've discovered an already established independent human colony." Picard looked at Troi. "We may not have found your Other-worlders, but what we've got may be just as important."

The captain turned to the teenage ensign at the Conn station.

"All stop, Mr. Crusher."

"Answering all stop, sir."

Worf's dark eyes scanned his board quickly. "Sir, we are being hailed."

"Put it on the screen, if you can."

The bridge viewscreen filled with the face of a human male in his mid-thirties, blond-haired, sternly handsome, with features that could have been carved from oak. He wore a military-type uniform with neat rows of insignia on his chest. Some of the insignia had tiny glowing lights worked into their designs.

"Starship," he said, "we have observed you and we know you come from Earth. You have entered the sovereign space of Rampart. We will have no quarrel with you if you leave the area immediately." He looked off-screen, as though consulting with someone, then back. "If you don't, we will be forced to attack."

Everyone on the bridge stared at the face, as each individual pondered how—and why—an apparent entire civilization of humans had developed here, unknown to the United Federation of Planets.

Troi noticed a vein pulsing in Picard's temple. She could sense his distaste. He always loathed the kind of bombast he'd just heard; but, as usual, he held his feelings in check. His voice was calm.

"Worf, open to their frequency. Audio only."

"Open, sir."

"This is Jean-Luc Picard, captain of the U.S.S. *Enterprise,* from the United Federation of Planets," said Picard. "We are here on an investigative matter. We mean you no harm. What is your name?"

"I am Major Ferris," said the man on the screen. "We want nothing to do with Earth or your Federation; that is why our ancestors left Earth and came here two hundred years ago."

Picard turned back to Worf, and said, in a low voice, "Give them visual of us."

Then he turned back toward the viewscreen.

He gave Major Ferris a long moment to look him over and absorb the placid, non-military ambience of the *Enterprise* bridge.

"The Federation does not wish to interfere in the affairs of your world," Picard said benignly. "Our Prime Directive prohibits our meddling with any society we encounter. We are here merely to investigate the disappearance of the U.S.S. *Huxley,* lost on or near your planet ten Solar years ago.

Ferris once again looked to his side, as if seeking and receiving counsel. Then he turned back, square-jawed. "Your investigation would be a waste. No ship from Earth, besides our own colony vessel, has ever been here. Our records are complete and accurate. There are no lies on this world. Your story of the *Huxley* is what we call a Code HC, a deliberately concocted fiction. Permission for investigation denied."

Picard's neck stiffened. "My duty requires me to look into this matter, Major Ferris. And I intend to see it through." Picard hand-signaled Worf to close the channel.

"What do our sensors tell us about the technology of this civilization?" he asked Data.

"Comparable to twenty-first-century Earth around the time of the Post-Atomic Horror. They have primitive technology: radiation guns, nuclear warheads—a lot of weapons, but no long-range warp drive, no—"

"Captain!" It was Worf. "Spacecraft are scrambling from the planet's surface. They are moving to surround us."

"Put our shields up, on full, and track them. Please go on, Mr. Data."

"Yes, sir. Scans detect a high density of video and audio sensors—probably surveillance gear, sir, permeating the population centers. The standard of living on the planet appears mediocre. A familiar syndrome. Their resources are used for munitions and covert operations."

"Looks like they've made a Post-Atomic Horror of their own," said Picard.

He looked at Deanna Troi.

"What do you feel about Ferris?"

The counselor replied without hesitation. "He's telling the truth as he sees it. I am sure he has never heard of the *Huxley*. I felt it when you asked him."

"Captain, guided projectile heading our way," said Worf.

"Evasive, Wesley."

"Yes, sir."

"Detonation," said Worf.

The viewscreen went white.

The crew braced for impact but there was none.

"Missed us by ten kilometers," said Worf, surveying his tactical panel, "Crude guidance and propulsion. Sensors show the ships don't have anything more refined. If so, we can outrun anything they throw at us."

"Yes, well, I'm not interested in playing that game with them," said the captain as he paced the command area. "Did the recorder marker from the *Huxley* show damage consistent with the type of weapon we just evaded?"

"Very consistent. Thermonuclear, sir. Their ships have taken up positions around us."

"Go to Yellow Alert, Lieutenant." Picard stood over Troi. "Maybe Ferris really knows nothing about the *Huxley,* but Ferris strikes me as far from omnipotent. The evidence suggests that we must check this planet for survivors, and one way or another I am going to do just that. Any of you have something to add?"

Young Ensign Crusher did. "Ferris looks like an actor playing a part. Like something out of an ancient war movie, or ancient Earth politics . . . but I guess that's not very germane."

"*Au contraire,* Mr. Crusher. Possibly very germane. Counselor Troi, any further impressions?"

"Ferris seems to be getting advice from some other authority. I think Wesley is right—Ferris is being presented to us for image purposes. We should try our questions on someone else."

"I agree," said Picard. "Worf, reopen the channel."

Ferris' face reappeared on the viewscreen. He looked like an army recruitment poster from the old days, when there were armies on Earth.

"Major Ferris, do you speak for your entire planet?"

"I speak for the Cephalic Security organization."

"And you do so alone?"

Troi could tell that Ferris was angry at the challenge, but only for the briefest instant, before his by-the-book persona snapped back into place.

The unseen companion to his side distracted him, and after a moment he rose and left the screen's field of view.

Another man took his place. He was older by twenty years, and completely bald. He appeared to be the victim of some crude surgery or irreversible malady. His face was scarred and frozen in an eerie, nerveless mask.

"I am Crichton, Director of Cephalic Security," he said. "Ferris is under my command."

"But you aren't the highest authority on this planet?" asked Picard.

Crichton's scarred face showed no change.

"The Council of Truth is the highest authority here, but I'm empowered to represent the planet in all matters of security. Now I suggest, Captain Picard, that it would be easier for all of us, especially you, if you take your ship and leave."

"Crichton." Picard's voice tightened up another notch. "Your weapons are no match for my ship. And even if you did drive us away or destroy us, other ships from our fleet would follow and find your planet. One way or another, the Federation will have its answer. Once our investigation is complete, we will leave in peace. Do you, Crichton, know anything about the disappearance of the U.S.S. *Huxley* and the fate of its crew?"

"Absolutely nothing."

He returned Picard's stare. The two men seemed to be testing wills with their eyes. Then Crichton looked down and pressed a button on his desk.

"You are going to limit both our options," said Picard, "if you continue to fire on us."

"I'm not firing. As you pointed out, it would neither destroy you nor deter your Federation. So I will allow your investigation. But I will tolerate no interference with the affairs of this planet. There is a disease, an epidemic going on here, and a violent insurgency as well. The criminals who disfigured my face are part of that insurgency. If you or your people help them, I will classify you as criminals as well."

"We have a directive which—"

"Yes, I heard. I would like to get this over with as soon as possible. Your search can begin now; all you have to do is allow us to inspect your ship first and assure ourselves that you are not bringing any infectious or forbidden materials to the surface of Rampart."

"I won't let you bring large numbers of people on my ship, especially not military personnel," said the captain.

"What would you say to just Major Ferris and myself, with our plague-detecting devices?"

"One moment." Picard had Worf cut the channel. He turned to Troi. "Your judgment?"

"He is truly concerned about the threat of contraband or contagion," said the counselor. "If he is satisfied on that count, I sense that he intends to let our investigation proceed. I can't read if he knows anything about the *Huxley*."

"We have no infectious diseases on this ship he need worry about," said Picard. "When he sees that, he may feel less threatened." He nodded to Worf. The channel was re-opened.

"Crichton, I will agree to your inspection of the *Enterprise*, as long as it excludes any areas of the ship I deem sensitive, and conforms to all other security procedures."

Troi stared with puzzlement at the helmets Crichton and Ferris wore for their inspection of the ship.

They were of a smooth, molded material and had, on their visors, two video rasters, like little television pictures, one covering each eye. Usually the rasters were semi-transparent and white, but on occasion they jumped and flickered with moire patterns, as if shielding the eyes behind them from something in the outside world. Each helmet also had a mouth-mike and headphones.

Troi guessed that the box floating on antigravs next to Crichton and Ferris housed a computer that controlled the helmets and linked them in communication. With its lens and antennae, it was also the device the two men used for detecting contraband or disease —or so they said.

Now, as Troi walked down the *Enterprise* corridor with the visiting party, she was aware of a low droning buzz, like a metal insect, behind her head. She turned and saw the metal box, which the men from Rampart called a one-eye, floating along close behind her. Its lens-eye stared forward, occasionally zooming in or out a bit. Above the lens the collection of antennae moved about, hunting, pointing at her, then beetling at Picard, who walked beside her as they followed Ferris and Crichton. Two *Enterprise* security men completed the group.

Troi knew that the one-eye device and ten others like it had been checked through the *Enterprise* transporter and deemed safe before they had been brought aboard. Still, the thing looked ominous. And she didn't think that Ferris and Crichton would go anywhere without weapons.

The search had gone on for two hours. Ferris had been curt and efficient, though Troi felt a primitive animal bellicosity lurking in him.

Crichton was harder to read; his mask-like face gave no clue to his inner state, and his mind itself seemed, to Troi, as if it were covered by something thick and opaque. His speech was peculiar—the words often seemed to jam together in his mouth like evacuees crowding an exit. And he had a compulsion to wash his hands every few minutes.

Troi was reminded of various brain pathologies she'd encountered in clinical training, but she had trouble classifying Crichton. She didn't think his problem was organic—physical damage to the brain itself. But something was definitely wrong; some uncontrollable mainspring was pushing him and testing his self-control.

He had just stopped the tour near the holodeck to wash his hands for the fourth time when Picard lost his patience.

"We've been at this long enough," the captain said.

"Is your sensing device detecting any communicable diseases, or not?"

Ferris and Crichton were silent.

"You've already seen that our personnel transporter is programmed to filter out any organism," Riker said pointedly.

Crichton answered with sudden bitterness. "My forefathers left Earth to escape a contagion. It has taken all the resources and manpower of Rampart to keep our planet free of that Allpox. I'm not about to rely on your equipment to do my job for me."

The group passed one of the holodeck doors. A crewwoman emerged laughing. She nodded at the captain and started down the corridor. Troi saw the antennae on the one-eye twitch in the direction of the crewwoman.

The two men from Rampart stopped to listen to some information coming over their headsets.

Ferris turned suddenly toward Picard.

"What was behind that door?"

"A room where we experience complete sensory illusions for training or entertainment," said the captain. "I myself have entered the imaginary worlds of Sherlock Holmes, Dixon Hill . . ."

As Picard went on, Crichton and Ferris suddenly tuned him out and listened instead to their headsets.

Troi sensed a tide of loathing building in the minds of Ferris and Crichton. She wondered what it was about the holodeck that the men from Rampart would find so odious.

Just then, the group was distracted by a crowd of adolescent students and their teacher, approaching along the corridor. In one child's hand was a small holo-statue, a three-dimensional color image of a Navaho sand painting. The teacher nodded to the captain but kept right on with her lesson as she passed.

"In Navaho mythology, the Rainbow Guardian represents the harmony of earth and cosmos, body and mind. He is a reward for those who follow hozho, the Path of Beauty, the way of unselfishness. In the holodeck I'm going to show you more Navaho sand paintings, some Tibetan *Thang-ka* scrolls, a Japanese rock garden . . ."

Troi sensed the two Rampartians' revulsion abruptly click into another track, a track leading to action. They both stood quite still as the students passed. Troi was about to try to get the captain aside and warn him, but now Picard spoke directly to the two men.

"Since you haven't found any diseases or contraband here, may we—"

"We have found it in abundance," said Crichton.

"Found what?"

"The disease of myth, fiction, imagination, blasphemy, religious heresy, the many forms of the Allpox," said Crichton.

Picard stood silently, absorbing these words as he watched the teacher and her students enter the holodeck. Then he turned back to Crichton.

"That is hardly what I would call a disease. We on this ship and in my Federation certainly seem to have gotten on in spite of our . . . infection. But if that's what you're afraid of, I assure you we'll bring none of it to the surface of your planet. We are interested only in finding the crew of the *Huxley*."

"Your story of the *Huxley* is a fiction," Crichton replied tersely, a quivering lip the only movement in his frozen face. "You can't help but spread the obscenity and filth of imagination wherever you go. It is in your schools, your speech, your actions, and your minds. Your children are brought up in a madhouse, taught by lunatics and devils."

"Oh, I see, I see," said Picard. "It's a good thing for

you that your people left Earth centuries ago," he continued. "Your kind has phased itself out, thankfully, on that planet. And what they once banned, we have right here on the ship. Every piece of work by Vonnegut, Joyce, James Baldwin, the beat poets, the Hollywood Ten, the Chinese student-poets, everything."

Crichton backed away from Picard. The captain was heating up.

"Let me make it simple for you, Crichton, and end this absurd search here and now. In our computer we have a complete copy of every notable piece of literature, art, and music ever produced by humankind, from the first paleolithic cave paintings right up to the present. Everything, no matter who banned it, in whatever country, for whatever reason. Not one word or image is missing. Got it?"

Troi's attention was drawn to Ferris. The major was looking over at the one-eye while Crichton and Picard had their words. Filling the one-eye with his intent, Troi was sure.

Now Ferris waited for an order, which came immediately from Crichton.

"It's time to return, Major Ferris," he said. "Procedure Rhombus."

"Yes sir. Procedure Rhombus."

A clicking sound and then a mounting whine emanated from the one-eye as it glided around the two men from Rampart and took up a position in front of them. Flanges below the one-eye's camera lens rotated and formed a hollow tube.

In the frontal lobes of security officer Timoshenko's brain, a recognition dawned: the tube was a waveguide, probably a weapon. His R-complex and limbic system became involved in the emergency. The alarm flashed out to a dozen different brain-loci of thought and action, bypassing any work on the problem of why, in favor of here and now.

Within the same second he was already drawing his phaser and shouting a warning to his fellow crew members.

But the one-eye had already intercepted his thought, acquiring him as a target, and the one-eye was faster. It fired.

A silent and invisible stream of radiation passed through Timoshenko's chest, destroying all tissues it touched. He collapsed like a stricken bull.

Frazer, the other security man, was already drawing his phaser. Another blast of radiation from the one-eye caught him in the head and upper body, and he fell.

Riker, who had been standing next to Troi at the moment the attack began, pushed the counselor to the ground and managed to get both of them partially into a recessed doorway.

"Stay here," he told her.

He peered around the corner of the bulkhead, just in time to see Ferris knock Picard cold.

A snarl escaped Riker's throat. His rage swept away caution as he moved to help the man to whom he owed his own life many times over.

But the one-eye instantly read the burst of energy in Riker's limbic system. It turned to face him. Riker realized he had no weapon. Frazer's phaser was still in his lifeless hand, under his body. Timoshenko's had skidded several meters away.

Ferris and Crichton watched Riker as they propped up the unconscious form of Picard.

Ferris let Picard go and came forward. It seemed to Riker as if he wanted to fight, wanted to abandon procedure in favor of a primitive need for enemy-blood.

Riker was surprised Ferris could do something so

stupid. He got control of his own anger and looked for a way to exploit Ferris' lapse.

"Major Ferris." Crichton's voice was like a bucket of cold water. "Let the one-eye do its job."

Ferris held Riker's stare for a moment and then stepped back. Riker could hear a whine build in the one-eye. He realized the one-eye was readying itself for firing. He searched around for a path of escape, and found none.

Suddenly Timoshenko, face white and sweating from the pain of his internal wounds, reached up and grabbed the one-eye from behind in a bear hug. His superb musculature momentarily overpowered the one-eye's antigravs, and he pinned it to the floor under his torso.

He looked up at Riker, his shout escaping through clenched teeth. "Go!"

The one-eye released another stream of radiation into Timoshenko's body. He bellowed.

Riker pivoted and ran. He ducked into the doorway where Troi still crouched. He grabbed her hand.

"Come on. Holodeck."

They ran, passing the doors the teacher and her students had just entered. Troi didn't look back. She felt the numinous emotions of death flowing down the corridor and into her mind. One stream, not two.

"Open!" shouted Riker as they reached the farthest holodeck room.

The sound of hard footfalls reached their ears as the doors whooshed open. Riker pushed Troi in first, then followed, the doors hissing shut behind him. The room was empty.

Riker tabbed his communicator.

"Lieutenant Worf."

"Worf here."

"Where are you?"

"Bridge, sir."

"The devices brought on board by the men from Rampart are weapons. Put the entire ship on alert. The captain has been taken hostage."

There was a pause, then Riker could hear the alert klaxon.

"We are tracking the captain through his communicator," said Worf. "He is unconscious. In the corridor outside your present location . . .

"Now his signal is moving. They are apparently taking him away, in the direction of transporter room four. The same transporter they beamed in on. Their other one-eyes are stored there, under guard by my men."

"Worf, I just saw a one-eye kill two security officers before they had a chance to draw their phasers. I don't want you to allow your men to endanger their own lives or the captain's by attempting direct action before we understand what we're up against."

"Acknowledged."

"All right, I'm coming to the bridge. Is the route clear?"

"Affirmative."

Troi touched her communicator. "Worf, when we left the security men, I sensed one of them might be alive."

"Checking . . . Timoshenko's communicator indicates life signs."

"Send a medical team but remember what I said about the one-eyes," said Riker.

"Yes, sir."

Riker and Troi silenced their communicators.

"Open," said Riker.

The doors parted. Riker and Troi peered out, then hurried back up the corridor.

When they came upon Timoshenko and Frazer, Timoshenko was breathing stertorously. Frazer was already dead.

They knelt over Timoshenko.

Riker stared at his face. The security officer had reported aboard only a few months ago, but had already approached Riker as a fellow jazz musician. Timoshenko was a bass man. Riker had jammed with him on a wild jazz tune with the backing of a holodeck band, and suddenly, without knowing how, they'd hit a sound of pure spontaneity—their egos had stopped playing and some great unknown river of life had taken over. The holodeck computer seemed to have known the moment was special; it had started changing the chord progressions, jamming along with them, adding its own spontaneity. Riker had never known such a state and he'd played rapturously until his lips felt raw on the trombone mouthpiece. Afterward he'd asked the computer to make him a permanent copy of the session.

Troi cradled Timoshenko's head. "Yuri, help is coming. Hang on."

His eyes, their pupils unevenly dilated, looked at nothing.

"Can't," he said faintly.

She could feel life leaving him.

"Yuri. Thanks," said Riker.

Riker and Troi waited, but there were no other breaths. They stood and looked down at the ruined body.

Worf's voice crackled from Riker's communicator.

"Commander Riker."

"Riker here."

"Sir, the one-eyes in the transporter room have overcome the guards we had on them. They're moving through the corridors. I've shut security barriers throughout the ship. I suggest you and the counselor get to the bridge while it's still safe. Take the turbolift aft of where you are now."

"On our way."

Chapter Five

SITTING ON THE BUNK in her quarters, Security Ensign Shikibu digested the bulletin Riker had just relayed to all crew. Human intruders and robotic devices infiltrating the ship. Already some fatalities among the crew. Orders were to shoot the devices, the one-eyes, if contact with them could not be avoided. Security personnel were asked to report to a staging area near the bridge.

Shikibu checked her phaser, then tied her long black hair into a ponytail. Her delicately arched eyebrows accented a face more appropriate in its elegance to the flowery, courtly games of tenth century Japan than to the *Enterprise* Security staff. Yet her equability in the face of danger, her absolute calm during the grimmest moments, were well known on the *Enterprise*. Rumors, quietly bruited about in the Ten-Fore lounge, attested to her almost freakish accuracy with a phaser.

Her gaze swept, without lingering, past the yumi, the seven-foot-long bamboo/waxwood/carbon-fiber composite bow leaning in a corner of her cabin. It was the instrument she used in the Japanese art of Zen archery. She had learned the art from a Master before entering Starfleet Academy. It was the reason for her oft-rumored abnormal accuracy with a phaser and tranquility in the face of danger. But she no longer consciously thought about her personal achievements or strengths. A sense of ego was anathema to the practice of Zen archery.

She tabbed her door panel. The door swished open. She entered the corridor, took two steps. Ahead, a box-like metal shape came careening around the bend and then stopped dead, hovering at eye level, a few paces away. It regarded Shikibu with a dark camera eye. Shikibu stared back.

The device matched Riker's description of the mechanical intruders. In Shikibu's mind it became nothing more than a target, no different than the straw targets she used for archery practice. She quieted her thoughts into a stillness like the smooth surface of a lake untroubled by winds. Her sense of self disappeared. There was no longer a separate Shikibu or phaser or target.

Her ears registered a rising whine coming from the metal box. This elicited no special emotion in her. Her hand had already closed of its own accord on her phaser button. Like snow dropping off a leaf, her arm seemed to find its own moment to move. She raised the phaser and tracked with the metal box as it made a sudden lateral movement. Her finger pressed the phaser button spontaneously.

Normally the one-eye could intercept the brain waves that signaled the intent and direction of a human's attack. But Shikibu didn't consciously think about her shot before it was fired, thus the one-eye could react only to what it sensed as psychomotor nerve activity and to what it saw directly. It managed to move but caught a bit of the phaser energy on its side, jarring its aim as it fired its own blast of radiation at Shikibu's head. It wobbled crazily and had to set itself down on the deck.

Shikibu collapsed; her limbs had turned to gelatin. She was still conscious but the half-dose of radiation had stunned and confused her by vibrating the water molecules in her brain. A paroxysm of nausea seized her. After it passed she still couldn't understand what had happened or what she should do. She didn't recognize that camera-eyed metal thing resting on the deck nearby, now rising to hover near her.

But she did feel a strong desire to go back to her cabin. She half-crawled, half-rolled back to her door. Her limbs wouldn't work properly. She ordered the door to open and dragged herself across the threshold. A moment later the door hissed shut behind her.

A minute later the one-eye recovered its "wits." Though still mechanically sound, it had lost the information in its temporary memory store, including all memory of Shikibu. It glided away and continued about its business.

Shiva danced the dance of the universe, his wild hair streaming about a face that was beyond bliss and pain. In one hand he held flames of destruction, in another, the drum symbolizing time and creation. His third hand was in a position meaning "elephant," the opener of the way, and with his fourth hand he gestured "fear not." In his streaming locks could be seen the crescent moon of birth, the skull of death, and the flower of the datura.

As Wesley watched this image from Hindu mythology, this dance of creation and destruction unfolding on his computer screen, he likened it to the dance of subatomic particles, with their births, deaths, and continual exchange of energy—the fire from the explosion that created the universe.

This comparison was not entirely his own. The computer had told him that as far back as the mid-twentieth century, physicists had found, in the concept of Shiva and in other Eastern ideas, eloquent metaphors for quantum and relativity theory, the uncertainty principle, and much else.

Wesley had been studying a lot of Eastern philosophy lately, not because he was naturally inclined to it, but because of Ensign Shikibu.

His first look at her face had sent his mind roaming into the ethereal. He was instantly captivated, but he soon found her to be difficult to understand, and the closer they became, the more he was intimidated by her. Though their new friendship had deepened, there had been no signs of romance so far, and already Wesley seemed to have reached an impasse.

It wasn't just that she was four years older than he. The problem went beyond mere, mundane chronological age. She wasn't like anyone he'd ever met. She was usually silent as a stone, especially when he wanted to talk, and just when he was about to give up and walk away, she would give him a brief smile that sent him into ecstasy for the rest of the day. But she would rarely talk about her personal life, or about Zen archery, and what she did say he often found incomprehensible.

Once, after he'd asked her for the umpteenth time to tell him about that ancient art, she took him to her cabin. She disappeared behind the partition and emerged wearing flowing robe-like garments of a simple style he'd never seen before, and a leather glove on one hand. She picked up her bow, the largest bow Wesley had ever seen, and fitted an arrow to the string. Lifting the bow, she drew the arrow straight back and pointed it at the wall. She held the drawn bow for at least a minute in a state of strange concentration, her breathing deep and even, her body elegantly poised. There was an ineffable beauty and mastery about her in this posture. She never shot the arrow; she simply put the bow and arrow away and silently opened her door to let Wesley out.

Hoping to understand her better by learning about her cultural background, Wesley started reading about Zen. As it turned out, most Zen writings were in the form of riddles and paradoxes called koan and mondo, which he didn't grasp at all, and which seemed to say that they shouldn't be grasped. He traced Zen's lineage back to the earlier writings of Chinese Taoism, but those writings said that words could not be used to describe Taoism. In search of something less elusive, he traced the lineage even farther back, to the ancient Hindu writings, and found Shiva, the starting point.

Shiva he could just begin to understand. Shiva reminded him of particle physics.

Now, as he watched the dancing Shiva and thought about dancing quarks and leptons, and also about the waves in Shikibu's raven-black hair, a sudden alert klaxon startled him.

He logged off the computer and waited. The klaxon kept wailing. After an uneasy interval, his cabin intercom came to life and he heard Riker announce that dangerous intruders were loose on the ship.

Then a different voice came over his communicator.

"Shikibu to Weh . . ."

The words sounded slurred, drunken.

"Wesley here. What's wrong?"

"Can't talk or think . . . truder shot me."

Wesley leapt up. He felt himself shaking. She must have been injured badly, disoriented—she was calling him when she should have been calling Security or sickbay.

"Where are you?" he asked.

There was no reply, just the faint ambient noise of a room somewhere on the ship.

Riker's voice broke into the channel.

"Mr. Crusher."

"Crusher here."

"I need you on the bridge. The devices haven't gotten up to your deck level yet, but they may soon. You have to come immediately."

"Sir, something has happened to Shikibu."

"Yes, we know about it. She'll be brought to sickbay as soon as someone from Security can get to her."

"But—"

"Ensign!" Riker became brusque. "The entire ship is threatened and the captain is being held hostage. Put aside your feelings. I need you at your station. Now."

"On my way, sir."

"Worf, where is the captain now?" asked Commander Riker.

He sat in the captain's chair, Troi to his left, Data and Wesley ahead of him at Conn and Ops, Worf behind at Tactical.

The entire crew presented the appearance of cool professionalism but Riker could see telltale tautness in their faces—even in Data's.

His own neck muscles had acquired a painful rigidity and he had to make a conscious effort to relax and avoid a spasm. Fateful decisions were arrayed before him like the forking paths of a labyrinth.

"They're taking him toward transporter room four —same one they came in on," Worf told Riker. "My people can converge and surprise—"

"No, Worf."

"But sir, we can't just sit here and let them take the captain off our ship."

"How do you know they won't simply kill all of our

people at the moment of first approach? Anyway, if all the Rampartians wanted to do was to execute the captain they would have already done so. If we interfere now we might force them to it."

"If I went down there myself, sir, I could—"

"You're staying on the bridge, Worf."

Worf emitted a low growl resembling that of a grizzly bear as he returned his attention to his console.

Riker wasn't alarmed by the guttural sound. He knew Worf well enough to recognize the growl as a way of venting Klingon steam. Worf would do his duty.

"They're at the transporter room door," said Worf.

The precise, clipped voice of Ferris came over the bridge speakers.

"Commander Riker, acknowledge. This is Major Ferris."

"He's using the captain's communicator," said Worf.

"This is Riker. Is the captain all right?"

"He is conscious and in good condition," said Ferris.

"Let me speak to him."

"Open the door to the transporter room first."

"Give me a moment."

Crichton broke into the conversation.

"Riker. I remind you that your captain is of use to me only while I have your cooperation. Stop cooperating and I will kill him."

Riker looked at Worf. "They controlled those doors to let their devices out. They can probably get back in too, but don't want us to know it. Anyway, we don't have a choice. Open the doors, and give us visual."

Worf's face twitched as he touched his panel.

A view of the transporter room flickered onto the bridge viewscreen. The same transporter room from which the Rampartians' one-eyes had launched their attack.

The unconscious forms of two security ensigns, one man and one woman, lay to the side of the platform. Transporter Chief O'Brien was sprawled near the console.

Ferris and Crichton entered with Picard between them. They held his arms at his sides. A one-eye glided over and hovered near O'Brien's head.

Riker kept his eyes on this scene as he called his ace in the hole, chief engineer Geordi La Forge.

"Riker to La Forge."

"La Forge here, Commander," came the reply over bridge speakers.

"Prepare to override the transporter circuits."

"Override is standing by. When can I get a look at the intruder devices?"

"Switch your viewer to the bridge channel. You can watch along with us."

"Aye, switching . . . Damn! They've still got the captain!"

"We may be able to change that. Stand by. Data, can you tell what that device is doing to O'Brien?"

"Some type of scanning, possibly for metabolic signs."

"What is O'Brien's condition?"

"Comatose, like the two security ensigns. Sir, it is possible that the device is reading the memory information encoded in O'Brien's brain tissue, and that it is also capable of reading the thoughts, the active brain waves, he'd have if he were conscious."

When there was no response, Data turned around to look at Riker. Riker was still pondering the remark.

"I think you have something there, Data," Riker said finally.

"It would explain a lot, Commander . . . why the

51

other one-eyes left O'Brien alive, for instance: to save information valuable to them. And, why they have been able to outwit and outshoot the personnel they have encountered."

On the screen, Crichton held a communicator—the communicator stolen from Picard—and brought it to his mouth. Yes, thought Riker, Ferris and Crichton would know all about our communicators if their one-eyes have been reading minds. And just think of how much else they would know . . .

"Riker."

"I'm listening."

"And watching us as well."

Riker upwardly revised his estimate of what Ferris and Crichton knew about the *Enterprise.*

"We are going to transport to the surface of Rampart with your captain," said Crichton, his mask-face a cipher. "We don't need your help to do so. Once again I caution you against interference if you value your captain's life. We'll return him when I am sure you'll leave my world alone."

"Believe me," said Riker, "I want nothing to do with your world. I'm willing to call off the search—at least for now. Just give me back the captain."

"No. I can't risk the safety and health of my planet's population based on your word. You think I believe your lie, your fiction about some ship lost here? I've seen that your *Enterprise* is laden with vile, deadly myths, entire books and computers and minds full of contagious insanity and blasphemy against the only true word of reason and of God. Your so-called imagination comes from a primitive, barbaric time. We on Rampart don't consort with dreamed-up creatures anymore. We don't draw pictures in the dirt or spend all day looking at the sky. We've already solved all the universe's mysteries."

"That's one way in which we differ," said Riker.

"Expectation confirmed," said Crichton.

"Commander," Troi whispered to Riker. "Could you ask him about the aliens; the Other-worlders?"

The doubt was plain on Riker's face.

"I've had time to observe him. I now suspect he's hiding information," Troi continued. "What he's hiding feels somewhat like the Other-worlders. I want to be sure."

Riker hesitated for a moment, but the determined look on her face convinced him.

He turned back to the viewscreen.

"Are you aware of aliens in this sector of space?"

Crichton stared back blankly.

"There may be aliens hidden here," Riker went on, "perhaps in another physical plane or universe. They could be a danger to you. Are you sure you don't want to talk about them?"

"My headset is filtering out your words."

"Crichton, this isn't fiction! This may be important to the welfare of your planet."

"All right, Riker, I'll give you a chance. Let's see if you can be rational."

Crichton switched off the fiction-filter on his helmet.

Riker repeated his remarks about the Other-worlders.

"Another fiction," said Crichton, as his nerveless mask-face tried to stretch itself into a grimace. "Science fiction, the worst of all. True science has determined that there is no alien life. Earth is the only planet where life arose. All life you see on Rampart we brought from Earth, because Rampart was a dead stone in space. Humans are alone in the universe. You and your people just can't face that. Your minds are full of fantasies about aliens, even aliens that serve on your own ship."

Riker allowed himself a short, ironic laugh. He was

standing near a full Klingon security officer and a half-Betazoid counselor.

"Injurious just to talk to you," Crichton went on, his cadence speeding up, an edge of hysteria becoming audible. "You're incurable, just like the criminals on Rampart, the Dissenters, with their diseased brains and hoards of deadly fiction. You plan to help their insurgency, don't you? That's really why you came here."

"Not true."

"So you say, but you're full of fiction. Just as the Dissenters are full of fiction."

"This isn't fiction. This really happened. Maybe my counselor's own description will convince you," said Riker, nodding at Troi.

"These aliens appear to invade one's mind," said Troi. "They may already know about your personal life, as they already knew about mine. They can take you to other planets—"

"Enough!" Crichton cried. "For God's sake, stop!" He was visibly traumatized.

As Troi watched Crichton's blanching mask-face she sensed with great force that her words had rung true for him. He had experienced the Other-worlders, or aliens of some similar kind. It was something he could never admit to, something powerful that permeated the dark fear-substrata of his mind—maybe the cause of his tics and compulsions, his hand-washing and his verbal stampedes. Maybe the key to his personality.

As she watched Crichton and Ferris set controls on the transporter, she turned from the viewscreen to tell Riker what she'd discovered. But Riker had other business to take care of.

"Riker to La Forge."

"La Forge here."

"The two men from Rampart are going to try to

54

beam down with the captain. Can you isolate the captain's signal and hold him here?"

"Stand by . . . Should be just a sweet little piece of cake . . . Should be but isn't . . . No, they couldn't know how to do that! Only O'Brien would know that!"

"Assume they know everything O'Brien knows."

"Then I can't override, the way they've rigged it. Not without cutting the power completely."

"Forget that. The fools might kill the captain. Based on what you've seen, do you know of any way we can neutralize the one-eye and storm the room?"

"Not yet. But I've just been looking at the transporter records of the one-eyes' structure, and there's one way we definitely can't neutralize them. Phasers. The one-eyes can be set to explode when penetrated by direct phaser fire. Could take out a whole deck. My guess is their booby traps will be set as Ferris and Crichton leave the ship."

"Worf, you heard all that," said Riker. "Relay instructions to all hands—no phasers. Geordi, what about using the transporter to beam the one-eyes out into space?"

"The one-eyes already have that covered. They're emitting the perfect interference frequencies."

Riker's eyes, like the rest of the bridge crew's, were locked onto the viewscreen. He saw Crichton and Ferris push Picard onto the transporter platform, then step onto it after him. The one-eye hovered next to them obediently. It was going to beam down with them. That meant ten were going to remain on the ship.

Picard now seemed fully alert, recovered from the blow that had knocked him out, an adamant expression on his face that said, "This is but a momentary setback."

55

"Commander," said Geordi's voice over the speakers, "their transporter sequence has started."

"I'm letting them go, Geordi."

Riker and his crew watched as Ferris tossed the captain's communicator pin against the wall of the transporter room. Then the figures of Picard, Ferris, Crichton, and the one-eye glowed, faded, and dematerialized.

"Data, do you have a fix on the beamdown point?"

"Yes, sir."

"Put it on screen."

Aerial view of a sprawling complex: blocky concrete buildings, spindly broadcast towers, white radomes, vast hangars for aircraft.

"Sensor information indicates this is the security force headquarters, sir. The only secure complex in the area. Highest density of surveillance gear and weaponry."

"This is probably where they'll hold him," said Riker. "Not a place we can beam right into."

Data cycled the screen through differing wavelengths, differing views. In one, large lettering on the side of the building became visible: CephCom.

In another view, underground topography showed itself in enhanced color.

"There!" Riker strode closer to the screen. "What are those faint radiating lines?"

"Underground tunnels or cavities. Too irregular to be man-made. But they do intersect with the foundation of the building."

"Any life signs down there?"

"Some, but not many. Too much interference to identify. No evidence of surveillance gear or weapons, though."

"Widen the view."

"Twenty kilometer radius. The same tunnels are visible."

"Okay. Select a likely beamdown point ten to fifteen kilometers from the building. Check it out thoroughly. You and Troi will beam down with me. We're going to find the captain and beam back up with him. Worf, what's the status of our mechanical intruders?"

"Confined to decks six and three."

"Any vital ship's operations threatened?"

"No. And we should be able to contain them where they are."

"Is there a secure transporter room I can use for beamdown?"

"Room Six, sir."

"We'll take it. Riker to La Forge."

"La Forge here," came the voice from Engineering.

"You'll command the ship while Troi, Data, and I are on an away mission. You can execute an evasive maneuver and drop the shields long enough for us to beam down. Away team, let's talk in the ready room."

As she sat with Riker and Data in the ready room, Troi felt a pang of guilt and responsibility. The tragedy of Timoshenko and Frazer's deaths, of the captain's capture, and of whatever might happen next, seemed traceable in a chain of causes that started with her original encounter with the alien Other-worlders. That encounter had caused Picard to stop the ship and search, and then to find the recorder marker. And Troi was sure she had somehow summoned the Other-worlders in the first place. Her amnesia still prevented her from knowing why.

Her rational counselor voice told her that she couldn't really be blamed since she would never have intended harm. She tried to push the guilt aside.

"The Rampartians have a primitive level of technology by Federation standards," Data was saying. "There is a question of why our security staff did not discover the one-eyes' capabilities before transporting them aboard."

"Our people checked them thoroughly," said Riker. "But I suspect that the Rampartians had the jump on us from the beginning; that they stole information on Starfleet technology from the minds of the *Huxley* crew, and after they somehow disposed of the *Huxley,* used the information to perfect their capabilities against future Starfleet ships—like us."

"Commander," said Troi, "Crichton knows about the Other-worlders, or at least about some aliens analogous to them. It's a secret he shares with no one. I felt it very strongly when I asked him."

"That might be significant."

"Might? I think it's the linchpin of his mind."

"Then it's significant," said Riker. "But right now I have to stay on my main track—retrieving the captain. I welcome your empathic impressions; in fact, we need them, but I don't have enough time now for a full psychoanalysis of Crichton."

"What about Oleph and Una, here on our own ship?" asked Troi. "What if they have something to do with the Other-worlders as well?"

"Worf and his staff are monitoring them. I didn't have the chance to tell you before, but Worf seems to be involved with Oleph and Una. He's got something secret going with them."

"Then I think we should question him."

"I already have, and found out nothing. But Worf's got their confidence, and a favored position to observe them—he'll report when he finds anything. We'll just have to trust him. Right now we have to think about the captain. We'll beam down in five minutes," he said, rising.

Troi thought Riker was missing the mark. But a counselor's view wasn't always in accord with the rest of the officers', and she had gotten used to that a long time ago. Her different view was what made her useful.

Her earlier feeling of guilt subsided as she experienced a surge of stubborn pride. After all, she was a top expert on the most complex phenomenon in the universe, the mechanism of consciousness. If the mystery of the Other-worlders was hers to solve, then so be it.

She followed Riker and Data out of the ready room and onto the bridge. Her gaze fell on Worf, who looked up and registered her stare. She sensed that Worf was concealing something. Whatever it was, there was no time to ask him about it now.

Chapter Six

RIKER, TROI, AND DATA beamed down into an abandoned ore-extraction factory. The site had been chosen by Data.

Crepuscular blue nebula-light spilled in through the top of the roofless building. Catwalks, snake-spiralling cables, and a delirium of metal pipes spread out above and below the away team's perch, a small platform along a wall of the building.

Data tuned his tricorder to a GEO setting that would help him find any shaft or duct that communicated with the natural tunnels underground. The threesome took a several-minute tour around the floor of the facility, returning eventually to the vantage point of the platform. Data wasn't able to pinpoint a way down, though in one area he had found a concentration of methane gas he pronounced "intriguing."

"Your taste in beamdown sites runs to the Spartan, Mr. Data," said Riker.

"Spartan?" asked the android, as he reviewed information on the small display screen of his tricorder. "As in Sparta, Helen of Troy's queendom?"

"No," said Riker, his gaze resting on a large cart

still containing its load of lead-colored rock. He imagined a populace that sweated and strained in futility. "Let me refine that a bit . . . Myth of Sisyphus, man pushing a boulder up a hill forever—endless, mindless toil."

"Your metaphor is cogently conceived," Data said, as he ran his collected measurements through the tricorder's programs, in search of the elusive passage down into the ground.

"Data, speed is of the essence here."

"Perhaps you can help me, sir."

As the two consulted, Troi stood a few steps away. She glanced at the chrome surface of a tank and saw her reflection, but perceived something else there as well. Another sentience. She opened her empathic perception a bit, then suddenly tried to seal it off, as she felt the presence of an Other-worlder. Too late.

The Other-worlder responded instantly. She felt it approaching. She'd initiated unintentional contact.

The reflections on the surface of the tank shifted and melted. She found she couldn't look away. Her face disappeared from the chrome. A new image expanded and became the reality surrounding her.

She was in a world of scorched ground, of billowing dark smoke and wild squalls of fire. She began to hear and then feel a deep gut-resonating throb, as though of an approaching aircraft or juggernaut.

An Other-worlder, the giant Mirror Man, emerged from the smoke, reflecting on his own burnished surfaces the conflagration around him. He was looking for something. The twin mirror-discs of his eyes shifted in unison. On his body surfaces Troi saw scenes of mechanized warfare, mammoth guns vomiting fire, aircraft diving and strewing bomb-clusters over a jungle, children running with mouths open in silent screams . . .

Suddenly the Mirror Man became aware of Troi. He

came closer, dragging the leg that had no foot. His eyes became intolerably bright, like flickering arclights.

"You called me," he said with a deep reverberant metallic voice.

"I didn't mean to."

He reached down and picked her up by the shoulders, held her high off the ground in front of him.

She felt as though she were enclosed by steel jaws. Her head was at the level of his chest.

"You want knowledge?" he asked.

She sensed a threat in the question.

"You want to know about Crichton?"

She stared into the fiery images on his chest. "Yes," she said. "You have contacted him?"

"He is now aware of life alien to himself," the Mirror Man said cryptically.

He drew her closer. He was pushing her face toward his chest.

"You want to learn more," he boomed as a sort of half-question.

Through the images of smoke and fire on his mirror-skin, behind them or under them, Troi could see something moving rhythmically. She thought it was his heart, and tried to shake her way out of his grip. She felt her limbs becoming numb and heavy. The paralyzing transformation again!

Then she sensed someone else's mind nearby. She recognized it as Riker's. She focused on it, and as soon as she did, she found herself back with him in the ore factory. He was holding her by the shoulders. The transition was instantaneous.

"Deanna, what's wrong!"

"It's okay," she said. "I'm back."

"You were in a trance."

She let out a long shuddering breath.

"I just had contact with one of the Other-worlders."

"Is it still here?" asked Riker.

"Yes. I can still feel it. It's here but not in our state of being."

"Data, check your tricorder."

Data switched it to the BIO setting. "Yes sir, but there is low probability we will detect the alien with this tricorder; even the *Enterprise*'s main sensors could not."

"Good point," said Riker.

"However, I have found something else . . . definitely not one of your Other-worlders . . . a humanoid outside the building . . . stationary."

Riker waved for silence and drew his phaser. Data put his tricorder away and drew his phaser as well. They looked about them at the corrugated-metal walls.

Riker moved in the direction of a door, but Data put an arm out to stop him. He looked back at his tricorder, moving it slowly. Then he motioned his crewmates backward. Riker understood that someone was going to enter. He ducked behind a huge oily metal gear and signaled for Troi and Data to do likewise.

The door swung inward, and steps came toward them, then stopped. Riker peered around the gear and saw, standing on the platform, a red-haired woman, about thirty, wearing somber-hued clothes. As she began to walk forward again, Riker stepped around the gear and into the open. The woman turned toward him, as though she were expecting him to be there.

She appeared to be unarmed but Riker kept his phaser trained on her. They confronted each other tensely.

"What about your two companions?" the woman asked. "Are they shy?"

She motioned toward where Troi and Data were hidden.

"Counselor, Data," said Riker. "Come on out."

The woman watched them keenly as they emerged. Then she seemed to make a decision.

"We're wasting time," she said. "I watched you and heard you talking. The CS could be out there right now, ready to arrest all of us. I think I know why you're here, but I have to hear you say it. You are Dissenters."

"We don't belong to any particular group," said Riker.

While the woman paused, trying to decide what to do, Troi assessed her. She felt the woman's rebellious spirit and keen intellect, explored her inner emotional mind-set. She decided the woman was an aesthete, a connoisseur of feelings and images. A poet, perhaps? A Dissenter—one of the anti-establishment rebels Crichton had mentioned?

"My name is Amoret," the woman said, then waited for a reaction.

"You don't object to my name?"

Riker looked at Data, who accessed his memory.

"Amoret is a character created by Edmund Spenser, sixteenth-century English poet," said Data.

"No," Riker told Amoret, "I don't object to it."

"You know the meaning of my name, and even spoke aloud of Sisyphus and Helen of Troy. You did that, committed a crime punishable by death, and you aren't a Dissenter? You ought to be."

"I'm sorry, but we can't be involved with you or your activities," said Riker. "If you could leave for just a minute or two, we'll be gone when you come back and you can do whatever it is you intended here."

"I can't risk going back out there!"

"You may not have to," Data said. "The CS are already here."

He pointed upward.

They all looked up. Thirty feet over their heads, silhouetted against the night sky, a group of six one-eyes hovered dead-still in precise hexagonal formation, looking down at them.

Riker reflexively pushed Troi and Data under an overhanging stair-landing. Amoret ducked in with them.

Riker touched his communicator.

"Enterprise, three to beam up now!"

He glanced regretfully at Amoret, sorry he could not help her.

But there was no response from the ship.

Riker tabbed again. *"Enterprise!"*

"Sir," said Data, as he moved a switch on the tricorder, "we are being electronically jammed, from several directions. The *Enterprise* can't hear us. It is as if the Rampartians knew precisely which wave patterns to use and already had equipment ready for our arrival."

He adjusted the tricorder again.

"Aircraft approaching."

They began to hear the whup-whup of hovercraft rotors.

Riker noticed a steel door standing open nearby. The room behind it looked like storage space.

"Counselor, wait in there," he said, then looked at the red-haired woman. "You can too if you like."

The two women stepped into the room and closed the door behind them.

Riker, phaser in hand, craned his neck to look upward at a maze of pipes.

The hovercraft's rotors became very loud and they could feel its wind. Its searchlights abruptly illuminated the maze of ducts on the floor below. Another craft could be heard landing outside.

Riker motioned to Data that he was going to climb into the network of pipes and catwalks overhead.

Data nodded and signaled toward the stairs that led downward. The human and the android went their separate ways.

In the small storage room, Amoret and Troi stared tensely at each other as they listened to the hovering craft.

"I still think you and your friends are Dissenters," said Amoret. "You were going to Alastor, weren't you?"

"Where is that?" asked Troi.

Doors slammed and curt voices muttered outside the building.

Amoret pulled a moldered, wrinkled, stained page from her coat.

"Can you read this and keep it in your memory?" she asked Troi.

"Why?"

"It's the only piece of genuine classic fiction I've ever owned. I found it when I was little. I've spent all my life trying to write the rest of the story. Someone has to keep it alive, either one of us."

Troi would have refused the request had it not been for the compelling emotions she felt in Amoret. The page was the focus of a tragedy—Amoret's impending death—and of a hope or wish as well. The page itself was an avatar of something immeasurably greater, something that could live on after the page was gone, or die and rise again even more powerful than before.

Troi looked at the page.

"Gulliver's Travels," proclaimed the heading at the top. Under it was a drawing of Gulliver himself, bound to a crude sled, surrounded by Lilliputians.

The page abruptly became dark.

Troi looked up and saw that something had moved over the hole in the ceiling. The lens of a one-eye looked down at them.

Troi put her hands out to show she was unarmed.

"Clear away from the door," said a male voice from outside.

Troi complied.

A CS officer wearing a white field jumpsuit and visored helmet kicked open the door and entered, gun at the ready.

"I hereby identify you as criminals and place you under custody of the CS," he said.

He handcuffed Troi, then went to Amoret.

Amoret looked at him defiantly. He pulled at the page in her hand, and she let it go.

He cuffed her, then locked the page into a metal cylinder slung at his side. In a moment a little puff of smoke from the cylinder signaled the destruction of the page.

"Someone will write that book again," Amoret said. Her voice was trembling.

"Sure," said the officer.

He turned his attention to Troi. She couldn't see his eyes behind the randomized jag-patterns of his twin rasters. He pulled the communicator pin off her uniform. As he put it in his pocket there was a bright flash outside the room, and the sound of an *Enterprise* phaser.

Riker looked out from his perch on the catwalk, six stories above the ground, and tried for another shot at the one-eyes. He had seen the CS man below, moving toward Troi's hiding place, but a one-eye rising up from nowhere had forced him to take cover.

Now the one-eyes were swarming all around him, dodging in and out of the pipe-maze.

A one-eye darted into the open dead ahead. Riker shot too late; it dodged the beam, which blew a hole in a great iron pipe.

Riker waited for his target to reappear. He squinted, eyes sweat-stung, into the blue-lit tangle of tubular shapes.

"Riker!"

He looked down. There, standing on the floor five stories below, was Ferris. Behind him floated several more one-eyes, and behind them stood several CS men, and Troi and Amoret, both handcuffed.

"I'm offering you a fair chance to give yourself up," Ferris called, his voice echoing among the steel pipes.

"Release your prisoners, and we'll talk," said Riker.

"Procedure says I have to give you this chance," said Ferris. "If you don't take it, you're not getting another."

Riker wondered where the hell Data was.

Maybe if he stalled for just another moment . . .

"Is intimidation the only kind of social interaction you know?" asked Riker.

"The record will reflect that you refused my offer," said Ferris.

Riker fired at a one-eye that dodged in front of him. He missed. The one-eye swung outward, and a moment later was obliterated by a phaser shot from the shadows below.

Data.

Another one-eye was hit, and dissolved into nothingness.

Then Riker heard a hum so close behind his head he could feel it on his scalp. He turned around slowly and looked directly into the lens of another one-eye. He dropped his phaser, put up his hands, and looked down at Ferris, six stories below.

Ferris raised his weapon, contempt on his face.

In an instant, Riker understood that Ferris was going to kill him, even though he had given himself up.

Ferris fired.

Riker had the sensation of his body falling apart, limbs beyond conscious control, as the cells of his brain were rudely vibrated. His sensory confusion was absolute and uninterrupted. He didn't even know he was falling.

On the floor of the factory, from a tangle of pipes, Data leapt forward, and with the speed and precision proper to androids, covered in giant steps the distance to Riker's impact point. He stretched his arms up and out. Riker fell onto them. Data absorbed the shock like a tempered spring, letting Riker nearly touch the ground at the end of his deceleration, then pulling him back up.

The CS men surged forward and in a moment surrounded the pair.

Ferris stepped toward Data, reached out and pulled the communicator pins off the uniforms of both men from the *Enterprise*.

Data carefully observed Ferris, the ring of armed CS men, and the hovering one-eyes.

Even Data, an android, could see the anger and frustration on Ferris' face. Ferris had wanted Riker to fall to his death.

"Put him down, robot," said Ferris. "Our weapons can destroy you as well as your flesh and blood masters."

Data set the unconscious Riker gently onto the ground.

"Throw down your weapon."

Data hesitated for just a wink.

He had deduced, during careful observation over the last several minutes, that the one-eyes could not read the super high-speed impulses in his positronic brain. Now, as he slowly removed the phaser from his belt and threw it to the ground, his fingers touched the phaser settings and the fire button in precisely calibrated movements.

The burst of phased energy was so short it appeared as though the phaser merely glitched or sparked on the way out of his hands. Its beam flashed for a microsecond at a far corner of the building, where Data, during his survey with Riker, had detected a flammable concentration of natural methane gas.

A round fireball bloomed in the air, and the shock wave knocked everyone over. The one-eyes were forced to the ground.

Troi was thrown backward. She rolled away from the fireball, and kept rolling until she stopped halfway into a large open duct pipe. As the fireball rose, Troi could see Data grappling with several CS men simultaneously. One of them reached over and pressed a spot on Data's back, a cutoff switch only a select few people on the *Enterprise* had ever known about— until the one-eyes came.

Data went limp.

Hands still cuffed, Troi leaned her whole body into the duct pipe and let herself slide a short way down. The pipe descended at an angle and she could control her descent.

The pipe had a square shape, one of those she recalled Data mentioning as a good candidate for access to the underground tunnels.

She let herself slide downward for several meters. The duct turned and joined with another, steeper one, and she slid faster, scraping and bumping, until she landed in complete darkness on a soft pile of dirt.

Ferris led his men toward the two white assault hovercraft that stood with engines idling. As he strode across the gravel several one-eyes kept pace, hovering in front of him, their lenses pointed in his direction, their lights throwing his rugged features and light blond hair into relief against the night sky.

Behind him, his men carried three unconscious criminals on stretchers.

Ferris strove to quell his frustration. He was a by-the-book military man, and he knew all about tactics and strategy. But, faced with this eternal rebellion, he sometimes got fed up with all the rules. Dissenters didn't go by the rules.

There were no clearly marked fronts and campaigns, and the CS, it seemed, could never know if it was winning. Could he be blamed for needing to pop his cork, for wanting to kill when he should only stun? Criminals, once arrested, were as good as dead anyway.

He'd seen some of his soldiers massacre Dissenters during skirmishes. He hadn't participated but God knows he'd come close. And he'd never disciplined his soldiers for it. They were good men, unselfishly risking exposure to the Allpox every day.

Now he climbed into the cockpit of one of the hovercraft and sat in the copilot's seat. On a small video screen in front of him, the face of Crichton was already waiting.

"We've been watching the video, Major. How did you find them?"

"We already knew the transporter frequencies to watch," said Ferris. "We weren't counting on the Dissenter woman showing up at the same spot, though. We'd been following her for weeks, waiting for her to lead us to the Dissenters' caves, but the *Enterprise* people's arrival made us blow our cover. Will we go in now anyway, sir?"

"Yes, we'll still carry out the cave mission. And we'll arrest the *Enterprise* woman in the process."

Crichton looked at the synchronized images on a bank of monitors behind him.

"The one-eyes gave us superb news video from

this, Major. We did a live feed straight to broadcast on some of it. The excitement out there is incredible."

Crichton's mask-face stretched slightly in a configuration Ferris recognized as pleasure.

"Just another operation, sir," said Ferris.

"I know you aren't always comfortable with these necessities of presentation, Major. But the people need you."

Ferris busied himself flicking a row of toggle switches over his head as the hovercraft prepared to take off. Crichton was right, he didn't enjoy being in front of the camera. The camera was Crichton's affair. Using the one-eyes to gather news video had been Crichton's idea, and Ferris thought it was untidy from a military point of view.

"I endure them by defining them within my duty, sir. When am I going into the caves?"

"I'm sending another patrol in."

Ferris paused for just a moment, a "why" on his face. But he quickly recovered with a snappy, "Yes, sir."

"If we force them out," said Crichton, "you'll make the actual capture. On video."

The hovercraft lifted smoothly.

"I have another mission for you now," said Crichton. "Some criminals have just attacked a Mental Hygiene clinic and are destroying the mind-cleansing equipment. You'll be—"

Crichton's mouth seemed to jam up. The color drained from his face. His eyes stared forward at something off-screen. He started to quiver slightly, like a slab of aspic.

Ferris cleared his throat.

"Sir, are you all right?"

Crichton leaned over his desk and held his head for several seconds.

When he came back up he seemed to have recovered.

"Sorry," he said, breathing like a man who's been held underwater. "My injury has been giving me trouble lately."

"Yes, sir."

Crichton, still looking very pale, launched into the details of Ferris' next mission.

The assault hovercraft—fitted with the most expensive ordnance available—flew Ferris on over miles of tenements, then over some mud flats strewn with old tires, rusting machinery, and household trash.

There, rising from the mud, was a cleverly assembled, monument-size sculpture. It was made of broken pieces of wood and sheet metal, and bits of colorful garbage. It was a caricature, a bust of a head seen often on Rampart, but here with features distorted to ludicrous effect, a mockery of manliness. The head was bent over, gnawing on another human head beneath it, in a rendition of a scene from Dante's Inferno—Count Ugolino, in the Ninth Circle of Hell, eternally gnawing the bloody head of his partner in treachery, Archbishop Ruggieri.

The man who was the object of this parody was spared the actual sight of it. The nose-mounted camera of the hovercraft that bore him through the night did in fact record the junk-sculpture, but couldn't display it on the hovercraft's screens because, as parody, it was both criminal and contagious. Instead, the screens simply indicated that a target had been acquired.

The hovercraft circled back in a wide arc and came in low. Twin pod-mounted guns roared to life, firing fifty explosive-filled rounds per second, and in one quick pass the junk-sculpture was blasted to pieces. It became just more old garbage.

Chapter Seven

TROI FOUND HERSELF lying in a darkness impenetrable except for a small, faint patch of orange glow on a rock surface. The glow seemed only a few meters away, but she had no visual frame of reference.

Bruised and still handcuffed, she rose to her knees and then, cautiously, to her feet. The glow ahead seemed a comforting color. All she wanted now was a place where she could rest for a few moments and decide what to do next.

She felt ahead with her foot. Soft earth. She began to work her way forward. The glow grew larger, visible as a curving stone passage, still many meters away.

Her shoulder nudged against a rocky protuberance. Unable to bring her cuffed hands up to steady herself, she leaned sideways against the rock. As her cheek touched it, she perceived that the rock had a peculiar texture. Leathery and pliant.

The object moved jerkily, and Troi lost her balance and fell to the ground. She heard a flapping sound and felt air moving. The flapping sound rose and moved about behind and above her, now audibly closer, now farther.

Worried that she might be in danger, she tried to sense consciousness but could discern only the most basic level of animal awareness. And more than one. There were several creatures flying around in the darkness, perhaps using echolocation to navigate, Troi mused.

She rose to her feet and moved urgently toward the light and the passage. The sound of the animals in the air behind her grew fainter and disappeared by the time she reached her destination.

The passage looked as though it had been deliberately hewn, like a mine tunnel. The faint orange light was coming from around a sharp bend. Troi moved toward the light, and turning the corner, found herself looking into an immense natural cavern. It showed her a diminishing perspective as it curved down from view in the distance.

On the floor directly ahead lay an underground lake. Droplets fell sporadically from stalactites on the ceiling. Peach-colored light emanated from grottos on the floor.

Troi walked forward into the cavern, until she came to one of the sources of light. It was a small, naturally glowing object, a rock.

Its orange-pink light had a calming effect on her. She became aware of her fatigue and sat on the sand near the pool, her manacled hands behind her.

The cavern matched the one described in a diagram she'd seen before beamdown: long, fairly straight, passing directly under the ore factory. It would lead most of the way to the area under the CephCom complex. But the away team had not known the specifics of the layout for the last three kilometers of that route. They would have explored it as they went.

If she attempted it herself and successfully entered CephCom through its underbelly, she'd still have to covertly locate the captain and a communicator for contacting the *Enterprise*. No way to know if Riker and Data were being held there, too. But if they were . . . hadn't Amoret implied something about capital punishment for those who violated the anti-imagination laws?

She looked at the situation as calmly as she could, and had to conclude that it was hopeless.

She thought of how she had sometimes told others that the boundaries of one's capabilities are self-imposed. She'd just have to push herself beyond her own limits. The counselor would have to counsel herself.

She was more determined than ever to discover the connection between the Other-worlders and Crichton. "He is now aware of life alien to himself," the Mirror Man had said. She wasn't sure if this meant Crichton knew specifically about the Other-worlders—but he certainly carried a secret. And it was the only handle she had. She decided her best course was to deduce all she could about Crichton and the Other-worlders before her arrival at CephCom. Then, if she failed to find a communicator and beam up with the captain, she would confront Crichton and learn what she could.

She summoned the energy to get up and work on freeing her hands from the cuffs.

Then her empathic sense made her aware of an approaching human. She quickly stood and looked about.

A small, disheveled man was walking toward her.

As he came closer she noticed the soiled rags which swathed his body, the dirt ingrained in his skin, and finally, when he was standing in front of her, his muddy, mildew-laden smell.

"And what sort of brave trespassing creature are you?" he croaked, looking her up and down, grinning.

"By Setebos, what a dark-eyed beauty. The master will want a look at you."

He commenced a detailed inspection of her person. Troi stood very still, sensing no malice or intent to harm, as he felt the material of her uniform between his fingers and tested it with his teeth, sniffed and gently tugged at her hair, and peered into her eyes as though he were a doctor.

When he was finished he stood back and said, with pride in his cracking voice, "My name is Caliban."

A Shakespearean name. Could he be a Dissenter? she wondered. If he was, the rebellion tottered.

"Mine is Deanna. I am pleased to meet you."

"Down," said Caliban, pointing to the ground.

"Beg your pardon?"

"Affix your hands to the earth."

She didn't comply until she felt a sense of what he wanted to do. He wanted to help her, which probably meant breaking her handcuffs.

Troi sat, and put her hands on the ground behind her. Caliban put a rock under the chain between the handcuffs, then picked up another rock and began smiting the chain.

"Are there others like you here?" Troi asked.

"Other people with different stories. But they're all Dissenters like me."

Troi began to think that she could use help finding her way to CephCom. Caliban didn't seem capable of providing it, but Troi began to wonder if there were other Dissenters, like Amoret, who might. She could only guess at the size of the insurgency, but from what Crichton had said it was a serious threat to his CS.

Troi still felt the Other-worlder aliens, not the Dissenters, were the essential factor for solving her crisis, but she'd take help where she found it.

"Can you take me to the Dissenters?"

"Let me think about it. Why don't you tell me your story first?"

"Well, I can't tell you everything. Is one of your Dissenters named Amoret?"

"Yes. You know her?"

"Sort of."

At that moment he broke the chain of the handcuffs. The metal bands remained on her wrists, but her hands were free. She stood and stretched her arms stiffly.

The beating of wings on air reached her ears. Troi looked up. At first all she saw was a small salmon-colored globule of light, circling near the roof of the cave. As it descended toward her, she made out the shape of a large flying creature, on whose back rode an adolescent girl with long dark hair. In one hand she held one of the light-stones.

The creature skimmed over the pool in circles. Troi realized she was probably seeing the same species of animal she had encountered near the cave entrance. It felt the same empathically. Again, Troi could feel nothing beyond simple animal awareness.

The beast was bigger than a horse. It took no notice of Troi, apparently content to let the long-haired girl guide it with a hand on its leathery neck. The girl glanced at Troi with curiosity.

"Crazy Rhiannon," Caliban said to Troi, "and her haguya-beast. Never happy unless she's flying with it. I like to keep my feet on the gruntworm-infested earth. What about you?"

"I think I know what you mean."

The haguya alighted on a rock near them. Troi noticed that its wings were jointed like a bat's. Its head and beak were reminiscent of a hawk's, but on a grand scale befitting the size of the body. Its eyes were shaped like a falcon's, but large and gold-hued.

Troi turned her attention to the girl called Rhiannon. The rider of the haguya seemed to be about twelve, with skin as pale as milk and a mouthful of crooked teeth.

Quite possibly both of them live in these caves, thought Troi. That would explain her paleness and lack of dental attention, and his smell.

Troi wondered if the girl led a life of loneliness and neglect. She peered into Rhiannon's emotions and found no such isolation, but instead, a warm family-feeling of shared adventures, and at the moment, a breathless exhilaration. The latter feeling had to do with riding the animal, Troi guessed.

Rhiannon seemed to have a special relationship with the haguya. Troi watched her bend close to its ear and whisper, while petting its great head and neck. The haguya tolerated her ministrations, but did not respond in any way Troi could perceive.

"My name's Rhiannon," she said to Troi. "Do you know the name?"

Troi had read the Mabinogi as a child, and remembered that the fictional Welsh Rhiannon was a beautiful grown woman, almost a goddess, who had a special affinity for horses. Rhiannon was clever, fearless, and more than a match for any man, while her horse had mystical powers and could outrun all others.

Troi paused before replying. To say yes was a calculated risk on this planet where fiction was a capital crime. She could feel no threat at all from the girl, however. In fact, Troi felt that Rhiannon wanted her to answer in the affirmative so she could be properly welcomed.

Besides, the girl's mythical name seemed a strong indication that she was a Dissenter, like Caliban and Amoret.

"From Celtic literature, isn't it?" asked Troi.

"That's right." Rhiannon seemed pleased.

"My name's Deanna. Can you take me to your friends?"

"I have to, since you're already here. But you'll like them. You are alone—no family?"

"No one is with me."

"Then you will be part of our family."

Rhiannon smiled broadly, with no embarrassment about her crooked teeth. Troi smiled back. She didn't want to hurt the girl's feelings by declining that last hospitality.

Spurred by some unseen signal from Rhiannon, the haguya flapped its wings mightily and lifted into the air.

"Follow Caliban!" Rhiannon called down at Troi.

Caliban picked up one of the light-stones and, using it as a torch, began to shamble across wet broken rock with surprising speed on his simian legs. Troi had to hurry to keep up with him. He mumbled to himself.

"Be not afeard: the isle is full of noises,
Sounds and sweet airs that give delight and hurt not.
Sometimes a thousand twangling instruments
Will hum about mine ears . . ."

Troi looked behind. Rhiannon and her mount were following, swooping and wheeling giddily among the stalactites.

The haguya, Troi supposed, was an indigenous animal, native to the planet. At any rate, it was not from Earth. It was the very thing the Rampartians said didn't exist—life alien to Earth.

As Troi followed Caliban away from the main lake and down the long natural passage, she noticed a small bubbling spring. Zephyrs of sulfurous, bacteria-ripe air reached her nose. By the glow of

Caliban's light-stone, she could see strange hydra-like animals moving in the waters. Caliban glanced at them.

So there were perhaps many non-Earth species here. And the Dissenters knew about them. The Dissenters had no problem acknowledging alien life. Did they perhaps know about the Other-worlders?

At that moment Troi felt a terrific jolt as she became aware that the Other-worlders were present—still in their own separate realm or universe, yet frighteningly close. Apparently her speculation had summoned them. They seemed to be getting more and more eager for contact with her.

Troi mentally closed them out, straining against the contact with all her will. Maybe she would have to "meet" them again to find out their secrets, but this was not the time for it.

She refocused her attention on the trail under her feet and managed to regain her equilibrium.

"Are we alone here?" she asked Caliban.

"Yes. We have a long way to go to Alastor."

She searched the feelings both of Caliban and Rhiannon, who was riding the haguya above them.

They did not seem aware of the Other-worlders.

As the feeling of the Other-worlders' proximity decreased, and Troi realized she had prevented contact, she reflected that the mystery was apparently still hers to solve. Were she and Crichton the only people on this whole planet who knew about the Other-worlders?

About an hour after Troi, Caliban, and Rhiannon passed the little sulfurous spring, a humming one-eye floated by, moving in the same direction.

The one-eye didn't register life-forms in the spring. It didn't register the nearby light-stones either, as they were powered by indigenous microorganisms. The one-eye couldn't recognize the bioelectric or infrared signatures of alien life; that is, of any kind of life not brought from Earth.

The humans had never discovered the indigenous life on their planet, because it all lived under the surface. Excess radiation from space had forced indigenous species to live and evolve underground. The Rampartians had neutralized the radiation with some simple filter-fields, but no indigenous life had as yet permanently returned to the surface (though over the last hundred years the haguya had developed a habit of making brief flights above ground, always hidden under cover of the darkest nights). And Rampartians didn't venture below the surface, since their underground mining and tunneling was done by machines. On rare occasions when Rampartians accidentally wandered or fell into caves, any resultant memories of indigenous life would be classified as "fictional" by the mind-cleansing computers, and the memories would be deleted.

So now the one-eye went on its way undisturbed, following its mission profile: to find the enclave of the criminals.

Behind it, in the great cavern of the lake, a squad of CS men, newly arrived through a forced-open duct at the ore factory, awaited the results of the reconnaissance, and the signal for attack.

Their eye-rasters were working overtime, blocking out the pool-dwelling animals and the glowing light-stones. The computers assumed that these "fictions" were illusions created by the Dissenters, like cheap magic tricks.

They walked for hours along the same natural string of caverns, one swift-flowing stream.

At a certain point Troi noticed an artificial dam

made from logs and piles of rock. Here the trail diverged from the stream.

After a bit more walking, Caliban stopped so suddenly that Troi almost ran into him. He was holding his light-stone against his body, leaving most of the surroundings in darkness.

The haguya alighted in front of them, and Rhiannon slid off its back. The adolescent girl whispered some words into the animal's ear and it took off and disappeared into the darkness.

Rhiannon turned toward the cave wall nearest them and said, "Alastor."

A voice from the other side of the wall answered, "Caer Sidi. What's today's word?"

"Minotaur."

After a moment, there was a grinding sound, and a cleft opened up in the wall. Rhiannon climbed through, then Caliban pushed Troi through and climbed in after her.

Troi found herself in a large round cave-chamber filled with stalactites and stalagmites. Interspersed among the natural columns were statues, a whole forest of them. The stone figures were variously rough-hewn and finely worked, of many styles made by many different hands. Troi recognized some figures—Polynesian, African, Hindu, Greek. Light-stones, set along the walls, provided insufficient light for the large space, and the statues seemed wrapped in their own shadows.

A giant strongman big enough for a circus moved the door-stone back into position behind Troi, then sat down to chisel with makeshift tools at one of the statues.

Another figure approached.

Troi found his age hard to estimate. He was broad-shouldered and had striking blue eyes, but his beard was flecked with gray and his face was well-weathered. His knee-length tunic was ragged. He spoke to the two who brought Troi.

"Rhiannon, Caliban, give yourself a meal," he said. "Call the Nummo twins to patrol outside."

"I'll wait so we can eat together," Rhiannon said to Troi, in a charmingly bossy tone that indicated Troi had better fulfill the appointment. Then the girl and her soiled companion disappeared into the statue garden.

The bearded man examined Troi with a cool stare.

She could sense his circumspection and self-confidence. A commander of some kind, she guessed. Her mental feelers sensed an indomitable will or guiding principle, strong enough to hold dominion over everything else within him.

"I'm Odysseus," he said.

He waited for her to speak.

"I'm Deanna," she said, and strained to feel his most private emotional strata.

She found a shamed, suffering man.

She was reminded of an incident on Rastaban III. She had been watching a performance of the royal pantomime actors. One of the actors' masks had fallen off, and she'd looked straight into the face of a cruelly beaten, humiliated slave.

Her feeling was quite sorrowful, and it had showed on Troi's face, then and now.

"What's the matter?" asked Odysseus.

"Nothing."

As their eye contact continued a moment longer she became aware of something else in him, a longing. It seemed to be directed at her, though Odysseus showed no outward sign of it. It was subsumed, like his suffering, under some great guiding force, a confidence and strength which she still didn't understand.

Two tall African men, apparently twins, came out of

84

the thicket of statues. They said something to Odysseus in a language Troi didn't recognize. The huge guard moved the door-stone so the twins could leave, then heaved it back in place.

Odysseus watched Troi as if gauging her reaction, and said, "They are the Nummo, named after mythological water-deities of the West African Dogon people."

"I see."

"This gentleman guarding the door is Nikitushka Lomov, the Volga barge-hauler of the Byliny epics."

Troi waited to see where Odysseus was leading.

"Are you a Dissenter?" he asked.

"No, but I assume you are."

"I am."

"Then I can't join your group. I'm a traveler, and I'm looking for my friends who are prisoners of the CS. I would be thankful for any information you might give me that would help. That's all I can say."

"Why aren't you looking among the CS? Why are you here?"

"I knew there were tunnels that would lead me in the right direction. I didn't know there were people down here."

"But you do now. You know the location of Alastor. That means we can't risk letting you go, because you could be a CS informer. You'll have to stay with us, at least for now."

He said it as though he were annoyed, but Troi perceived that he was actually glad she would have to stay.

"I don't think you understand," she said. "Lives depend on me. The CS will execute my people if I don't help them immediately."

"What did they do? Are they Dissenters?"

"No—but they have violated the same laws that your Dissenters do."

"But you still can't tell me who you are."

"That's for your protection as well as mine."

"Then for my protection, you'll have to stay," said Odysseus.

"But you saw my reaction when you mentioned those mythological characters. You were testing me."

"I was. It meant little. The CS have tricked us before; you could be another trick."

"You don't believe I'm a trick. And why should I believe you? If you're Odysseus, where is your ship and crew? And do you have a wife named Penelope, and a son named Telemachos?"

His face grew as hard as the statues behind him.

"I don't want to talk about my wife and son. All you need to know about me is that I'm Odysseus. I'm different than the other people who live here. They're experts in many stories, but I actually am a story."

Now Troi could sense his emotions in greater detail. She understood that the mythical Odysseus persona, with its strength and determination, its quality of being 'never at a loss,' served as a support, a guiding principle on which he leaned the full weight of his life's suffering.

And his suffering had something to do with his wife and son. She'd sensed that quite clearly when he spoke of them.

"If I were from the CS," she said, "would I have asked you that question—with those mythical names?"

"You're tired," he said, ignoring her question. "Let me show you where you can rest."

He started to walk.

Troi didn't let herself become angry, but kept her emotional distance from the situation. She was trapped for the time being; there was no way she could get past that huge guard and the door boulder. Assuming there was no other exit—and she intended to check that if she could—then the best she could do was to figure Odysseus out and get his cooperation.

She put herself in her clinical frame of mind—something she did so often in her life it was reflex—but now, for some reason, it produced in her an unfamiliar aching melancholy. She didn't stop to think about her unusual mood, and kept her mind on the task at hand.

"Wait. Odysseus didn't imprison anybody," she said. "Why can you?"

"He trapped, in his own house, those who plotted against him," said Odysseus. "Anyway, even if I let you leave, you'd stand no chance on your own. No chance without our help, and for that you'd have to become a Dissenter."

He started to walk into the crowd of stone figures.

He looked back and saw that she hadn't moved.

"Are you going to stand there all night?" he laughed.

She followed, wondering if he ever let this mask of self-confidence fall, and if he did, would the man beneath be any more manageable?

They proceeded up a little stair and left the great chamber of statues. Neither of them noticed the lens staring from the small hole in the ceiling of the stairwell.

The one-eye had homed in on the infrared warmth from Alastor, and found its way from the main cave passage to this vantage point. It had hovered near the hole like a bee, the rocks around it blocking its hum but also its ability to intercept brain waves. Still, its lens and shotgun-microphone had gathered a lot of good data.

Now it floated away from the hole, back to the main passage outside Alastor. There, in the shadows of the mighty stalactites, it reported back by radio transmission to the waiting CS squad.

Odysseus showed Troi into a private little cave-room and left her there to rest. After a few minutes she snuck out, and, finding no guard, wandered along a narrow passage, looking for an escape option. Instead, she found Odysseus' own cave-room.

He wasn't aware she was peering in at him. He was standing in front of a wall papered with old torn illustrations and book covers, images from the story of Odysseus: the Cyclops Polyphemus, the Trojan Horse, a Bronze Age many-oared ship in a dark sea.

Near him, on a stone table, was a bowl of water. He broke his gaze away from the pictures, dipped his hands in the water, and splashed the water on his face. Then he stared some more at the picture of the Bronze Age ship.

Troi perceived his feelings. She understood that he was nourishing his Odysseus character. The sensation of the water on his face helped him to imagine himself on the many-oared ship.

So this is how he sustains the Odysseus persona, she thought. He uses all these accoutrements as artificial memory-props. She'd once read about method actors doing much the same thing.

He picked up a large rock and hefted it repeatedly over his head. A sort of strength-exercise, Troi assumed. She realized he would have to work constantly to maintain his heroic musculature.

Suddenly Troi heard the low voices of Dissenters coming up the passage. She stole unobserved back to her room.

Chapter Eight

"SHIP'S LOG, Lieutenant Geordi La Forge recording. We have lost contact with all members of the away team, because of electronic jamming on the planet.

"I'm not prepared to send any more people to the planet's surface until we have an idea where the original team is, and we can guarantee countermeasures against the jamming. Hard to know how much the Rampartians stole from the minds of the *Enterprise*'s crewmembers, and maybe the minds of the *Huxley*'s too, but as commanding officer I'm making a worst-case assumption. So any countermeasures we already have may be anticipated by the Rampartians. My Engineering staff is therefore working on new modifications to away team equipment.

"We have no recourse in using the *Enterprise*'s main weaponry. Crichton contacted me and said that if we fired on any of his ships or anything on his planet, he would harm the captain.

"Meanwhile, the one-eyes on the ship have escaped from Security containment and are spreading out. I'm working with my staff to find a way to counter them."

Geordi rubbed his forehead. The prosthetic VISOR that covered his blind eyes and gave him visual perception—but not normal human sight—was making his head throb. The omnipresent pain seemed worse than usual.

Looking around at good old Engineering seemed a comfort, although Geordi's VISOR-acquired view of his environment would look, to a sighted person, something like a video-thermographic version of a surrealist painting.

But this was no place from which to command the ship. He touched his communicator.

"La Forge to Worf."

"Worf here."

"My cabin fever's running high."

"It is still not safe for you to attempt transit to the bridge. The route cannot be guaranteed secure from one-eyes."

"How about the battle bridge?"

"Same problem. I can't ensure your safety anywhere outside Engineering."

"Worf . . . we have to balance the risks. Some risk will be necessary."

"The consequences," the deep Klingon voice said, gaining a decibel, "if a one-eye were to scan you, or kill you, are unacceptable. You are the only key officer whom the one-eyes have not yet scanned. You have more engineering knowledge than anyone on this ship. Your—"

"Okay, Worf."

"Thank you. One moment, I'm getting some new reports."

While he waited, Geordi's VISOR showed him a sudden increase in heat of a hundredth of a degree reflected off a nearby bulkhead. Someone or something was coming into the room.

The constant threat provided by the intruders on

the ship had made him jumpy. He found himself rising quickly out of his chair and turning to confront the visitant.

"Chops!" he said.

For that was who had entered. Dorothy "Chops" Taylor, Geordi's most valued maintenance engineer.

As always, she looked a little wild. Her hair was as freeflowing as regulations permitted and there were hints of improbable colors in it, along with the first hint of gray. Her hands, with their metallic finger pads, flexed with everpresent, almost manic energy. The unconventional picture was completed by the dark visor which covered her eyes.

Chops was blind. Because of the particular type of congenital damage to her brain, she could not be fitted with a functional VISOR like Geordi's. Instead, she "saw" through the sensor pads on her fingers.

Her freewheeling personality was a deliberate attempt to offset the despair of her childhood.

Nearly forty years ago a race known as the Sadalsuudians, from Beta Aquarius V, made exploratory contacts with ships from the Federation. The Sadalsuudians appeared friendly. What they really wanted was not diplomatic relations but some living human reproductive cells. After the Sadalsuudians had stolen the cells they wanted, they withdrew to their own planet, got the human sperm and human egg together in vitro, and grew a human embryo as a means of observing alien genetic principles, though they had a poor understanding of genetics in general, including their own.

The result of the experiment was Dorothy Taylor. She turned out blind. The Sadalsuudians hadn't intended that, but they treated her as cruelly as their own native blind. On their planet, there was a huge population of birth-defect handicapped natives who had been forced into underclass status.

Dorothy Taylor was exhibited publicly. She was degraded as a new kind of "inferior" being, an alien with a "mutation."

But one of the scientists who studied her saw things differently than other Sadalsuudians. He was far ahead of his time. He was the only one who had realized that the first life on his planet, the first tiny chain of nucleotides and sugars, must have been a kind of mutation on the random patterns around it, and that all subsequent evolution was also a result of mutation—of some organisms accidentally turning out a bit differently than their forebears and finding an advantage in their difference. If there had been no mutations on the first form, then all life on Beta Aquarius V would be nothing more than tiny replicating chains of nucleotides and sugars, no different than the very first. Life itself was mutation.

The scientist had tried to publish his findings but was ignored. The Sadalsuudians couldn't bear to relinquish their attitudes about their "mutated" undercaste. The scientist found he couldn't change these attitudes of ignorance but he managed to set one handicapped person free. He turned Dorothy back over to the Federation during a diplomatic contact.

When Geordi met Dorothy she was completing a five-year voyage as a maintenance engineer aboard the U.S.S. *Feynman*. Her reputation had preceded her, and Geordi took the opportunity to transfer her onto his staff.

When he was much younger he might have been uncomfortable working or socializing with another physically challenged person, particularly a blind one, as it would draw attention to his own condition. But as he became an adult, he lost that self-consciousness. He was now at ease with his blindness and with being around other blind persons. Transferring Chops Taylor to his staff was an expression of that maturity. It

didn't hurt, of course, that she was the best maintenance engineer he'd ever met.

The name Chops came from her hobby. She played
28-string duotronic-enhanced guitar. "Chops," in the
earliest rock-and-roll days, meant the ability to play
well—a hot musician was said to "have chops."

Chops Taylor was a phenomenally good musician,
easily good enough to go professional. In fact, she had
been on some tours with a band that included a
boar-faced Tellarite drummer, a tall blue Andorian
bassist, and an elegant Vulcan on keyboard.

She didn't perceive her guitar in the normal visual
manner. She formed a spatial image of it through the
information near her fingertips. The guitar filled her
entire field of consciousness. She saw each nuance of
string and fret with microscopic clarity. She saw
things other musicians didn't see, like heat and har-
monic vibration. Above all, her manual dexterity was
unmatched, both as a musician and as a maintenance
engineer. She lived through her hands.

Now, Chops came over to Geordi and put a sensor-
augmented hand on his face; her way of seeing him.

"You're looking tired, sir. Lot of fatigue in the
forehead, the jaw, hmmm, down on the neck . . ."

"You're tellin' me. How's it going on those communicators?"

She held up a partially-assembled communicator
with her other hand.

"Incredible," said Geordi. "State-of-the-Chops."

"And guaranteed un-jammable. All I have to do is
the final assembly."

Geordi didn't let himself indulge in relief. The
special communicators might allow him to send another team down to the planet, but there would be no
guarantee they would be able to find the first team. His
guts would be grinding until the moment he got the
captain, Riker, Data, and Troi back, safe and sound,

on the ship. And until the moment he got rid of the damned one-eyes. Right now his stomach felt like it had been tied in a reef knot.

He was also tired as hell, having been up for a good twenty-four hours. Even if he had no time to sleep himself, he could at least exert command authority and make her sleep.

"Chops, you've been up as long as I have. Don't you think you should take some quick winks before you go on?"

"Why? I'm toolin' along fine."

"Our communicator task is only one of several. When you're finished with it I'm going to put you on the team that's devising weapons to use against the one-eyes. Somewhere in there you're going to have to get some sleep."

There was enough sternness in his voice to convey what amounted to an order.

"Okay, but I'll do it here. I slept in worse places when I played in clubs on the road."

She went and sat on the floor, in a corner, and fell asleep instantly.

"Lieutenant La Forge."

Worf's voice. Geordi put his hand over his communicator and tiptoed into the next console bay.

"La Forge here."

"How many other crewpersons are in Engineering at the moment?" asked Worf.

"Five besides myself."

"Two of the one-eyes have split off from the others and appear to be working their way over to you. They may attempt to enter Engineering itself."

"Worf, how are they getting past us like this? At least some of our security measures should be stopping them—at least once in a while."

"We've been observing them whenever possible,"

said Worf. "It seems that of the two heading in your direction, one is specialized; a kind of locksmith. It uses electromagnetic energy to enter codes and open doors. It already knows many secret procedures—because of information gathered from the minds on the *Enterprise,* or from the *Huxley,* or both. Its companion is a guard, a one-eye armed like the others. It's been fending off attacks from our security people."

Geordi saw that poor Chops had woken up in the next room, and was standing, leaning unsteadily against the wall. The alarming conversation he'd been having with Worf had roused her. She'd gotten no more than a minute of sleep, but her eternally active hands were flexing, ready to be used.

"Sir," said Worf, meanwhile, "I have an idea how we can take out that locksmith one-eye."

There was little navigation for Wesley to do at the moment. The *Enterprise,* surrounded by Rampartian ships, automatically held the synchronous position Wesley had set above Rampart. As he looked at the curving blue horizon on his viewscreen, and simultaneously kept an eye on the console under his hands and an ear open to the soft crew-talk around him, an unsettling memory danced around in his mind.

It had been about a week ago.

The visit to the Holodeck had been Shikibu's idea. She had programmed it for the rock garden at Ryoanji, Kyoto, in a softly falling morning rain.

They sat on the floor under an ancient wooden eave. After Wesley unsuccessfully tried several times to start a conversation, they lapsed into quiet. Wesley realized she wanted it this way, as usual. He became aware of the complexity of sounds created by the rain falling gently on the bamboo and the conifers, on the ancient tile roofs and on the rocks and sand of the garden itself.

Wesley couldn't tell if the islands of rugged rocks in the large rectangle of raked sand had been there before the garden was built. The whole garden, in fact, was a careful blending of the works of man with the spontaneous works of nature, crafted so that the visitor could not tell where one left off and the other began.

Beside him, Shikibu was gazing at the garden. Her hair was the blackest he'd ever seen. It fell about her shoulders in an arrangement that told both of deliberate design and the chance of wind and movement.

He felt a sudden impulse to touch the fine black hair. For quite a while he sat there next to her, several times almost doing it, but always chickening out. She could embarrass him; she could be offended, scold him like a child and walk out. She could laugh, and tell him that he was clumsy, that he was doing it all wrong. Or maybe she would respond with some wild scary Kama pleasuring technique he'd never even dreamed of.

Dumb thoughts, he told himself. Those things were all out of character for her. And all he would do was touch her hair. That was no crime. They were friends. Stop stalling and just do it.

He reached out and let his fingers run through the soft jet-black hair, just once. Her head moved slightly, in what felt to Wesley like a reflex. But still she stared at the garden and said nothing.

Puzzled, Wesley withdrew his hand.

Shikibu got up and asked the Holodeck to show her the door. Wesley followed her out and she bade him a short, polite good-bye. She did not seem to be offended.

He was just as mystified as he had been by her wordless demonstration of Zen archery postures. He had the definite feeling she was trying to tell him something, but he had no idea what it was.

It had been the last time he'd seen Shikibu.

Just a few moments ago, as he sat at his station on the bridge, he'd heard his mother relay her report on the status of her patients in sickbay, among them Shikibu. It seemed Shikibu was sleeping under sedation, and had no permanent injury.

Now he stared at the bridge viewscreen; at the curve of Rampart, and the thick nebula beyond it, veiling Rampart from the rest of the cosmos.

Wesley wasn't sure if he were in love with Shikibu. But he began to think—what if he were, and what if both of them lived on Rampart? It was a love-against-adversity scenario. He imagined the two of them on the run, hiding in abandoned buildings or alpine wilderness.

What exactly did the sexes do with each other on Rampart, he wondered. How could they fit sex and love into their lives of rigorous precision and fact? It would be like a watchmaker trying to build an apple.

Maybe a Rampartian would tell his intended, "My attraction to you is expressed in this bar graph, using fractional courting algorithms for a male and female at sea level, noon standard time."

And she would say, "Thank you. You have just increased by two percent the secretions of my endocrine glands."

Wesley saw they would have to reject all those things which were impossible to put into words or even thoughts but which, for him, made women—like Shikibu—into magic.

The Rampartians would have to block it all out. Make it into two animals mating, or two machines docking.

In his mind he pictured the one-eye that shot

Shikibu, and the other ones running rampant on the ship. He hated them; he hated the people that made them, because they thought they knew everything.

In Wesley's field, physics, such people retarded the growth of knowledge, and were invariably wrong anyway. The great discoveries had always been made by those with the most imagination.

Behind him he could hear Worf talking, relaying to Geordi a plan for neutralizing some of the one-eyes. Tactical stuff, none of his business really. But he itched to participate somehow.

Some time ago, Dr. Crusher had analyzed Security Chief Worf's musculature and found the muscle tissues so strong, efficient, and fast to respond, that she had wanted to write an article about him.

"You'll appear in only the best medical journals, I promise," she had said with a wry smile.

"A Klingon does not submit to the fussing and coddling of doctors," he had replied gruffly, getting off the table, impatient to get back to work. "One is bad enough, but all the doctors in the Federation—the dishonor would be unthinkable."

"Some football scout might get it off the data nets and decide to try you out," replied the pleasant, auburn-haired doctor. "You'd probably make an ideal tight end."

"I agree, except the opposing players would not survive the intensity of my play."

"I was just joking, Worf."

"I was not."

Now, Worf ran, the footfalls of his six-and-a-half-foot body booming along the corridor. His eyes shone with the adamantine flame of a Klingon entering combat. There was no greater glory for Worf than defending his ship, his crewmates, and the Starfleet organization, which had rescued him when he was a child.

He also knew in the back of his mind that everything that happened to him now could later figure in his own secret attempt at personal glory, his clandestine quest made possible by Oleph and Una.

But that would come later.

Now, entering a service crawl space, he reviewed what he would have to do inside. He would station himself at the intersection with a certain Jefferies tube the one-eyes would probably use to get to Engineering. There he would wait in ambush.

The plan depended on the armed one-eye preceding the locksmith one-eye as they made their way along the tube. He and Geordi were of the same opinion— the soldier would go first to protect its unarmed specialist.

When the soldier one-eye passed his hiding place Worf would move a metal cover-plate into the Jefferies tube, separating the soldier one-eye from its companion. Worf was then to touch the unarmed locksmith with an electric probe, giving it a healthy megawatt to think about.

The Klingon felt inclined to take on both of the intruding robots right now, no matter what his odds against the armed one, but Geordi had flat-out refused such a suggestion. Stopping the locksmith would be enough for him.

As Worf crawled along the conduit-lined crawl space, his communicator came to life. No voice, just an audible signal—three clicks—from Lieutenant Regina Wentz, who had the bridge. It meant the one-eyes had been observed, and were on their way.

Worf moved quickly on hands and knees, and stopped at the plate that separated him from the Jefferies tube.

He heard two clicks from his communicator. It

meant the one-eyes were proceeding toward the ambush point.

He looked at the short-range sensor he'd brought with him, which now had an exact fix on both intruders. Twenty meters for the leader; the other was at twenty-four. He put his hand on the control for the cover.

Ten meters. Worf felt the wine-dark Klingon combat hormones pumping into his blood. His muscles itched for immediate use.

Five. Two. Zero, said the rangefinder. The first one had passed.

Worf touched the control under his hand. The cover moved.

Suddenly he saw white, and heard a sustained roar. It was as though a bomb had gone off in his head. His limbs refused to work. His hand fell from the control, stopping the cover in a halfway position. His other hand dropped his electric prod, which fell, irrevocably lost, into a cluster of conduits, but he was only dimly aware of the loss, or of anything else.

It was Worf's bad luck that, commencing a short time ago, the one-eyes had started emitting blasts of radiation as they had moved down the Jefferies tube, to prevent the ambushes they had decided were likely.

The metal plate that would have protected Worf was stuck halfway down, leaving him vulnerable.

Detecting a hidden living consciousness, whose brain waves were too distant to be decoded, the soldier one-eye emitted another blast of radiation before going behind the cover for a close-up inspection. The radiation dose was measured to incapacitate a human for several hours but render him available for brain scan. The soldier one-eye wanted to know what other plans might be afoot.

The second blast knocked Worf out completely. But his Klingon nervous system had responded a bit differently than a human's. Its water molecules hadn't been vibrated as violently. It was already recovering.

The soldier one-eye backed up and joined its companion. Like two curious boys peeking over a backyard fence, they hovered half hidden by the metal cover. Their antennae bent toward Worf. Their lenses zoomed and focused with little servo-motor whirs.

They knew no context for identifying Worf. His brain waves could be received but not accurately decoded. Aliens, the programming of the one-eyes told them, did not exist, but this being in front of them was close enough to Homo sapiens' form to be classified as a strange kind of mutant deformed human. They would follow the procedure for humans—the only procedure they knew.

The locksmith one-eye stayed back, while the soldier one-eye moved right up to Worf's head for a scan of his brain waves.

The slow, non-rhythmic "delta" activity in Worf's brain resembled human coma or deep sleep. But the soldier was misreading the signals. It could not tell that Worf was coming around; did not know that Worf was enraged, and that the proper response to an enraged Klingon was to leave the area immediately.

Worf's arms moved with explosive speed. He grabbed the one-eye at its base, getting a good grip on its antigrav housing, turning the one-eye so it couldn't fire its radiation directly at him. Although not all of his strength had returned, he could feel his arms overcome the pull of the antigravs.

The one-eye fired a blast from its gun, bouncing the radiation helter-skelter around the crawl space. Worf absorbed some of it, but managed to hurl the one-eye against the wall with a sparking clang. It slipped away from his hands like a darting fish. He aimed a prodigious kick at it, sending it tumbling back over the side of the metal cover and into the Jefferies tube, where its unarmed partner had already retreated to safety.

Worf felt himself losing consciousness. In a confused state, he dimly understood a duty: Geordi would insist that he preserve his life. Another part of him, a Klingon part, wanted to keep fighting and die with glory, but at this moment duty took the fore. He managed to tab the control and close the metal cover, separating him from the one-eyes. Then he blacked out completely.

In the Jefferies tube, the one-eyes resumed their progress toward Engineering. The crew on the bridge were able to tell, through the life-monitor in Worf's communicator pin, that Worf was injured and unconscious. They advised Geordi that the one-eyes had not been stopped, and that he should prepare his department for their arrival.

The little storage cubicle was not made for storing living beings.

That was much in evidence to the six who were presently in self-imposed cellarage. The insufficient oxygen (all six were oxygen-breathers), the excessive body heat, and the awkward positions they had to maintain made for much misery.

The construction of this door might save our lives by hiding our brain waves from the one-eyes, thought Geordi, but it might also kill us by starving us for air.

He winced as he listened to the destruction from outside. Wildly arcing electrical energy, frying circuits, warping and shuddering panels.

He tried to discern some pattern to what the one-eyes were doing, but found he was baffled. He wondered if Chops might understand more. Through his VISOR sight he looked at the patterns of warmth and cold on the surface of her head, as if that could tell him something. Seen in infrared, Chops was very psychedelic. Suddenly he felt the whole situation so absurd that he had to chortle. He was deliriously punchy. He wanted to hug Chops or slap her bottom.

A word floated before his eyes. Hypoxia.

What the hell was that? He started to laugh again.

Oh yes, lack of oxygen to the brain. Delirium. Every Starfleet crewperson knew how to recognize it. His training now made him act automatically.

He picked up the hand of Skoel, the Vulcan ensign next to him, and in a silent gesture, put it at the juncture of his own shoulder and neck, then at the same spot on the other crewpersons in the closet.

Skoel, the Vulcan, had been anticipating such a decision. The most logical one. The only possible way to save oxygen.

One by one he nerve-pinched all of the humans in the closet, rendering them unconscious, a state in which they would use the minimum amount of oxygen.

Skoel then put himself into a trance and his green Vulcan blood slowed until it was barely moving.

Skoel roused them many minutes later. Wentz had called from the bridge; the one-eyes had left Engineering and were pursuing new opportunities for ship sabotage.

The six of them spilled gasping out of the closet. The air was thick with acrid vapors, but to the six it tasted delicious.

Chops quickly went from panel to panel, her sensitized fingertips "seeing" the scorched circuitry in microscopic detail.

Geordi went right to the main status board. It had enough function left to tell him that the warp engines were in bad shape. They could still produce power, but not much, and not safely. He'd have to take over manual control of the mix itself, the temperature and pressure controls, and the frequency range of the emissions.

The one-eyes had known what they were doing. They'd disabled the ship to the point where Geordi could barely defend it and keep it in orbit. All he could rely on now was impulse power, and if that went, forget it.

Skoel set to work securing the entrances to Engineering but found they were already secure. The one-eyes, not detecting anyone inside, had closed the doors and shorted the switches to keep everyone out.

Geordi touched his communicator.

"La Forge to bridge. Report."

"The one-eyes that just left your area are on their way up to the impulse engines," said Wentz. "We have no way to stop them."

"Damn it!" Geordi cursed. "Do we ever need a deus ex machina! Has any help gotten to Worf yet?"

"He's been evacuated to sickbay. Doctor Crusher says he'll be out cold for a few more hours at least."

"Let me know when he wakes."

He saw that Chops and the others were already into repairs on the most vital controls. At best it would take many hours. Now he began to see his crew's lack of sleep as a critical problem, and he knew that he and Chops were the worst off. But nothing could be done about it.

At Science Station Two on the bridge, Wesley faced the small display screen.

He knew Geordi had his staff working on the one-eye problem, but he wanted to contribute something useful if he could. He decided to go to the heart of the matter.

"Computer, I'll be using the particle physics library."

"Would you like to start where you left off?"

He didn't remember what he'd last used the library for, and was not yet sure where he wanted to start.

"Fine."

The screen showed him the Dance of Shiva. Underneath it scrolled a list of metaphorical references to the subject by physicists over the last five hundred years.

"Oh . . ." he said, "not what I'm looking for now. Show me some high-energy proton collisions."

Chapter Nine

"THIS BIBLE SETS FORTH the only true religion. All other religions and philosophies are hereby declared false and criminal.

"Everything contained in this Bible has been verified as factual truth, and is to be accepted as such, and in no other way, by the reader. Any interpretation of this Bible as metaphor, literature, or mythology is expressly forbidden.

"Violators will be subject to the full penalties as determined by the Council of Truth and enforced by Cephalic Security.

"To report criminal violations call this number toll free . . ."

Picard leafed farther into the book. It was recognizable as a Rampartian revision of the Christian Bible. The Rampartians had annotated it throughout with "proofs" as to the "factual" nature of its "events."

What confused people, he thought—they take what should be understood as a metaphorical story and they try to make it into science and history. They see a hand pointing a moral direction, and instead of looking to see where it points, they spend their time sucking on its finger and declaring to themselves, "It's a finger, a finger, a finger."

Picard closed the book solemnly and put it back where he had found it, on the table by his cot.

He looked up at the camera lens and brain wave antennae in the upper corner of the small white room.

That's right, he thought defiantly. You heard me correctly.

Or maybe they hadn't. Maybe his thought was trapped somewhere, like lint, by a metaphor-filter.

He lay back on the bed, tired but unable to sleep.

The white room that now served as his home was as stark as a prison cell but also reminded him of a primitive mental hospital. It made him think of some of the sadistic "mental health" practices of centuries long past on Earth, the time of lobotomies, forced electroshock, "lock them away and forget them."

The bed had thick straps and buckles dangling from its frame. On the wall above it were several jacks for electronic gear. The lens and antennae in the upper corner were similar to those carried by the one-eyes. Built into the wall at the foot of the bed was a video screen, which was on all day and dimmed automatically at night. There appeared to be no way for the room's occupant to shut it off at will.

So far as Picard could tell, the screen showed only news reports and commercials. He guessed he was seeing the same broadcasts that all other Rampartians watched. A studio anchorman who looked like a store mannequin introduced each news piece. The anchorman never speculated; the stories were always factual.

"Yesterday," the anchorman now intoned, "CS Major Ferris captured three armed criminal conspirators."

The name of Ferris caught Picard's attention.

"The incident occurred at the old Dumont ore factory."

Wide shot of the interior of the factory: blue-washed maze of ducts and catwalks. A group of white-suited CS men pointed to something up on a catwalk.

Close-up: a man on the catwalk fired a phaser.

Picard leapt to his feet. The man was William Riker, his own first officer.

Riker seemed desperate as he spun around and fired again.

Flattering close-up of Ferris: The stalwart Major took two steps forward, looked upward, raised his pistol. With two-handed combat grip, he fired.

Medium angle of Riker: He fell from the catwalk, tumbling toward the camera.

Tight close-up of Ferris: the very picture of avenging justice, the "good guy" that won, the military man that did his duty in the face of whatever danger, that risked his life for the sake of those snug at home, watching from couches and around dinner tables.

Long shot, exterior: Under the blue nebula-shrouded night sky, Ferris led his men toward two assault hovercraft with rotors that now began to turn. The men carried three bodies.

With a sick feeling in his gut, Picard got as close to the screen as he could, straining to see detail.

One of the bodies was Riker. The heads of the other two were hidden by several walking CS men, but Picard knew by the uniform and shape of one that it was surely Data. The third wore dark clothes, not Starfleet issue, and appeared to be female.

Medium angle: Ferris climbed into the copilot's seat of one of the hovercraft.

Dramatic long shot: The two white craft were aloft, their red running lights blinking as they flew toward the dark horizon.

Back to the anchorman: His face clearly showed that he was moved by what he had just witnessed. He paused, as if the sight of such heroism had put a lump in his throat and he needed to compose himself. After an appropriate wait, he moved on to his next piece.

"The CS has developed a new-generation truth-inducing drug which will be used in the field when factual information is being withheld by criminals. Deployment will come within the next day. Our Tom Martin was at CephCom today and has the details . . ."

Picard sat slowly down at the foot of the bed.

So Riker and Data had come, presumably to search for him. The sight of their limp bodies was devastating. They were his family, or the closest thing he had to one.

He swallowed his emotions. He reminded himself that the announcer had said "captured," not "killed." He himself had been captured even though he could have been killed. Wouldn't all of them be most useful alive, as hostages?

He looked up at the antennae again. Strange feeling —he could think about his crew, his ship, his own imprisonment, and even about trying to escape, and the CS could listen in to all of it.

The single windowless door opened noiselessly. Picard tensed. He felt an animal reflex for escape poise him for action.

An armed and helmeted CS orderly, followed by an armed guard, came in with a tray of food. Their eyes, partially visible behind the glowing twin rasters on their visors, watched Picard warily, and the guard kept a gun trained on him.

"I wish to communicate with my ship," said Picard. "Tell Crichton that. And tell him if he and I talk we can settle our misunderstanding and the *Enterprise* won't have to retaliate."

The orderly set the tray down, and the two of them backed out, without a word, and shut the door.

Picard had to begin considering escape as an option. He feared that if he couldn't reason with Crichton and he was forced to remain here, then the Rampartians, with their brain wave technology, might be able to alter his thoughts and actions. He could be forced against his will to betray his own ship.

He looked again at the camera and brain wave antennae. Planning an escape was impossible; the antennae would pick up the plan. The only feasible options would have to occur as spontaneous inspirations. He would have to act on them without deliberation.

"Deal with that," he said to the antennae.

Picard watched the screen for another hour but there was nothing more about Riker or Data, and though he half expected to see it, there was nothing about himself.

As he watched more news images of Ferris and other CS officers in their exploits, he reflected that here on Rampart, where fiction was a capital crime, the people were forced to twist their own psychological needs and cast real-life public figures as pseudo-mythical heroes. Ferris was not, in reality, a hero, he was a monkey who did what he was told, but because the people of Rampart had no other outlet for their minds' unconscious needs, they made Ferris a hero (after all, he looked like one) and the Dissenters an evil force for the hero to vanquish.

On Earth, in the present twenty-fourth century, a man like Ferris would be an object of ridicule, thought Picard. He had been satirized there for three thousand years; even in classical Greek comedy the goose-stepping soldier had been made into a buffoon.

Picard's door opened again. Three CS men and a one-eye entered.

The CS men all had weapons drawn.

"Time for your sentencing," said one of them.

Picard was handcuffed and led out of the room.

He made them stop.

"I must speak to Crichton," he demanded.

There was no reply; the CS men simply heaved him along.

They flanked him as they took him along several hallways lined with cells like the one he had just left.

At one point Picard noticed a group of CS men with a woman who also wore a CS uniform, though on hers the logo was red rather than blue. She was unarmed, and wheeled a cart full of electronic gear.

Picard had already noticed that in CephCom certain jobs were reserved for men while others were only for women, as though here equality between the sexes had still not been accepted. He supposed the Rampartian settlers all left Earth before equality was achieved, and once they were here, no speculative thought on changing the situation had been allowed.

The equipment on the woman's cart had switches, meters, and CRT tubes. It could have been anything. On top was a rounded cap-like dome with color-coded wires sprouting from its electrodes. He was sure the cap was meant to fit on a human head and somehow interface with a human brain.

As it happened, the group with the CS woman entered a room in front of Picard and his guards. As Picard was brought past, he stutter-stepped to slow himself and was able to catch a glimpse of an adolescent girl on the bed, restrained with straps. As the cart was wheeled in she cried out hysterically. Her panic washed over Picard in a wave. It made the fine hairs on his neck stand on end. Her cry reminded him of an animal caught in a trap.

111

The CS men roughly pulled Picard back into line with them.

As they continued to walk, Picard began to understand the staggering size of the place. The corridors went on forever, filled with CS officers, soldiers, administrators, and one-eyes traveling alone or in patrols of a dozen. He saw doors inscribed "Psychosurgery Division," and "Interrogation," and "Chemical Corps."

Two high-ranking officers emerged out of the latter and walked along behind Picard and his escorts. He could catch only parts of their conversation.

". . . new kind of pharmacological attack on the brain . . ."

". . . scopolamine, methamphetamine, atropine sulfate . . . classic goofball effect . . . provide every officer a truth-kit to use in the field . . ."

Picard's guards brought him to a sudden stop. There was a commotion ahead. A CS soldier had suddenly been surrounded by a dozen one-eyes. Within instants the soldier was arrested and taken away.

The incident confirmed something Picard had already guessed. He'd noticed antennae and cameras mounted along the corridors. Now he knew what they were for: One of the CS's tasks was to spy on its own staff. Subversion could happen anywhere, even here. Maybe especially here, where the CS was in constant contact with the enemy—the Dissenters they'd arrested.

Picard's forced march ended in front of black double doors. A nameplate read "Director of Cephalic Security." The CS guards who stood on either side opened the doors and Picard was taken in.

Crichton was shuffling papers on his desk. He was wearing a protective helmet but the rasters were clear enough for Picard to see his eyes.

Picard was made to stand at a spot in front of the

112

desk, like a naughty schoolboy. He noticed that in this spot he was covered by several camera lenses and antennae situated along the walls.

Crichton stood. He seemed to be avoiding Picard's stare.

He read aloud from a document.

"For the high crimes specified in the Code of the Council of Truth, pursuant to and as a result of documentation gathered and on record, the detainee before me, Jean-Luc Picard, is hereby sentenced to death, such sentence to be imposed without delay."

Crichton sat down. Not once had he actually looked Picard in the eye.

"That's all," he said, and began to collect some of the papers on the desk.

The guards began to pull Picard toward the double doors.

Picard dug in his heels.

"Wait!" he cried, twisting around to see Crichton. "You have two of my officers as prisoners—what's going to happen to them? What is happening on my ship?"

"Your two officers, your ship's crew, will all receive the same penalty as they have committed the same crime. Everyone on Rampart who commits that crime is likewise penalized."

Picard's face reddened with rage. "Don't you have trials here? Aren't people told the nature of the charges against them? Don't they have a right to defend themselves?"

The CS men pulled him again.

"Get off of me," he growled.

"Let him stay a moment," said Crichton. He still looked at the papers on his desk. Sweat trickled down the scars on his mask-like face.

Finally Crichton looked up partway, at the level of Picard's chest. Picard had the impression Crichton was hiding something, which eye contact might make him betray.

If I provoke him, thought Picard, perhaps I can make him reveal something, or entrap him. If fiction is a capital crime here, then Crichton can't actually lie to me.

Crichton began to speak. The words emerged from his mouth like hard, dry pellets.

"We deal only in facts here," he said. "Irrefutable facts. For what, then, do we need trials, lawyers, or judges? A person either committed a crime or they did not. There are no ambiguities for argument. All crimes are clearly documented on this planet; that is what Cephalic Security is for. If you were to commit a crime right now, as you can see," he said, pointing in an arc at all the lenses and antennae, "your crime would be a matter of record. In fact, your crimes were a matter of record as soon as our one-eyes first intercepted your brain waves, on your ship. This sentencing is merely a completion of the file."

"Then sentence me," said Picard, "and let my crewmembers and my ship go. I'm the captain, I'm responsible for their actions. They were just following my orders. You have no cause to prosecute them."

"You are all guilty of high crimes," said Crichton. "It's a matter of record."

"And exactly what are these high crimes?"

"You already know."

"Maybe I just want you to look at me and say it. The crime of having an imagination and using it? The crime of speculating, of creating, of thinking at all, is that it?"

"We manage to think quite a bit. Enough to get along without the help of anyone from Earth, which was in a pretty sorry state when my ancestors left."

"What you do is not thinking any more than the pronouncements of a mynah bird. And I'll tell you something else, Crichton. Earth is in fine shape, and we got there by doing exactly the opposite of all this. Crichton! Aren't you going to look me in the eye just once?"

Picard advanced a step. The CS men grabbed him roughly. One of them raised his hand to strike.

"No," said Crichton. "Don't harm his body."

As if unable to resist some inner temptation, Crichton lifted his eyes to meet Picard's.

It was just a quick glance, and then he returned his attention to his paperwork. He immediately went pale, and then grabbed his head with both hands, pressing as if to keep it from exploding. Through clenched teeth he groaned, "Get him out of here."

As the CS roughly shoved Picard out of the office, he heard someone from inside say, "Call the medical staff!"

"No!" he heard Crichton reply. "I'm going to see my own doctor."

Picard was taken under heavy guard back to the little white cell. On the way he tried to make sense out of his interview with Crichton—but couldn't. He didn't believe all persons who used their imaginations on this planet could be executed without trial. Eventually there would be too few people to keep the machines running. Eventually there would be no people at all.

By the time he was locked back in his room, he thought he might have hit upon the answer. It wasn't simple capital punishment, it was worse.

Riker awoke in a small white room. He had a devastating headache. Gradually the memory of the fight at the ore factory came back to him. He figured that the radiation gun Ferris shot him with was responsible for the pain. It was so bad he couldn't move a muscle.

He lay for a long time, watching news reports on the video screen. He was in one of them; it was a piece on his capture at the ore factory. And there was Ferris and the CS.

The funny thing was, the report had been edited in such a way as to distort what had happened. Riker saw how he was shown unfavorably while Ferris was presented as a hero.

Riker thought perhaps he should complain about it. The idea made him laugh in a gallows-humor sort of way. Laughing made his head hurt worse and he had to stop.

The pain was still very bad when the CS came and took him. He was led past Crichton's office to a smaller door inscribed with Major Ferris' name.

Inside, Major Ferris, helmeted and in white dress uniform with twinkling medals, sat behind his desk.

Riker gritted his teeth and tried to speak.

"Where—" he began, but stopped as the pain flared like a welding torch burning into his head.

"Keep your mouth shut," said Ferris. "The prisoner isn't allowed to speak until sentence is read."

Ferris then sentenced Riker to death, using the same words Crichton had used with Picard.

"And my friends?" asked Riker slowly, with great effort.

"I'm not required to speak to you about them, or anything else," Ferris said stiffly.

Riker pictured Picard, Troi, and Data in small white rooms awaiting execution. He thought how disappointed poor Data must be at the behavior of the humans on this planet. But then he thought, Data'll throw these fools a curve or two.

Ferris listened to his headset for a moment.

"I am informed," he said, "that you just committed another crime of fiction-making. You just thought

116

of your android as a person, when he is merely a device."

"No, he is a person, and that person, and all the rest of my friends and crew, will defeat you," said Riker. "You can't imagine how because you can't imagine anything, but they will."

Ferris almost replied but stopped himself. Riker could see the hate on his face. Ferris still hadn't fought him one-on-one and drawn the primal blood he wanted so badly.

"Return the prisoner to his cell," said Ferris, thick-voiced.

After Riker had been taken away, a CS officer entered and saluted.

"Major Ferris, sir. The Director of Cephalic security is on his way back to his office."

"Is his health better, Lieutenant?"

"Yes, sir. I talked to him myself. He requests you carry out the executions immediately, starting with the prisoner Picard. The android is already being dismantled."

In the type of lab known as a "clean room," with controlled atmosphere to filter out even the smallest dust particles, several men in lab coats and mouth-masks prepared to permanently disassemble Data and learn all of his mechanical secrets.

The technicians were unarmed but wore CS helmets to filter out fiction or blasphemy the android might try to utter. A trio of one-eyes hovered in the background as guards.

Data was lying at an angle, held onto a tilting lab table by several steel restraints. Above him clustered cameras and other recording devices. The dismantling would be well documented.

The CS already knew a lot about Data by what they

stole from the minds of the *Enterprise* crew. But they didn't know as much as they might. Many of the theories behind Data's design and construction had been censored by the one-eyes and were never input into the central CS computers. Such theories were unverifiable given current Rampartian knowledge, and had to be classified as criminal science fiction until they could be proven true by actual dismantling of "the Data unit itself."

The supposed account of Data's genesis, of the inventor Soong and Data's "brother" android Lore, and of Data's entire personal history also had to be censored out of the Rampartian information-pool. The story had the qualities of a fairy tale, especially of a certain abominable children's story about a wooden puppet who wanted to be human.

"Press its switch," said one of the technicians. "We'll take some measurements with the unit powered up. Our schedule allows for some observation before disassembly."

A white-gloved hand slid under Data's back and pressed the switch.

Data's eyes jerked open. He looked about.

Some of the technicians watched him, while others peered at dials and meters on their equipment.

"Excuse me," said Data. "May I inquire where I am?"

"Great voice emulator system," said a tech, looking at an oscilloscope.

"Where are my friends?" Data asked. "May I communicate with them, or with my ship?"

The techs ignored his requests, which he repeated in various forms as they performed tests on him. By their comments to each other, uttered as though Data were not even there, he understood that they were preparing to dismantle him.

An idea occurred to him—a weapon he might use against them. He didn't have enough information to know for certain what effect the weapon would have, but its theoretical base was sound.

In a voice that would have carried out to the last row of a theater, he said:

"Cries of carbuncle ecstasy when you perfume her with Chyme de Voltaire;
Mary Queen of Callipygian Beetles rubbed against gallstone-pattern wallpaper scream scream;
Monkey milkshake squirting from her tear ducts in the quiet dawn so fun-sized;
Podiatrists smell like wet dog resonators, so they called him Bob Crowned With Savory Carbon Atoms."

The techs looked at each other, baffled. One of them tittered, then put his hand over his mouth.

"You hear all that?"

"Some of it. My headphones cut out some parts but let me hear others."

"Mine, too. Something's mixed up."

"Hey, Jack, look at the one-eyes. I just gave one a thought order and it didn't respond."

"Looks like they're frozen up."

Data saw that the one-eyes were hovering immobile, as he had postulated. Intriguing.

He strained with all his strength against the solid steel bars that held him against the table; he was able to flex them a bit, but they were too strong even for him to break.

Maybe under different circumstances, he thought, the strategy could have been used for escape.

The techs were momentarily clustered around the trio of motionless one-eyes.

"There. Back on line. Just a little glitch."

"All right, let's keep to the schedule and start the disassembly. Shut the unit off."

Data felt a hand reach behind his back.

In the space of a microsecond, Data thought of each living being he'd ever known and said a silent good-bye to them all.

Chapter Ten

THE SMALL CAVE-ROOM wreathed Troi in its cold dampness. She sat leaning back against the wall, the stone drawing the warmth from her flesh, making the flesh feel like stone, too.

Since she had found no escape option, she had decided to use her time in these caves as best she could. She was going to invite contact with the alien Other-worlders and try to unlock their secret, which she hoped would unlock Crichton's secret as well.

She had considered what had happened during her previous contacts with the Other-worlders, and concluded that since only her mind, not her body, had been transported into their universe or state of being, she should be in no physical danger.

Still, the thought of confronting them was terrifying. The fear was causing waves of nausea to wash through her. She told herself that she didn't have to lose control of the encounter; she had broken it off voluntarily the first time, and she could do it again.

Troi shut her eyes and opened her empathic sense. The Other-worlders were all around her. She sent out a mental invitation to them. A moment passed and nothing happened, so she opened her eyes.

The walls and roof of the cave were gone. She was in the midst of an oceanic multitude of Other-worlders. Under a sky filled by a huge spiral galaxy they covered the ground from horizon to horizon.

Those near enough to show their detail were greatly variegated—some humanoid, others of inconceivable shape and dimension. Among them Troi recognized the Mirror Man and the Lioness, but they were only two faces in the infinite horde. This was not the situation she had expected and she didn't know how to initiate any kind of dialogue.

She noticed that she was up on a raised platform. The horde was scrutinizing her with such intensity she had to look down at her body. She found she was nude. Her skin felt strange. It was changing, hardening as she watched, developing small sparkling flecks.

Then she became aware that the inside of her body was changing as well. She felt heavy. Her body temperature began to drop.

She tried in vain to move or speak. They were trying to put her through that same bodily metamorphosis they had attempted during her earlier contacts. Now it was going further. It felt like freezing or dying. In spite of her earlier determination to stay in control and not panic, her fear was too great and she couldn't help but try to break the contact in an effort to return to her familiar world. But this time she couldn't. She tried to cry out but her mouth and throat were no longer capable of it. Troi had the feeling that some hidden piece of fearsome knowledge was about to be revealed to her.

Someone spoke her name. She felt herself being rocked like a heavy object, as though she were a boulder.

Then she suddenly unfroze and found herself sitting in the cave, back in her proper universe.

Rhiannon was squeezing her arms.

"Hey! Hey! Deanna!"

Troi was covered in a film of sweat, yet shivering.

"Felt sick."

"I can see that. I thought you were dying or something."

Troi wiped her forehead on her sleeve, then rubbed her eyes. Rhiannon watched her with concern.

Troi knew, with a feeling of dread, that if the vision had continued, the metamorphosis would have been completed. Yet she knew she would have to let it complete if she were going to discover the hidden knowledge of the Other-worlders. It seemed they would not communicate with her in any other way.

"Do you want me to get you anything?" asked the girl.

"No. I'm okay now. It was just a dream."

Rhiannon glanced at Troi's wrists, which still bore the metal bands from the CS' cuffs.

"I can get Nikitushka Lomov to cut those off."

"Maybe later."

Rhiannon smiled at her with a mouthful of crooked teeth.

Troi could tell Rhiannon already had one of those fixations an adolescent girl can get for a big-sister figure.

"How long have you been living here, Rhiannon?"

"Since I was this high."

Rhiannon lowered her hand to the level of her chest.

"Where are your parents?"

"I don't know. They were declared criminally incompetent. The CS took them away and I had to live in a group home. That's not the only thing that made me run away, though. It was school. My teachers.

They wouldn't let me do anything I really wanted or learn anything I really wanted. I wasn't allowed to ask, 'what if this,' or 'what if that.' No telling stories. No drawing pictures unless I traced them from a stupid photograph. They made me get my mind cleansed every week. Didn't that stuff happen to you, too?"

"No, my childhood was a lot different. What do you do all day down here?"

"Don't you know about our library? We have tons of books. I'm reading all of them."

Rhiannon went on to list what she was reading right now. Troi began to realize this wasn't just a frivolous young runaway. This was a literate young mind in development, following its own inspirations. The scope of her reading was amazing. She was becoming a scholar in the early Welsh and Irish stories, especially the story of Rhiannon and the other branches of the Mabinogi.

Rhiannon wasn't beautiful in conventional terms, but Troi felt a quality of magic about her, a mysterious source of female strength and independence that echoed the mythical Rhiannon. And though her haguya-friend, the flying beast, was hardly the beautiful pale horse the mythical Rhiannon rode, still she spoke of it with reverence, as more than an equal.

Troi was going to ask her more about that, but suddenly Rhiannon decided she couldn't look at those ugly metal bands on Troi's wrists any longer, and summoned Nikitushka Lomov.

The huge strongman sang Russian Bylina songs as he began to file away at Troi's cuff-bands, and Rhiannon hummed harmonies with him.

Outside the caves of Alastor, in the larger caverns, the Dissenters known as the Nummo crawled around deep inside the huge boulder pile that comprised the man-made dam. They had built the dam themselves long ago. Like the mythical African water-beings after whom they had named themselves, they were always involved with water; with all the streams, pools, springs, and weirs in the caverns.

But at this moment they were hiding from a one-eye, which hummed and hovered above the rocks, trying to find the humans it had detected from a distance. The Nummo had seen the one-eye coming from far away and had had time to worm their way deep into the dam. Now the Nummo reached a space in the middle, like a beaver lodge, where they could be safe, shielded by the water and the rocks.

While the Nummo twins were forced to hide, the rest of the CS squad passed by the dam and began to set up for their assault on Alastor.

Rhiannon and Lomov led Troi into the cave used for dining.

Around a great round table hewn from stone sat two dozen people eating, laughing, and talking in many languages. They were all clothed in parti-colored, dirty castoffs.

Odysseus sat away from the table, on a step in a rough stairwell, following Troi's entrance with interest.

The diners fell silent.

Odysseus stood and addressed them.

"This is Deanna," said Odysseus. "She seems to have arrived in our midst by mistake. I'm afraid we can't let her leave, but other than that she can be treated like any other Dissenter."

With that he withdrew to the background and let Troi fend for herself.

Rhiannon motioned Troi toward a rough wooden stool next to a white-haired, ebony-skinned elderly woman. Troi sat.

"My name is Gunabibi," said the elderly woman, as

her face, which Troi recognized as the Australian aboriginal racial type, crinkled in a smile. "Have some of my stew, won't you?" She pushed a bowl toward Troi.

Troi still felt jumpy inside and wasn't sure if she could bring herself to partake of the lumpy green and brown stew. She recognized some of the plant leaves in it; she had seen them growing around the sulfur pools farther up the caverns.

Aromatic fragrance from the stew reached her nose and her mouth began to water. She was suddenly hungry. Rationality dictated caution but her stomach seemed an independent unit. Picking up a wooden spoon, Troi tasted the stew.

It was delicious. She ate it all.

After dinner, everyone left the table and sat on stones set around a pile of glowing red embers.

Troi noticed that Odysseus didn't join them. He stood near the entrance to the dining cave. Staring out, he seemed intensely vigilant, as though he sensed an imminent danger.

He looked at that moment so much like an ancient Greek epic hero that Troi found she had to stop herself from believing that he was one. She remembered the character "exercises" she'd seen him do. Now he was fully in his character.

She approached him.

"You think we're going to be attacked, don't you," she said.

That got his attention. He seemed fascinated at the way she'd guessed his feeling.

"What makes you say that?"

"That's not important. Is it true?"

"The Nummo never returned from their patrol. That might mean the CS are out there."

"Then why can't you let me leave? Why do you want me to be arrested along with you?"

126

"I don't. Neither of us is going to be arrested. The CS are stupid, like a cyclops. We'll protect you from them."

She didn't know what to say and couldn't see how they could protect her.

He seemed to understand her feeling and looked her directly in the eye. "I give you my word as Odysseus, son of Laertes, that I, and my people, will protect you with our lives."

She mumbled some kind of thanks and walked away, taken aback by the intensity of his determination. At that moment she was caught in ambivalence; on the one hand these Dissenters seemed so idealistic, so caught up in their stories, that she thought she should seek escape and strike out on her own, and on the other hand, she found herself wanting their help and able to believe that they could somehow provide it.

In this frame of mind she went to sit with the other Dissenters near the glowing embers. The old woman named Gunabibi came over and sat next to her, explaining that it was storytelling time. She said that all of the Dissenters were experts in their own myth-heritages. She herself was an expert in the stories of aboriginal Australia and had named herself after a Fertility Mother myth-character.

"But tonight Coyote will tell stories," she said.

An elderly white-haired American Indian man stood up next to Troi. It was clear to her that in spite of his age, he was youthful and strong in mind and body. He reminded Troi of a picture she'd once seen of Red Cloud, the great leader of the Oglala Sioux many hundreds of years ago. In fact, both he and Gunabibi, the two oldest people here, gave Troi the impression of quiet power held in reserve.

Troi had noticed him earlier at dinner. She had caught him staring fixedly at her, as though he were trying to determine her true character. But now he was smiling at her, and Troi felt as though he had accepted her. He spoke.

"For our newcomer I will explain that I am a Miwok Indian. My ancestors lived in California, and many of them were utentbe, professional storytellers, long before the Europeans came. You might say I'm an utentbe too. I'm named after a hero of many Native American stories, and I'm going to tell some of them now."

He wove several stories with grace and artistry.

The mythical Coyote in these stories was a Trickster, but often for the benefit of mankind. He gave people fire, like Prometheus, and the power of words.

His trickery was often eloquent. In an Apache story he showed the invading white colonists how greedy they were, convincing them to buy a burro which defecated money. He even showed them how the burro "worked," how it had to be fed first. Of course it was one of Coyote's tricks, he'd created an illusion, and when the excited colonists got the burro home they fed it and prodded it, and waited for money to come out the other end, but all the burro would do was break wind.

When the stories were concluded, Troi asked if the mythical Coyote was an animal or a human, or something beyond either.

"Each person may interpret the stories as they choose," the white-haired Indian said. Troi liked that answer and thought to herself how different these people were from the Rampartians above ground.

Troi asked if someone could explain more about the Dissenters and their chosen stories. Gunabibi stirred up the embers with a stick and began to talk.

"My own culture was forty thousand years old when the white colonists came to Australia and tried to stamp it out. I'm sustaining it in my stories of the aboriginal Dreamtime, as the others here are sustaining their own stories. The people who follow the Rampart way, all facts and regulations, will never have the connection with life, nature, universe, however you want to put it, that the people with stories have. The Rampartians haven't the imagination to see worth in a tree or a mountain. The universe is just so much meaningless stuff to them. They are worthless in their own eyes, just a lot of pitiful animalcules who will work, buy lots of things, grow old and die, while their facts and regulations won't ease their loneliness or their suffering. If old folks like Coyote and I were up there now on Rampart, we'd be regarded as just some useless senile nobodies waiting to die, and if we were like the other old Rampartians, that's just how we would feel.

"But, see, in a culture with imagination, old people are respected—they're the ones with the most understanding, the most stories. They've had the time to use the stories and metaphors to identify themselves not with the greedy ego that clings to life yet must die, but with the infinite living universe.

"The Rampartian Bible claims as an objective fact that the infinite is some real man with a white beard sitting up in the sky, separate and distinct from us. But that is such a sad misunderstanding, such a cause of needless alienation. Infinity is here and now, all around us, and we are part of it, from moment to moment."

Gunabibi made an expansive gesture with her arms and hands, taking in her surroundings.

"And stories can bring one to that feeling," she concluded.

Troi watched the embers. She began to understand why there was a feeling of comradery among all these Dissenters of different ethnic groups. The Dissenters didn't reject each other's stories and mythologies as false. All were metaphors, and all were valid if they worked as a means for personal insight.

She wished she could take these Dissenters to twenty-fourth-century Earth. They could be whatever they wanted there, tell whatever stories they wished. But she still didn't understand how they conducted their rebellion here on Rampart. How did they defend themselves against an overwhelming police state?

"Do you possess weapons?" she asked. "Do you have anything to fight with?"

"We use our stories for that," said Gunabibi. "That's why we name ourselves after myth-characters. We use the power of the stories. We don't believe in using guns. A gun has never imparted knowledge to anyone."

"But are you people the only rebels? Is this the whole Dissenter movement right here?"

"No, there are lots of little groups around. We have to stay small to stay unnoticed. There isn't much structure to it. Odysseus is the leader of this group in matters of tactics and fighting, because he's good at that, but we're all equal. And we get new members once in a while. People who are sick of having their minds cleansed every week, sick of not being able to read and think what they want. I don't know where you lived up there, but you must have seen people going crazy, all those murders and suicides."

Gunabibi's description of Rampart life made Troi remember the early experiments on Earth where people were deprived of REM sleep. The mind goes mad when it can't spontaneously dream. Maybe depriving the mind of stories and imagination had the same result.

"Are you going to join us?" asked Rhiannon, who had sat down next to Troi. "It doesn't matter what you were up there. Coyote was a plain old postal worker. Caliban was an oxygen salesman."

Troi wondered how best to respond. As she stared past the fire she saw a small white object fall from the darkness above and land near the embers.

Suddenly Odysseus leapt into their midst out of nowhere, diving at the white object. "Grenade!" he shouted, as he threw it toward the entrance to the cave.

He then pushed Troi to the ground, among the rocks.

"The stones will help shield you," he said.

She waited for an explosion but heard only a sweet little peeping sound. Instantaneously, she felt the effect of the grenade as an overwhelming wave of mental numbness, as though her brain had been immersed in novocaine. She stared around in a daze.

The effect seemed to wear off quickly, though Troi had no way of knowing how much time had passed. Her lucidity returned like a rush of air into a vacuum. Odysseus helped her stand.

"Thought-grenade," he said. "The CS are here."

"Save the books!" she heard someone shout.

Around them, the other Dissenters were getting up, recovering their wits. Odysseus led them toward an annex-cave, from which Troi could hear frantic fumbling movements and anxious whispers.

Odysseus and Coyote came out of the annex first, whispering to each other. They each had cloth bundles bound to their backs with cords. The rest of the Dissenters came out behind them, all bearing similar bundles on their backs.

Odysseus led everyone through the stairwell and into the great statuary cave. Troi followed them through the shadowy stone throng toward the door-boulder, where the strongman, Nikitushka Lomov, stood with a fearless, distant expression. Odysseus positioned the Dissenters along the wall near the door-stone, while Coyote disappeared into the galaxy of statues. Then Odysseus pulled Troi to stand beside him against the wall. They waited.

Troi could hear voices outside Alastor, from the other side of the door-stone. The door-stone began to shift heavily.

Troi quickly tried to run through her options. What if there were a confused skirmish and she had the opportunity of escaping either alone or with the Dissenters? Which would she choose? Wouldn't being with the Dissenters increase her chances of being arrested, as they were always targets? On the other hand, wouldn't she be vulnerable in the vast caves by herself?

The door-stone moved, then moved again, then fell forward onto the floor with a thunderous boom.

Six white-uniformed CS men holding radiation guns ran over the fallen stone and into the statuary room, followed by a pair of one-eyes.

The CS men all wore imagination-proof helmets.

They looked around at the great chamber, then quickly took up positions in front of the Dissenters. One of the CS, the one standing nearest Troi, brandished his weapon.

"This place has been identified as a criminal hideout. The facts are already a matter of record. All of you are under arrest."

He looked young, and Troi felt his skittishness without needing to see the eyes obscured behind the jagged, moire-quivering rasters on his helmet visor. She read the nametag on his uniform: "Lieutenant Daley."

"We are going to scan you one by one, starting with you on the end," he said, pointing to Caliban. If—"

A pebble struck him in the back of the head. He glanced behind him and saw Coyote, far out in the middle of the statue garden, dodge from one statue to

132

shelter behind another. The multitude of stone images created confusing shadows and false perspectives.

"I'll take care of him," Daley said to his men.

He aimed his gun at a statue of Mahu-ika of Polynesia. The gun whined, the stone glowed, and Coyote leapt from behind the statue just before it burst like a bomb. He took cover behind the voluptuous curves of Venus Callipyge.

Again Daley fired, and again Coyote escaped to the protection of another statue. Troi was astonished at the old Indian's agility.

"What are the one-eyes picking up from his mind?" Daley asked the CS man on his right.

"They're not getting much from here, sir. What they're getting, they're censoring. Must be all fictional. Unrepeatable. No usable information. Send the one-eyes in after him?"

Daley nodded. "I'll go, too."

The pair of one-eyes drew up and flanked him as he walked toward the host of statues.

"Hoooeee!" Coyote shouted with elan from the middle of the crowd of stone figures.

Daley threaded his way with difficulty through the statues. His eye-rasters were filtering the statues, making them into vague globular shapes.

He reached a small open space near the center of the room. He stopped and looked about for Coyote. The one-eyes hovered overhead, sweeping their scanners downward, moving about, trying to get a line-of-sight fix on the elusive Indian.

When the one-eyes were aligned in a pair over Daley's head, Coyote reached up from behind a statue of the Chinese deity of literature, Wen-ch'ang, and tugged at a rope that was anchored to Wen-ch'ang's fat pencil.

Troi heard a ripping sound, then saw a heavy dark

mass fall from above onto Daley and his two machines, knocking them all to the ground.

Daley yelled and thrashed about on the stone floor. The one-eyes rose back up, circling in a wild mazurka, covered with muck.

One of the CS men ran toward Daley. Coyote's foot shot out and tripped him. He fell right into the mess.

An ammonia-like smell reached Troi's nose. She realized the substance that fell was excrement. It looked like bird guano—or perhaps haguya guano.

She stood poised, ready to take advantage of the confusion and make a break for the door. But three CS men still had their guns pointed at her and the Dissenters, and another still blocked the door. Troi saw no safe way to get out of the chamber.

One of the CS men, apparently seeing her intent, suddenly pointed his gun directly at her.

Odysseus stepped in front of her, protecting her with his body. He shouted one word, "Nummo!"

The CS man fired, and Odysseus pitched forward onto the rock floor.

Troi felt the ground begin to vibrate under her feet.

The CS men felt it too. They began to back away from the Dissenters. Daley, by now on his feet though smeared with guano, looked about for the source of the vibration. The one-eyes pivoted and hummed about erratically, their sensing devices and weapons guano-clogged. One of them shook itself violently, like a dog trying to shake off water, but the guano stuck to it like mucilage.

"What's going on!?" Daley called urgently to his men. "Did the one-eyes pick up anything else—from anybody?"

"Just snatches of myth they censored out," said the nearest white-suit, listening into his headphones. "Their interception capabilities are . . . not so good right now."

"Hooooeeee!" shouted Coyote from deep in the forest of statues. He laughed as though he were riding a wild horse.

The CS did not try to get to him. They were looking at the vibrating ground and walls, and at the darkness above, from which they heard a growing rumor of hiss and spray.

The waters burst downward into the chamber, cascading off the floor and leaping wildly, knocking Dissenters and CS alike off their feet. Troi braced herself against the wall next to Rhiannon. They locked forearms and held onto one another as the water slammed into them.

The CS man guarding the door braced himself against its sides with his feet and one hand while holding his weapon with the other. Water gushed out around him, through the doorway.

Several Dissenters, with the packs of books still on their backs, swam forward to fight with the other CS men. A melee developed in the forest of statues.

Troi saw two dark shapes carried like a pair of fish into the chamber with the cascading waters. They swam near her, then ducked under the swelling tide. She recognized them as the Nummo, the West African water-being twins. She realized that they must have released the dam she had seen outside Alastor.

The CS man at the door started to kick at something in the water. The Nummo's heads came up around him, their arms already entangling, eel-like, with his. They loosed his hold and all three were swept out of Alastor.

Something jostled Troi from behind. She turned and saw the huge Russian, Nikitushka Lomov the Barge Hauler, with Odysseus slung unconscious on his shoulder, and an immense pack of books on his back.

Without warning Daley the CS man leapt up and

135

grabbed hold of Lomov's head from behind, savagely twisting it sideways.

Lomov looked no more than mildly annoyed. In fact he seemed strangely pleased. He set Odysseus face up on the surface of the water, then reached up with one hand, lifted Daley by the collar of his uniform, and held him at arm's length. The CS man swung at Lomov but hadn't the reach. Lomov stepped over to a half-submerged statue of Orpheus and wedged Daley's head and shoulders into the Orphic lyre—just parked him there to flail helplessly—then picked up Odysseus.

"Time to go!" Lomov boomed cheerfully at Troi, through his heavy accent. He inclined his dripping dark-haired head toward the now empty doorway.

Troi and Rhiannon were already letting themselves drift in that direction. As they were carried through the doorway, Troi caught a glimpse back into the chamber of statues. She saw a one-eye looping crazily in the air with Caliban riding it. The little man was laughing and spouting Shakespeare, his grimy hand in front of the one-eye's Cyclopean lens.

Troi held onto Rhiannon as the newly diverted river plunged them along the great passage outside Alastor, where no light-stones cut the darkness.

The water slowed quickly as it leveled out, allowing Rhiannon and Troi to drift at a leisurely pace. Rhiannon kept to the side of the channel and felt along the banks with her hands. At a certain point she pulled Troi, leading them both through a small natural tunnel deep into the bank, where the water level gave them just enough space overhead to breathe.

They emerged on the other side into the company of several Dissenters, some with light-stones, who were standing around the terminus of the tunnel. The Nummo twins helped Rhiannon and Troi climb out of the cleft and onto dry rock. As Troi caught her breath, she looked around.

The caverns were smaller than the others Troi had followed to Alastor. She knew she was now out of the main passage that would have conducted her to CephCom. She had no idea where these smaller caverns led.

Nikitushka Lomov, still carrying Odysseus, climbed out of the water and set the unconscious Dissenter down softly. He checked to see that the man was still breathing, and seemed satisfied that he was.

Coyote came out of the water next and exchanged looks with the other Dissenters. Nobody spoke. Troi perceived a mood of foreboding.

Finally Coyote said, "Maui and Isis have been captured. Caliban is dead."

There was a prolonged silence. The Dissenters stared down into the water.

Finally Coyote said, "We can't stay here. We have to move deeper into the caverns."

Then he spoke directly to Troi.

"Now it doesn't matter who you are, because we've lost Alastor and will have to wander until we find a new home. You can go your own way or stay with us. But the main passage we left is not safe anymore."

"Can you show me how to reach CephCom through these caves?"

"Only Odysseus knows that, and he won't awaken for many hours yet. But he no longer has a reason to keep it from you. There is no Alastor left to protect."

Troi thought for a moment.

"I'll go with you."

Chapter Eleven

AT SCIENCE STATION TWO on the bridge, Wesley had searched through physics files for hours. Nothing he'd seen so far suggested a solution for stopping the one-eyes. In fact, he felt he was intuitively closer to the solution when he had started his search.

"Computer, what was the first file I saw?"

The screen displayed the image of the Dance of Shiva, the Dance of the Burning Ground, a symbol of the universe-dance of creation and destruction. Shiva's four arms and four legs moved in a hypnotic pattern. Wesley could even hear the computer-generated rhythmic tap-tap of Shiva's drum of Time and the roar of the hoop of flames surrounding him.

Below the image, the screen displayed a list of references to Shiva, as a metaphor, made by physicists over the past several centuries.

Wesley almost told the computer to move on to something else, as he hadn't meant to call this image up. But he restrained himself. He felt the germ of an idea starting.

The dance of the physical universe, the endless round of light/dark, creation/destruction, life/death;

the on-off vibration without which there is no sound or light or life or universe at all . . .

Wesley knew that even at the subatomic level, the smallest particles, the stuff of which everything is made, oscillate through many states. Matter itself is a dance. He pictured to himself various phases of the dance, the phases of light matter and dark matter—

Dark matter.

A huge proportion of the universe's total mass is dark matter, the neutrino matter that permeates the void, emitting no light or electric charge but with enough mass to keep the universe from expanding forever. Enough mass to eventually reverse the expansion and collapse the universe into itself, into a singularity. And perhaps out of that singularity would come another explosion, and another universe. Like the endless creation/destruction Dance of Shiva.

Wesley kept thinking about the dark matter, the neutrinos.

He thought maybe in neutrinos there was a weapon to use against the one-eyes, but he wasn't sure what it would be.

Chops handed Geordi a sterile tech-wipe. He swabbed the sweat from around his VISOR, and then they fell back to work on a burnt console. Chops' sensor-padded hands moved over the console with pixilated speed while her blind eyes, behind their dark visor, looked off in some random direction.

The warp engines, running at low power, had almost gotten away from them just now. This couldn't go on much longer. They'd eventually have to force a shutdown to avoid a matter-antimatter catastrophe. But a shutdown would mean no shields and they'd have to use the impulse engines to attempt an escape from the surrounding hostile ships.

If they still had impulse engines. The one-eyes were about to knock those out as well.

Geordi figured the Rampartian ships around the *Enterprise* were waiting so quietly because they wanted a sure thing, an easy target. Battling an enemy that still had options would make the Rampartians nervous; there would be intangibles, and the Rampartians certainly couldn't like intangibles—couldn't even *think* about intangibles.

Wesley's voice issued from Geordi's communicator.

"Crusher to La Forge."

"La Forge here."

"I've been working in the particle physics library. I think I might have something, but I'm not sure what it is."

Geordi turned toward his monitor.

"Computer, put me at Ensign Crusher's location in the library."

An image of the Dance of Shiva appeared on the screen.

"Uh, Shiva was my inspiration," said Wesley.

"Time's a little short, Wes. What's your idea?"

Wesley asked if it would be possible to make a weapon that would convert the one-eyes into neutrinos. He admitted he couldn't think of a way himself.

Geordi was silent for a moment.

"Well, it was just an idea," said Wesley. "Sorry to—"

"No, wait."

Geordi stared at the Dance of Shiva.

"Let me think about it, Wes. La Forge out."

Geordi worked quietly beside Chops for a few minutes, then suddenly it came to him. A special recipe of high-energy particles could be used to smash the atoms in the one-eyes in such a way that only neutrinos, and no other particles, would be produced.

Vast numbers of neutrinos would fly out from the site of the event—but neutrinos, which had no positive or negative charge, would pass harmlessly through anything; through living bodies, through metal, through a whole planet, without any interaction.

Conversion of atoms into neutrinos, into dark matter, was a natural part of the dance of matter/energy, but from what Geordi had seen, Rampartian technology hadn't achieved that level of understanding of the dance . . . the level of understanding that encompassed both the light and the dark.

Geordi called Wesley back. He told the ensign that a weapon could and would be built. He was putting Chops in charge of building it, but Wesley would be given the pleasure of operating it.

Since his sentencing an hour earlier, Picard had watched the video screen in his room, trying to pick up useful information.

The images had the smooth consistency of baby food. Mind pablum.

He thought about what he'd seen in the flesh with his own eyes: Crichton's physical problem. Some kind of seizure. Maybe it had to do with his scarred, mask-like face; maybe it was one of the injuries the Dissenters had given him. Whatever it was, the staff in his office had been taken by surprise. It was a new infirmity.

Picard looked at the camera lens and the antennae in the upper corner. He spoke directly at them.

"How can a man in Crichton's condition be allowed to pass judgment?" Picard asked, though he supposed they could just as well read his thoughts. "I know somebody is listening. Let someone else try my case. Crichton could have been wrong. An error, a falsehood, may have been committed."

The door opened, and several CS men and one-eyes

141

came in. Without preamble they came over to Picard, forced him down on the bed, and with the gentle firmness reserved for the condemned, began to fasten the restraining straps around him.

"I have proof on my ship," said Picard, hearing a new note of fear in his voice, "that Crichton is wrong. I have evidence that the *Huxley* did disappear here, and that Crichton must have known about it. I have a recorder marker from the *Huxley*. Crichton is perpetrating a fiction."

The CS ignored him.

They finished, leaving Picard immobilized on the bed, and made their exit.

A short time later, a woman entered with a mobile cart full of electronic gear, on top of which sat a round cap with wires and electrodes. It was the same setup Picard had seen in the hall earlier. He had guessed what it was for.

The woman wore the protective CS helmet. Twin flickering rasters on her visor partly obscured her eyes and headphones screened her ears. No prisoners would be allowed to tell her any fictions in their last moments.

Her uniform had a red CS logo, and a nametag, "Smith." Her hair was trussed up under her helmet. Her movements were practiced and impersonal, like a nurse's.

She positioned the cart in a corner, then took an electric razor from a drawer in the cart and came over to Picard. Although he was for the most part bald, she shaved areas of his skull to remove all hair and fuzz.

The shaving seemed to go on forever. He could feel the warmth of Smith's body as she leaned over him. She was a living being, and she was going to annihilate another living being. If he was right in his assumptions, his body would still be alive, and would eventually be given a new personality, but he, Jean-Luc Picard, would be dead.

He looked at the woman's green eyes which were only partly visible behind the flickering rasters. Strangely, her eyes seemed sad, full of regret. At first she avoided his stare, but then she paused for a moment and looked right at him.

Picard thought he saw pity there, the first he'd seen since he'd been in CephCom.

"Yes, you are different," Picard said. "You *don't* believe in what you're doing."

She didn't react at all, and Picard wondered if her protective headphones were filtering out what he said.

She continued with her work.

Her shaver buzzed like a steel fly.

He caught her eye again, for just a moment, but she looked away quickly. She clicked her shaver off and put it away.

Picard focused all of his perception on her, the last living being he would ever see.

She didn't belong here. She had a visible insecurity, a vulnerability. She knew that she didn't know everything.

Picard thought she might be his means of escape, at least from imminent death, if only she would take her damned helmet off. But what good would that do if the sensing gear in the room picked up everything they said?

Smith slowly rose from Picard's side, went over to the cart, and put the shaver back in the drawer. Picard couldn't tell if her motions were indeed slow or if his sense of time was playing tricks on him.

She pulled the cart by its handle. It rolled on hard black rubber wheels. Now it was right next to him, filling his sight. He saw the dials, oscilloscopes, and switches. He even saw the numbers on their graduated scales.

She took the jack-ends of two cords and plugged them into sockets in the wall near the bed.

Picard felt his breathing speed up.

He stared at Smith's face, prayed for her to look at him again.

She flicked a switch on each of the rack-mounted components. Picard could see the scopes light up, hear the little cooling fans starting to blow.

She picked up the cap-like thing, and paused. Picard willed her to doubt what she was doing, and for a moment he thought she really was wavering. Then he realized she was just inspecting the electrodes.

She smeared conductor on the electrodes and then she put the cap on his head, seating it firmly. Through his scalp he could feel the sticky conductor, and the hot electrodes themselves. She picked up a roll of thick white tape from the cart and tore off a strip.

She met his eyes again, just for a moment, then she put the tape over his mouth, and turned toward the cart.

She hadn't seemed affected by the plea Picard knew was in his eyes.

A terrible thing occurred to him. What if Troi had been right all along, more right than she knew, about the way he kept his emotions in check? What if now in this last moment he was too cold to make this executioner feel enough pity to spare him? Maybe this was his hamartia, his doom waiting for him all along like an unnoticed face in a crowd in some huge painting . . .

Picard closed his eyes, heard himself breathing, heard his blood roaring.

Then he heard the sound of a switch being pulled, and, immediately afterward, a buzzing sound.

He waited. He felt no change.

Smith pulled the tape off his mouth and went back to her machines. The buzzing stopped.

Had it already happened? Was it instantaneous?

Maybe it wouldn't work on him.

He needed a way to test his brain. What would never have survived a Rampartian brainwashing?

A line, the final moment of Leopold Bloom's fictional journey, a story so often censored, came to him.

"Going to a dark bed there was a square round Sinbad the Sailor roc's auk's egg in the night of the bed of all the auks of the rocs of Darkinbad the Brightdayler."

It was as reverberant as the day he first read it.

Picard knew he was still Picard. Somehow the brainwashing hadn't worked. He was still alive.

He watched Smith remove her helmet. She was at that moment the most beautiful thing he'd ever seen.

She pointed at the antennae and camera in the corner.

"They'll register that I'm carrying out the sentence. They're fooled by interference when I have the machines in this mode. They can't hear us. We only have a moment to talk."

"Why? Before what?"

She sat on the edge of the bed.

Her green eyes, unobscured by the helmet, showed her anguish.

"I've been doing this for years," she said. "I've blanked thousands of people. But this time, I don't know, something went wrong with me. What did you want to tell me?"

"That you're different," said Picard. "You see how this is an atrocity. You know the people here try to kill imagination because it comes from deep in the psyche, and they fear what's deep in the psyche. They can't even bear to look at it. And the more they try to keep from looking at it, the more fearful it becomes. They would sooner kill than look at it."

Picard moved his eyes to indicate the machines in the rack beside him.

"All their science is wasted," he said. "They've decoded brain waves but still know nothing about their minds. I can prove all this to you. I can show you things that imagination has done for the human race . . . things that no one on this planet would believe possible, and yet which came to be, because someone once imagined them and was free to tell others. I can show you, if you just stop this killing. You can come away with me to a place of total freedom. I can't guarantee we'll escape, but I will give us a fighting chance."

Smith's brow corrugated in a frown. She nodded slowly.

"It's so strange . . . I've been hearing the opposite all my life, but what you say actually sounds right. Which means either I'm going insane, or everyone else is insane. It doesn't really matter. I'm going to have to carry out your sentence anyway."

"Why?"

"Because there's no way to stop all this. Someone else would carry out the sentence if I didn't. Even if I set you free, we'd never make it out of here alive. Never."

"Then at least help my crew," said Picard. "Two of them are imprisoned here. You could give them their communicators. And help my ship. The CS is trying to destroy it. Please tell me you'll at least try."

She put her hand on his chest, but kept her head turned away.

"I'd like to."

Picard realized she was crying.

"I know there's something special about you," she said. "They don't tell me anything about the people I do this to, but I just know . . ."

She took a deep shuddering breath, then stood up quickly.

"Sorry," she said.

She put the piece of tape back on Picard's mouth, and replaced her own helmet, hiding her eyes behind the rasters.

Then she went back to her cart, and with a quick, angry motion, flipped a red switch.

Later, Smith stopped at the doors to a computer room, dialed a personal code into a combination lock, and entered.

She took off her helmet and clipped her red hair in a tight whorl.

If you asked her right now if her name had always been Smith, she would say that it had. However, she would be wrong; it had been Smith only for the last two days. For many years before that, it had been Amoret.

When she had been captured along with Riker and Data at the ore factory, she had been taken to this building, put in a cell, and her mind had been wiped completely blank. On this planet, such blanking satisfied the legal demand for capital punishment, for the original person was indeed dead and gone. The body became a new citizen with a new identity.

This new citizen's memory was filled, by computer, with real-life incidents from other people's lives, all verified as true, and sanctioned by the CS. Only the names and faces in the incidents were changed to make them fit the new citizen's new personal history.

Though the new memories weren't really true for the new citizen, they had been true for someone, and the Rampartians had declared that these re-used memories were not fictional. They did not carry the Allpox of imagination. A lot of tortured logic was used to justify this practice, but the real reason for it was pure necessity. Without it there wouldn't be enough sanitized new minds.

The practice allowed for instantaneous placement of the new citizen back into society, wherever there happened to be a need. In this way, the large number of arrests and capital punishments didn't decimate the population or disrupt the operations of the CS or the commercial sector.

Once in a while there were problems. The Rampartians had decoded brain waves and neural memory codes, but there was much about brain physiology that they didn't know. Sometimes the blanking and refilling didn't work completely and the original memories and "criminal" tendencies remained. In such cases the intransigent brain was written off as a loss and the body was killed by injection.

However, when successful, the brainwashing provided ideal citizens for Rampart society. The people who were most recently brainwashed were actually the "safest" of all Rampartians, and were often employed by the CS, which constantly needed more sanitized minds.

Smith, though she didn't know it yet, was turning out to be one of the failed attempts at mind blanking. A thread of the Dissenter spirit had persisted through her blanking, on some deeply buried stratum. She still thought she was someone named Marjorie Smith who had blanked thousands of people, but when she had tried to blank Picard, her Dissenter spirit had twitched and groaned remorsefully in its sleep.

And now, as she reflected back on her life as Marjorie Smith, a comfortable life among a lot of bland people, it seemed an unreal montage, an interminable, colorless, sleepwalk. She felt that this meant she had lived a meaningless life, having no idea the memories weren't of her life at all, but rather sanitized memories from the minds of others.

The CS was already aware of some of her doubts. They hadn't heard her conversation with Picard, but they had read some of her brain waves before and after, and identified her as a possible miscreant. They were simply waiting to see what she did next.

Now she checked the computer room's bulletin board for memos, an act she thought she had performed thousands of times. She found one from her boss, Bussard.

It read: "Smith: The Picard disk should be left in the safe. I will process it tomorrow. All other disks should be processed as usual."

She looked at a row of disk-cases on the rack in front of her. The disks were made automatically of all the material drained from each mind during the blanking process. At the end of the day, she was supposed to use a computer to cull any usable information off the disks—any facts about the Dissenter rebellion, for instance.

Once the facts were in the computer, the disks were always erased. What use did the CS have for the ravings and hallucinations of criminal minds?

Now, one by one, Smith put each disk on her rack into a disk drive and let the computer pull off the files it wanted. Finally, the computer erased the disks— the final death and disposal of each personality.

The CS administration were going to do something special with the Picard disk. They probably needed specific information from Picard's mind, and Smith assumed her boss Bussard would search the disk manually for it. Then it would no doubt be erased like all the rest.

Late in the afternoon, Bussard, a baby-faced, double-chinned, middle-aged bureaucrat, leaned his head in the door.

"I'm leaving for the day."

"Okay. I still have work to do."

As she loaded another disk on the main drive, she felt his eyes still on her for a good minute.

"I'm leaving my door open," he said finally. "Can't seem to find my key. Have to get a new one made tomorrow. Good night."

"Good night."

When she had disposed of all remaining disks except for Picard's, she opened the temporary safe. The case containing Picard's disk felt cold and heavy as she placed it in the safe.

She began to close the safe door, but stopped. She had a sense that she had done something terribly wrong and felt an imperious need to atone.

Then, like a leviathan rising up from unplumbed waters, a plan surfaced in her mind. It would be considered a high crime, of course, if she were caught.

Luckily for her, Bussard had left his door open. She took Picard's disk in and latched the door.

On Bussard's desk was a disk drive hooked up to a video screen and keyboard. Bussard had left it powered up.

Not like him, thought Smith, to be so scatterbrained.

The drive was used for manual searches of disks, in cases where the main computer couldn't find something. This manual system actually imaged the deceased person's memories on the screen. A bank of switches marked "enable" and "disable" was used to censor out all material of imagination so that the operator would not risk self-infection while searching for facts.

Neither Bussard nor any other trusted CS employees who had this job would operate the system in fully open mode. That would be like deliberately driving a car off a cliff. Rather, they would selectively disengage various of the filters, letting needed facts through, and if by error some material of imagination was viewed, immediate mind-cleanse would be used to remove it. Bussard had a small mental hygiene unit on his desk for such contingencies. It looked like an electric toothbrush with an electrode where the bristles would be.

One by one, Smith toggled all the switches to the "disable" position. A red warning light flashed: System Fully Open.

She locked the disk on the drive and typed a command. Images began to form on the screen.

Late into the night she sat there, exploring areas of Picard's memory. On the video screen she saw incidents from Picard's public life as a Starship captain, and images of his private thoughts as a quirky, creative man. She saw experiences she had never imagined and imagination she had never experienced; outlandish aliens Picard had met and incredible stories he had read.

As she watched she began to accept that the universe was teeming with intelligent life. It didn't matter that Rampart science had told her the opposite.

She watched without condemning anything as impossible. She just let the images unfold. They clicked; they felt more right than anything she had experienced in her gimcrack-plastic life as Marjorie Smith.

She saw how Picard handled a double of himself. She watched Picard's response to a supertyrant failed-god named Q. She experienced with Picard an encounter with vicious little rat-men for whom profit was everything. She saw through Picard's eyes intelligent life that looked like a grain of sand, a lizard-man, a pool of black tar, a moving ball of light. She saw two colossal jellyfish creatures embracing in connubial bliss. She saw a Dali painting called "A chemist lifting with extreme precaution the cuticle of a grand piano."

She saw the holodeck image of Sherlock Holmes and Picard's own mental images as he read *The Tempest* and *The Mahabharata.*

She saw images of Picard's most private, creative musings, and unspoken jokes. She noticed that he had a great deal of affection for his crew but she could not catch him in any direct statements of those feelings. She chanced upon several love affairs, and many profound losses, such as the deaths of his crew on his former ship, the *Stargazer.*

She kept skipping around the disk, sifting randomly, compulsively, unable to stop. The intensity of the exhilaration, of the terror-joy of discovery, kept her going.

What finally made her stop was an excruciating realization. She, Marjorie Smith, had blanked a thousand people, a thousand personalities. For all she knew all of those personalities could have been as extraordinary as Picard's. Since she'd never looked at them, she'd never know. Murder, over and over.

She made up her mind what she would do.

Raising her eyes from the screen and keyboard, she saw gray morning light around the edges of the window blinds. She had been here all night. Bussard and the rest of the department would soon arrive for work.

She made a duplicate of Picard's disk, putting the original disk back in its case and the duplicate in another case. After moving all the switches on the viewer back to their original settings she left the power on, as she'd found it.

Back in her work room, she put the original Picard disk in the safe, and sat holding the duplicate disk in her lap. She'd taken the first step. The next would be a lot harder.

The sound of footsteps told her that Bussard was

arriving for work. He was a good half-hour early. Maybe because he'd had to get a new key made . . .

She got up and carried the disk into the long storage hall, far back between the shelves and file cabinets.

After a moment she heard someone enter the work room, open the safe, close it, and then shuffle through papers on her desk.

"Marjorie?"

It was Bussard.

Holding the disk in her hand, she stepped into a large steel storage cabinet and silently shut the doors.

She heard the click of Bussard's steps, and the hum of a one-eye passing the cabinet.

Then she heard Bussard's voice coming from the direction of her own desk. She pressed her ear to the cold steel.

"Bussard for Mr. Hazlitt . . . How are you, Rob? . . . No, she's not here—I'm standing at her desk. She couldn't have left the building, though. . . . She looked at the disk all last night, unfiltered. . . . Yeah, I left my door open to see if she'd take the bait. A one-eye patrolling outside was attracted by the light. . . . She must have seen a lot; we'd already had the disk rated as High Crime. Bad as it gets . . . and after only one day. Looks like the blanking didn't get rid of her Dissenter memories. She must have been a real sicko. We'll have to put her to sleep for good. . . . Yeah. I'll tell her she has to fill out some paperwork for a vacation. . . . Thanks."

He hung up and went back into his office.

For many minutes Smith stood in the cramped closet, assimilating the news that she was once a Dissenter, and that she was now scheduled for bodily destruction.

She wasn't Marjorie Smith. The realization exposed some buried memory fragments: sitting in a roomful

153

of books, with other people who called her Amoret. Fleeing down a dark street, tracer bullets from a CS hovercraft flashing past her head. Writing something by the illumination of a penlight, a story she could no longer remember—a thought that made her oddly sad. And, as a little girl, chasing a ball into some bushes and finding a single wondrous ancient page, the contents of which were now lost to her . . .

Everything dovetailed neatly. Her doubts when she blanked Picard made perfect sense.

The death sentence gave her a feeling of freedom. She could do anything she wanted, because she was already dead. If she had been a Dissenter named Amoret, then her life was merely completing its proper trajectory. Although she would never remember most of that life, she knew what she could do to end it properly.

There was an electric van parked at the back entrance to the storage room. Her Marjorie programming told her that. There could still be a one-eye lurking in the room, but she'd have to make a dash for it. Delaying would get her nowhere.

She burst out of the tall cabinet and ran the few steps to the back entrance. The van was there. She opened the door and got in. She put the disk case under the seat and floored the pedal.

Ferris entered Crichton's office.

"Morning, sir."

"Morning, Major."

"Glad to see you're feeling better, sir."

"Thank you. Just the old injury. Facial nerve. You've been briefed yet on what we're doing with the captain of the *Enterprise?*"

"No, sir."

"He was completely blanked clean yesterday. But

154

we're going to put back some parts of his original mind. Just facts about the *Enterprise* and his crew, his speech patterns, and so forth. Just what we will need to fool the *Enterprise*.

Crichton's laugh was short and mechanical.

"You wouldn't believe the amount of obscene garbage in that man's mind. The computer put it at ninety percent of total content. Fantasies about space-beings and all that. All gone now, though, thrown out except for what we need."

"What about the other captives, and the ship?"

"The ship will probably be destroyed by the one-eyes, even without the help we'll get from Picard. But we'll take extra protection wherever we can get it. The other captured man will be blanked today, and the robot is being taken apart as we speak. Don't worry about them, Major. I want you rested and ready when those Dissenters from the caves make their move."

Ferris didn't hide his surprise.

"Where'd the intelligence come from?"

"A super-stealth miniature one-eye got close to them after they left their stronghold. It's since lost them but it did find out about a plan. They're going to come out of the caves and attack CephCom. If they do, we'll let them, and arrest them right on the front steps."

Ferris didn't like it. He was a by-the-book military man, and this plan was not by-the-book. This was another of Crichton's video spectaculars that made the war harder for the soldiers who actually had to fight. But the Council of Truth thought Crichton was a born genius with video, and they'd shepherded him up through the ranks.

Still, Ferris was determined to voice his objection.

"Sir, that's tactically a bad plan. They should be arrested at a safe distance."

"I want to show the public how these criminals are a real threat, Major. The Council of Truth has approved my plan. They agree that this could be the best news video ever."

Chapter Twelve

"TOO HIGH AND TOO FAST!" said Troi breathlessly. Rhiannon had promised her the ride would be short and conservative. But the haguya's gravity-pulling turns around the stalactites were like an old-fashioned thrill ride. The animal was a virtuoso aeronaut.

"Hold on to me," said Rhiannon.

Troi held on. Rhiannon seemed to have no fear of heights at all. Troi figured it was because of long acclimation.

Eventually the haguya slowed its flight, made a sharp turn, and headed back over the walking Dissenters.

"Did you tell it to turn around?" asked Troi.

"No! Saushulima knew."

Troi could feel Rhiannon's defensiveness. The girl wanted to believe the haguya was intelligent.

"What did you call him?" Troi asked.

"Saushulima. I named him after a being of sky and wind in a Zuni story. Chief of the zenith domain."

"Is the haguya a friend only with you?" asked Troi.

"No, he likes us all. So do the other haguya that live in these caves. Sometimes they sit around with us when we have storytelling time, and listen. They bring their babies to listen, too. When we're in dangerous places they watch out for us. Once Gunabibi almost fell off a cliff, and one of the haguya caught her."

Troi thought Rhiannon might be projecting her own wishes onto the haguya. Making it into a fantasy companion, like the mythical Rhiannon's light-footed horse.

"Do the haguya ever come out of the caves? Do they go up above ground?"

"Once in a while, but they stay away from the people. They go up to the mountains."

"Aren't they ever spotted?"

"Anyone sees a haguya up there, the memory will be cleansed right out, because the haguya aren't supposed to exist. But I don't know how people explain the weird guano lying about!"

Another haguya pulled up alongside and flew next to Saushulima. Troi watched closely, trying to see if any form of communication would occur between them. But nothing happened and the visitor parted company.

"Where are your people going?" asked Troi.

"A secret cave a couple of miles away. We have to wait for Odysseus to wake up."

Troi wondered what frame of mind he'd be in—would he cooperate and tell her how to get to CephCom? There was no Alastor secret left to protect, so why shouldn't he?

If she got the information she needed, she decided she'd leave without seeking anything else from the Dissenters. On her way there, she would try one more contact with the Other-worlders, one more attempt to understand what they were. She vowed to herself not to succumb to fear this time. She would let them communicate however they might.

She could still feel their presence. They lurked beneath the surface of the physical reality around her like serpents in a shadowy sea.

Troi's musings were interrupted by a sadness she felt coming from Rhiannon.

Troi hazarded a guess as to its cause.

"I'm sorry you lost some of your people back at Alastor."

"Well . . . the way I see it," said Rhiannon, "they aren't really gone. No one can kill Caliban, or Maui, or Isis. Isis is already five thousand years old. See what I mean?"

Troi understood the literal meaning. But the words seemed to have a special significance Troi couldn't pinpoint.

"Do you like Odysseus?" asked the long-haired girl.

"Why do you ask?"

"I was hoping you did, so maybe you'd decide to stay with us. Like, if you married him."

Troi laughed.

"I like all of your people, especially you, Rhiannon, but I can't possibly stay."

Below, the Dissenters were entering a narrow cleft in a rock wall.

"We're here," said Rhiannon.

"Come in," said Gunabibi. Troi entered the little cave and sat against the wall.

Odysseus was lying on his back, his head on a crude pillow made from rags. Gunabibi was applying a wet cloth to his forehead.

Troi checked to see if he was near waking up. He seemed quite unconscious, but as Troi leaned over to peer at him closely, his eyes moved beneath their lids.

She studied his sleeping face. A very masculine face, weathered but handsome, framed by a gray-flecked beard. He looked like a man on a hegira, a penitent.

Sitting so close to his sleeping form, she had to acknowledge that she felt an attraction to him. Maybe it was just a bodily feeling, an instinct. She couldn't picture any kind of real-life intimacy between them.

Still, his tactics, and his Dissenter group, had been more effectual against the CS soldiers than she had expected. They'd saved her from the CS, just as he'd promised. She wasn't going to let that draw her into the conflict emotionally and derail her from her own mission, but as an outside observer she wished the Dissenters victory and freedom.

Gunabibi took the wet cloth away from Odysseus' forehead.

"He should be waking soon," she told Troi.

Troi wondered about the effects from the stun he'd received. When he awoke, would he be in any kind of shape to talk?

She put her hand on his cheek. It was warm but not feverish.

She decided to see if she could read his feelings while he dreamed.

Averting her gaze, Troi unshrouded her consciousness and let in his feelings. He was indeed dreaming. She expected to find that in his dream he would not be Odysseus, he would be that defeated, shamed man that hid underneath the fictional character.

But she was surprised, because he was still Odysseus, even in his dream. The fictional character he worked so hard to sustain had pervaded his mind even to the stratum of dreams. She let the feeling of his dream wash over her, the feeling of an odyssey across a vast place full of adventures, both dark and bright, across the limits of the known and the unknown, and how he survived it through his resourcefulness . . .

She felt there was a woman in the dream, just out of his reach, and she felt his wanting—

She quickly brought her gaze back to Odysseus' face. His eyes were open. He was looking at her. Her hand was still on his face; she had forgotten it was there. Withdrawing it with a jerk, she felt herself blush and silently cursed the involuntary response.

"Beautiful way to wake up," he said. He shifted his attention from Troi to Gunabibi.

"Welcome back," said Gunabibi, laughing with joy. She gave Odysseus a motherly hug and helped him sit up.

The sitting position was obviously painful for him. He held his head in his hands for several moments, breathing through clenched teeth.

"Where are the others?" he asked Gunabibi.

"Getting food."

"Did we lose anyone at Alastor?"

"Isis and Maui were arrested. Caliban is dead."

He said nothing. With his hands still covering his face, he slowly let himself sink back down to the rock floor. He put his head on the pillow and turned away from the two women.

Troi sensed quite clearly that he wanted to be alone. The Odysseus character was faltering, and, underneath, that other man, the old, failed one, was hurting.

She went outside.

The Dissenters had bedded down.

Troi had no way of knowing if it was night on the surface of Rampart, but she had fallen into the same circadian body clock as the rest of the Dissenters, and was ready for sleep too. But she wanted to question Odysseus first.

Most of the light-stones that the group had carried were covered with clothes or bundles of books. In the insufficient orange glow of the remaining few, the cave the group had chosen for a rest site looked like the stone-ribbed gut of a sinuous animal.

Troi picked her way around the stalagmites, pools, and recumbent forms of the Dissenters. She sensed clearly that some were joined in the act of love. She gave them a wide berth, but admitted to herself some curiosity about who was with whom. There were so many interesting possible pairings.

She found Odysseus sitting awake, apart from the others, on a ledge that gave him a view of the entrances and exits to the cave.

He acknowledged her with a nod, and offered her a cloak as she sat next to him. She accepted it gladly, since the cave air was mercilessly cold.

Troi immediately perceived that he had recovered from the losses in his group, and regained his confidence and strength. He was once again the much-enduring mythical Odysseus.

"I was hoping you could tell me how to get into CephCom from these caves," she said. "Or am I still a suspected CS spy?"

"No. We've decided you're no more CS than any of us."

"So you'll tell me?"

"You can't get in by yourself."

"I have to at least try."

"No, you don't. You can come in with us. We have a mission to accomplish while there are still enough left in our group: a last try at putting CephCom out of commission. We've been planning it for a while. You don't have to be part of it. You can just sneak in with us and go your own way."

"You're going to take on the entire facility?"

He nodded.

Troi was incredulous. This seemed too farfetched to

be real. Had the recent battle pushed him off the deep end?

"Do you want to come with us?" he asked, watching her closely.

"Are you sure you aren't being unrealistic . . ."

"Why would I be unrealistic? When have you seen me make a misjudgment?"

She was momentarily at a loss.

"You are no more infallible than anyone else," she said finally. "You've suffered some big losses in your past."

"Not true."

"Yes it is. It's your wife and son isn't it? You lost them, you feel that you failed them somehow."

Troi felt she'd stabbed into a deep wound and winced. But his Odysseus persona wasn't too badly shaken this time. In fact, he seemed to have been expecting her remark.

"I knew it," he said.

"Knew what?"

"I knew it from the beginning. You can read my feelings, like a seer—like one who sees into the mind. You aren't of this world at all. More like someone out of a myth. You don't even look like other women—your eyes are different. Why is it you've never said a word about where you come from? Why is everything about Rampart new to you?"

She was astonished at how he'd led her into this trap. Wily Odysseus. She wanted to terminate the conversation before her cover was blown. But he kept right on.

"You're the most mysterious, beautiful woman I've ever met. But either you deny your own feelings or you don't have any feelings."

"That's absurd. You know nothing about my feelings. What you don't seem to remember is that I have friends in trouble, and it's going to take everything I've got to help them. I don't have time for anything else. I don't have time for an affair with you, and I know that's what you want. I may decide to go with you into CephCom, but that's it."

"What I have to do is at least as hard as what you have to do," he replied, "but I don't turn myself into a stone to accomplish it."

She thought it was a ridiculous statement. Troi wanted to tell him why he was wrong, but stopped herself. How had the conversation become an analysis of her? She was supposed to be analyzing him.

Odysseus put his hand on her arm.

"Don't," she said, and moved out of his reach. "That's out of the question."

Troi took off the borrowed cloak and stood up to leave.

Then she paused and examined the situation rationally. She didn't want him upset. She needed to let him down without hurting his feelings. In fact, if she was going to accompany him into CephCom, she still needed to know more about him—if she could rely on him, or if he might suddenly go off the beam.

"Sorry," she said. "I do like you, but it can't be the way you want. This is hardly the time or place for such a thing."

"I'm glad you put it that way," Odysseus said. "Because there will be another time and place. I'm going to make sure of it."

"All right," Troi said. "Someday I'd like to know you better. I admit to curiosity about what happened to your family. In fact, it might make you feel better if you just got it off your chest now."

"That's just what I was thinking. See, there you go again."

Troi wouldn't be drawn along any farther and

waited to see if he would unburden himself on his own.

"I was married when I was in the CS," he said after a pause. "I was a rising star in the service and had the highest arrest record of any officer. Worst of all, I was dead serious about what we were doing; I thought we were fighting for our lives and the lives of Rampart.

"One day I happened to have a one-eye with me when I came home. I found out my own wife, and my son, who was fifteen then, were Dissenters. They were hiding fiction in our own house. I did what a CS officer had to do—I had them arrested, and they were given the maximum penalty, they were blanked.

"I never saw them again; I wasn't allowed to. I told myself they'd been put out of their misery. But then I started to have trouble on the job. I kept blowing arrests. The CS pumped me full of military psychogens to keep me going, but I started to hate myself anyway, and I wandered off in a depression and never came back.

"Turns out some of the fiction my family'd hidden was still at the house. I found it and couldn't stop myself from reading it. The stories helped me cut through the pain. I had to have more of them, and I took up with Dissenters, just to get the stories, at first. When I actually became a Dissenter, I was Odysseus, because that was my son's favorite story.

"There have been other defectors like me. Through them I found out my wife's blanking didn't work, and they had to destroy her body. The body that was my son's belongs to a CS officer now. He wouldn't know me if he saw me. He thinks someone else is his father."

Troi felt that he was relieved to have talked about these things, and that his Odysseus persona was still strong as ever. His fascination with her was part of that Odysseus character—in order to fully live the myth, he wanted a woman from the myth-world, and she was that woman.

But he might, after all, be able to get them into CephCom. He'd once worked there, and he had a strong motive for atonement and revenge.

She asked him some questions about his mission, told him she'd accept his help getting into CephCom, and then bade him a cordial good night.

As Troi walked away she thought she had, as a counselor, figured him out pretty well. But she found herself beset by an unusual melancholy. She didn't know if it was the effect of talking with Odysseus or some spontaneous mood of her own. She remembered it had happened when she had first met him. Such strong pangs usually were symptoms and shouldn't be ignored, she knew. But she had to put it out of her mind, because there was just too much else to do.

Troi lay alone in a rough wool blanket, listening to the fugue of dripping and trickling waters, the snores and sighs of the Dissenters around her, and the occasional flapping wings of haguya high overhead.

She would be at CephCom by tomorrow. This would be her last chance to have contact with the Other-worlders. She would either find out what they were now or face Crichton without understanding what he was really about. Just getting into the CephCom building with Odysseus was not enough; she wanted options once she was there.

She lay on the cold stone, asking the Other-worlders to come, though she was sure they would put her through that icy transformation again. This time, she would let them—and maybe then she'd learn the truth.

Her teeth chattered and her body shook as she waited for the Other-worlders. She could feel their proximity; they were no farther than a footstep away, but still in their own state of being. The boulder next to her might have been the Mirror Man, the stalactite above her the Lioness, but Troi could not make them reveal themselves.

She lay awake all night, waiting.

The Dissenters had walked for several hours along a rushing underground river. They were tired and thirsty.

Odysseus halted them, and went off to look for something in the rocks nearby.

The Nummo Twins climbed down to the river itself, and in a moment were passing cups of cold, clear river water back to the other Dissenters. The draughts were accepted gratefully. There was an atmosphere of ceremony and finality to the act.

Troi was the only one who carried no books. Even the elderly Gunabibi had a sizable bundle, which now rested on the rocks next to her, along with a light but long tube of wood, apparently the hollowed branch of a tree. Though Troi didn't know what it was for, she thought the smooth, strong, ageless dark wood matched Gunabibi perfectly.

Gunabibi saw what Troi was looking at. "That is my dijiridu. A musical instrument. I'd play it for you now, but Odysseus has already told us we're getting close to the surface and we have to be quiet."

Gunabibi worked a couple of books from her bundle.

"Look at this," she said to Troi. "Look at how they're soaked from the flood at Alastor. We won't have a chance to dry them."

"You aren't taking them . . ."

"Into CephCom? No. We're going to hide them here. That's what Odysseus is looking for; a hiding place. Even if the CS read our minds they'd have trouble finding some nondescript pile of rocks down here."

She opened one of the books to see if the pages could be unstuck. It was a richly illustrated volume on Egyptian mythology and art. Troi glanced at one of the pictures and felt as though her heart had stopped.

For several seconds her shock at what she saw prevented her from speaking.

The picture was of one of the Other-worlders. The Lioness.

Gunabibi, unaware of Troi's stare, started to turn the page.

"Wait!" said Troi. "Who is that a picture of?"

"Sekhmet, the mythological Egyptian lion-goddess. She is a symbol of the heat of the desert sun, life-taking and life-giving."

Troi asked Gunabibi to tell her more. What she heard left no doubt that the mythological Sekhmet, and the Other-worlder Troi had called the Lioness, were one and the same.

Troi felt as though she were on the verge of discovering something she'd known, unconsciously, all along. She suddenly wanted to know if all the Other-worlders could be found in the waterlogged books.

She asked Gunabibi about the Mirror Man and the Matriarch-voice.

Gunabibi brought out a book and found Troi a picture of Tezcatlipoca the Dark Mirror, who was from Aztec myth and personified the savage, shadowy, militaristic side of humans—a sort of heart-of-darkness warrior who appeared to the night-bound wayfarer. Tezcatlipoca and the Mirror Man were one and the same.

The Matriarch and her mate, Gunabibi suggested, were the symbolic Mother Earth and Father Cosmos —Gaia and Ouranos of the Greeks, Maka-akan and

Nagi Tanka of the Lakota, Awitelin Tsita and Apoyan Ta'chu of the Zuni.

There were small differences between all these myth characters and the beings Troi had encountered as the Other-worlders; but fundamentally, in their meanings and actions, they were the same.

Troi remembered the vision of the Other-worlders she'd had in Alastor, the vision of the great crowd of aliens. Now she realized that they, with their outlandish appearances, their many species and forms, might have all been characters from human imagination.

She started looking through other books that Gunabibi had laid out on the rocks. Once, every few pages, she would see an image that corresponded with an "Other-worlder" she'd encountered. As soon as she finished with one book, she went on to the next. She felt driven to understand as much as possible before the books were hidden.

Altogether, she went through dozens of books without being aware of time or of the other Dissenters.

At a certain moment she looked up and saw the huge pile of books that she'd looked through and cast down next to her.

Gunabibi and Coyote were putting more books down for her to look at, assembly-line style. Troi hadn't even been aware of their help.

Then she realized that all the other Dissenters had gathered around to watch her.

Odysseus laughed. "I'm sure we're all glad that you've taken such an interest in the literature of Earth. Is there something we can help you find?"

Troi looked at the scattered books, some of them wet, some of them falling apart but for makeshift string bindings, some of them just falling apart.

It took another few moments for her to remove her attention from the question of the Other-worlders and place herself mentally back with the people around her. They waited patiently.

"I'm sorry," she said finally. "I should have remembered how precious these books are to you. I hope I didn't damage them."

"Don't worry," said Odysseus, "Coyote was watching you as sharply as a . . . coyote. He made sure you weren't hurting anything—at least no more than was necessary to find what you needed."

"But I shouldn't have hurt them at all."

Coyote, who was standing next to Troi, spoke up.

"Deanna, what good would they be if nobody read them? Now did you find what you needed, or will it be necessary to unpack everything?"

At first she thought he was being sarcastic. Then she realized he was quite serious; the Dissenters were ready to let her look through every book they had, no questions asked.

"I think I've seen what I needed to see," she said. "There was something I'd misunderstood, but now I think I understand. Thank you."

"You are welcome, as a fellow Dissenter," said Coyote, as he and Gunabibi started to pack away the books.

Troi waited for them to finish. She hadn't told them the whole truth. Actually, she didn't fully understand what she had just discovered.

If the Other-worlders were mythological characters that had somehow gotten stuck in her mind, characters of great vividness that she was compelled to remember and imagine, then why?

Perhaps they were actual living beings of some kind that had a will of their own?

And what about Crichton? If the Other-worlders were not aliens, and were in fact characters from literature and mythology, then was Crichton, the Director of Cephalic Security, guilty of the supposed crime he was charged with eradicating—the "crime" of imagination?

Troi again strained to remember what had happened that day on the *Enterprise* with Oleph and Una, just before she first experienced the Other-worlders. But her amnesia still covered that memory like a blanket of fog.

The Dissenters finished hiding the books and were ready to go. They stood for a moment, their stillness in contrast with the rush of the river.

Troi guessed they were saying good-bye to the caves. Some kind of era was ending. Dissenters had lived down here for two hundred years. Maybe these were the last.

Odysseus was the first to move.

The group followed the broad-shouldered, bearded man. After some slow climbing through broken scree, they emerged at a flat place, where the river rushed past a smooth concrete wall, the nether-surface of CephCom itself.

There would be no more time for Troi to solve the mystery of the Other-worlders.

Chapter Thirteen

THE BLIND WOMAN standing before the assembly bench played its microwelder like a musical instrument. Geordi stood nearby to check her progress.

It was a sonata of love and fury, as intense as her ecstasies with her guitar. The Cyclops-buster machine was taking shape with time-lapse rapidity under her sensor-tipped fingers. Geordi knew this struggle to save the ship had a personal dimension for Chops.

For her, a progressive musician, Rampart was the great destroyer of all art—the Censor. She'd been known to put her life on the line to defy it. Once, before she joined Starfleet, her band accepted an invitation to play on a non-Federation planet where food and eating were considered shockingly obscene, and by law, eating had to be done in private.

When Chops' band played there she made sure all lyrics of food remained uncensored in their songs. Some members of the audience attacked the band and the Vulcan keyboardist had to use the nerve-pinch to defend Chops. The band were all arrested and taken to trial, where the Tellarite drummer defiantly answered all questions with luscious descriptions of gourmet dishes, and even smuggled in a sandwich which he produced and tried to eat while on the witness stand. The Federation had a difficult time negotiating the band's release.

Chops hadn't laughed when she told the story. She said that censorship just as ridiculous had been applied to artists, writers, and rock musicians in the twentieth century and that some of them had even been targeted for death because of it.

Now, as Geordi watched the frenetic movements of her hands, he knew no one on the ship could build the Cyclops-buster faster than Chops, but he doubted it would be fast enough. A call from Wentz, on the bridge, supplied confirmation.

"The one-eyes almost got into Impulse a minute ago. I think it's the same pair that got into Warp Engineering, the same locksmith and escort. We can tell by the dents; the soldier-escort has had dents since Worf tried to ambush them."

"You're telling me Worf actually laid hands on it, Lieutenant?"

"Don't know, sir. He hasn't been awake to tell us. But it looks like they're about to make another try and I think this time they'll get in."

"Have you tried fluctuating the temperature around them?"

"As much as we were able. Didn't bother them a bit."

"Try cycling power through the life support grid around them, set up a magnetic field."

Geordi went back to work on a damaged console while he simultaneously controlled the engines. The myriad pains and tensions in his sleep-deprived body had achieved an ever-changing complexity that rivaled the engines themselves. His command was turning into a battle with his own biology.

"Wentz to Lieutenant La Forge."

She sounded excited.

"La Forge here."

"We're being hailed from the planet's surface—it's Captain Picard, sir!"

"Send it down to my screen here—but I want you and the bridge crew to see it, too."

Geordi went over to his monitor. Picard's face was already there.

"Lieutenant La Forge!"

"Captain, sir! Are you all right?"

"Yes, I've been treated well since I've been on the planet's surface. I've been talking with Crichton and he now sees this was all a misunderstanding. We're close to an agreement on finishing our search for the *Huxley*."

"Well, why, then, are his one-eyes still trying to sabotage our ship?"

"Apparently he can't communicate with them from the surface. They have their own on-board command and control systems. You know, it's like the missiles used on Earth during the Post-Atomic Horror—fire and forget. But don't worry. I'm going to tell you how you can neutralize the one-eyes. How much damage have they done so far?"

"Just a moment sir, I'll check the current status."

Geordi switched to a private channel.

"Computer, tell me if that's really Captain Picard."

"Working . . . positive on all parameters."

Geordi still didn't like it. He decided to be safely nonspecific. The real Picard would understand.

He switched back to the outside channel.

"Captain, we're still afloat, but we're going to need a lot of time in drydock when this is finished. We'd love any tips for stopping those little vandals."

"What you have to do right away, Lieutenant, is change the beam-collimation on your phasers. Use the Rollins Collimation Standard. Otherwise, in present

174

configuration, the phasers' energy would cause the one-eyes to explode. Rollins Collimation will allow the phasers to destroy the one-eyes without the explosions."

"That's it?"

"That's it."

"We'll jump on it."

Geordi was really sweating over whether it would be prudent to ask the next question. But Picard anticipated it.

"The away team you sent, Geordi, they're all fine. I think I can even say they're enjoying their stay. And I've asked Crichton to pull his ships back from your position as a gesture of good faith."

Sure enough, Wentz called from the bridge.

"Sir, the Rampartian ships are backing off."

That didn't do much to assure Geordi. The *Enterprise* was still vulnerable. And the communicator-jamming had continued on the surface.

"Keep the shields up, Lieutenant."

Before he switched the channel back to Picard's, he took one more moment to think it all out. There had to be one test, just the right one . . .

"Captain, I need to ask you a question to verify you are who you appear to be."

"You can ask one of the standard code questions."

"No, I had something else in mind, something to suit the occasion. What is the book you sometimes keep in your ready room, from which you most often quote? The book that was in your ready room before we got to Rampart?"

"Lieutenant, this is no time for improvisation. Use standard procedure please."

"What is the book, and who wrote it?"

"I can't remember. Lieutenant, this isn't a recognized procedure."

"Who wrote it?—your favorite, Captain."

"I say, and this is an order, Lieutenant—"

"Can't you give me a phrase from it? It doesn't have to be a fictional phrase. Just one of the titles. A type of storm, for instance. Or, you know, that certain small wild animal that has to be tamed."

"No. There is no such book! You're babbling nonsense."

Geordi could see that Picard really meant it.

"I can't accept that you're Captain Picard," he said, "unless you can give me something from that book."

"Lieutenant, I'm going to have to relieve you from duty," Picard said darkly.

Geordi cut the channel.

For a moment he stood there, appalled. Something abominable had been done to the captain's mind.

He called Wentz on the bridge.

No answer.

"Wentz, are you there?"

"Yeah, I'm here. We . . . oh, God."

"Talk to me!"

"We just lost someone. Someone from Security. They were trying to stop the one-eyes."

Geordi had to lean on the console to stop his shaking. Nightmare without end.

"The one-eyes have broken into impulse," said Wentz.

"Lies, disgusting myths, obscene stories. They're all over the place in there. Don't give me some garbage about not finding them."

Crichton sat in a treatment chair, while a rotund, middle-aged mind-cleanse doctor stood over him with a probe. It was a hand-held device with a shiny gold pod on the end. It could electronically search and destroy fiction in the brain, clean it out and replace it with inert filling, as one would treat a dental carie.

This was known as "cleansing," and Rampartians had to do it all the time. The filling might consist of the number "six" repeated a million times, or a report on the history and technique of sandblasting.

The doctor moved the pod around the top of Crichton's head, searching.

"But I really can't find them, Director Crichton. It is possible that they're present but just not active at the moment."

"You'd better look harder. I've suffered spells of near-insanity because of these hallucinations. I've just been lucky that a one-eye didn't pick them up. We can't just wait for them to happen again. They're getting out of control."

"I could call in another doctor—"

"No, out of the question. You're the only one I trust to keep this in confidence, Henry. Of course, I have voluntarily sought help, and that would be a matter of record, so my guilt would be small. But think of the consequences to the CS. The Director of Cephalic Security, himself a carrier of the Allpox!"

"I do understand the problem, sir."

The doctor moved the probe around the top of Crichton's skull, while his eyes peered over their fat-pouches at an oscilloscope on the table.

Crichton looked at his watch. Then he grabbed his handset phone from his jacket pocket, dialed a number, cleared through CS voice-check, and got his office.

"Are the Dissenters . . . just outside the sub-basement? . . . No, don't let them in. I want them forced to the designated zone in front of CephCom. Where's Ferris? . . . Not like him, but let him finish. Just divert all the men and one-eyes you need to keep the criminals occupied, get them good and tired. No arrests. We'll have Ferris do that, but outside, where the wide angles will look good. CephCom towering in the background. Make sure you have plenty of fill-light for the shadows."

Crichton hung up and let the doctor continue his search.

"Sir, you're under an awful lot of stress. Did you ever consider quitting the CS? Seems like you would be good at directing TV news shows or commercials."

Crichton sighed. "Probably what I should have done all along. Now it's too late. The Council will keep me where I am."

The orderlies had come in an hour ago and strapped Riker onto the bed. He had spent the intervening time in unendurable anguish, not because he seemed to have reached the end of his days, but because he seemed to have failed his friends. The away team mission had been a disaster, had accomplished nothing.

From this position he could still see the video screen on the opposite wall.

He saw images of Ferris and a squad of CS men, jumping from hovercraft onto the roof of a Rampartian building. They threw concussion grenades into the building, then cleared away from the windows as the explosions showered glass and thick smoke into the air.

Then the camera moved smoothly in, taking up a position behind Ferris' shoulder, following him as he leapt through a shattered window and sprinted down a hallway. In an office at the end, behind a door marked "Mental Hygiene," three rag-clad rebels had some lab technicians tied and blindfolded. Ferris burst in at the head of his team. The insurgents were quickly subdued and handcuffed. Ferris went over to one of the technicians and removed her blindfold: expression of undying gratitude on innocent face.

Oh yes, thought Riker, Ferris the liberator, Ferris the patriot, Ferris with all the emblems and decorations . . . If Riker hadn't been tied down he would have kicked the screen to pieces.

The door to Riker's room opened. Two CS men entered, followed by a woman in white uniform with red CS logo, wheeling a cart full of electronic gear. A cap with electrodes sat on top of the cart.

Ferris and another man, both wearing helmets, followed them in.

"Take your helmet off," said Ferris to the man with him. "Let him see you."

The man took his helmet off. It was Picard.

"Captain!"

"Hello, Will."

"I didn't even think you were still alive!"

Picard stood over his first officer with an expression of pity.

"Will, it would be hard to explain it to you in your present state of mind."

The woman started shaving areas on the top of Riker's head.

"But Ferris wanted you to see me," Picard went on.

"That's right, Riker," said Ferris. "I wanted you to see how your captain turned out. How we burned the evil right out of him. Like what we're going to do to you."

Riker had a terrible desolate feeling as he looked at Picard. The Captain's whole demeanor had changed. He was a patronizing schoolmaster.

This, he supposed, was what awaited him too. He kept himself calm, and focused the totality of his concentration on finding a way out, for both of them. His senses felt heightened, as he saw everything with an almost painful clarity. It was as though a layer had been peeled from his eyes.

The other CS men were regarding Ferris with curiosity. It got Riker's attention.

Riker could see that Ferris was agitated. Not operational, not by-the-book. Ferris had come to win a fight while the enemy was still an enemy, and the only way he could signal victory was by showing off a brainwashed Picard. What Ferris really wanted was a true fight to the death, a struggle—complete with ritual blood at the end, not this kind of unwinnable battle against ideas.

Ferris was like a certain type of soldier that had committed brutalities in the twentieth century. The two "oldest" parts of his brain—the R-complex and limbic system, the parts humans have in common with pterodactyls and wolves, the parts that evolved hundreds of millions of years ago—were overstimulated, exploited, driven to distorted aims by his society. His conditioning gave him only aggression, territoriality, blind loyalty, and the hierarchy of the CS as a means for expression.

Riker searched for an idea, some way to trick Ferris into becoming his own victim.

Picard seemed to want to cut the silence.

"What is going to happen to you, Will, is a kind of rebirth. You are insane right now; you have a serious and progressive mental illness that compels you to do criminal acts. I am not able to remember much from the time when I was mentally ill, but I'm sure it was terribly unpleasant, as it must be for you.

"What I want you to understand is, the transition is not painful, or difficult. These people will do it humanely. And the relief when it's over!—when you see the world rationally, with no guessing, nothing unknown, or strange, or frightening. No mysteries, no stories to lie to you and distract you from the facts. The only enemies we really have, Will, are external—those people who want to perpetuate all the falsehoods, all the heresies against truth and the true God."

The woman had finished shaving Riker's head. She smeared conductor on the electrodes, pushed the cap down onto his head, plugged the jacks into their wall-sockets, then powered up all the components on the cart.

She ripped a thick strip of white cloth tape from her roll, and leaned over to apply it over Riker's mouth. Riker moved away from it. In a futile gesture of defiance, he pulled with all his strength against his restraining straps.

Picard seemed to want to say something else to Riker. He frowned, searching for words.

"Will, I promise your fears are groundless."

The technician tried to put the tape on Riker's mouth but he spat it off violently.

"You aren't Jean-Luc Picard," he said. Then he looked at Ferris and played his last card.

"I'm a Federation Marine, Ferris," Riker lied. "I've been in combat worse than you've ever dreamed of. I've had my legs blown off and rebuilt and I've gone for weeks without food and water and still had the strength to kill." Riker spoke the lies with all the false fervor he could muster.

Then Riker tried the bait. "You—you're not a fighting man. You're a housecat. You've never had a real fight in your life. I can take you or any of your soldiers one-on-one no problem. Right now. We'll use the same weapons, you choose them."

Ferris nodded slowly.

"I'd like to take you up on it. Maybe you're a good soldier, maybe not, but one thing this soldier knows is how to finish his mission."

Ferris turned to the technician.

"That's enough time wasted. Let's go."

Ferris motioned for Picard to stand back. Picard

seemed concerned yet hopeful, like a man about to witness an organ transplant.

There was a knock at the door.

"Go ahead," Ferris told the technician. "Blank him. We'll take care of the door."

The technician flicked a switch. Her equipment made a buzzing sound. Riker's eyes were clenched shut.

The knocking at the door continued. One of the CS men opened it. An object flew in, hit the wall, and landed on the floor. It was a small white canister emblazoned with the CS logo.

"Damn it!" shouted Ferris. He dove for the canister, but by the time he'd touched it, the grenade had gone off with an insipid peeping sound.

Ferris' movements became slow. His expression turned imbecilic. He picked up the canister and stared at it uncomprehendingly. He turned it over in his hands, then shook it like a rattle.

The other CS men, the technician, and Picard all looked at each other torpidly.

"I was . . ." said the technician vaguely.

One of the CS men covered his mouth and started to giggle.

Amoret came into the room cautiously. She saw that the grenade had taken full effect. She saw the cart full of equipment, heard it buzzing. She slapped all the switches to their off positions and the buzzing stopped.

She pulled the cap off Riker and struggled with his restraining straps. Sirens started outside. Her sweaty hands slipped on the smooth leather and the chrome buckles.

She jerked Riker to a sitting position. His eyes roved like twin hobos. It was solely the effect of the thought grenade. She'd turned off the blanking equipment in time. His mind would be intact after the grenade-effects wore off.

She pulled him up. Then she grabbed Picard with her other hand and heaved them both toward the door. They were as docile as sleepy toddlers.

She looked up and down the corridor for a moment, then ducked back in the cell. She unhooked a thought grenade from her belt, tripped the safety and the activator, then leaned back out and threw it.

She waited for a few seconds after she heard the little peep. Then she pulled Picard and Riker out the door. The van she'd liberated from the disk-vault was parked right outside. A bit farther down the corridor, a group of CS men stood blinking and scratching their heads, stopped in mid-assault. The thought grenade lay at their feet. One of them started to play with it as though it were a soccer ball.

Amoret opened the back of the van and pushed Riker and Picard in, then ran around to the front. As she climbed into the cab, she saw a phalanx of one-eyes come whipping around the corner behind her.

She floored the power pedal and the electric van took off.

She careened around the bends in the corridors and kept her head low. She knew the van itself would partially protect her and her passengers from the radiation guns, at least from fire coming from the rear.

But the van couldn't protect itself. The radiation from the one-eyes behind her crackled and arced across the metal surfaces inside. Her poor passengers huddled together in the back like animals bewildered by lightning.

A CS man stepped into the van's path and raised his weapon. Amoret ducked. A bright sheet of errant voltage rippled inside the cab. Amoret's hands jerked off the wheel, shocked by the energy, and the van banged and scraped against the side of the corridor.

She swerved around another corner and saw her destination. Down this ramp . . . The long descent allowed her to pick up speed and gain distance from the one-eyes.

Before her were doors stenciled "Clean Room 3." She kept her foot jammed on the pedal, braced herself, and slammed into the doors.

The van ended up inside the lab. Several technicians backed away from the van. On a table near them, Data was strapped down, lifeless.

Amoret activated her last thought grenade, opened the van window, and threw the canister. She ducked down. When the little peep sounded she caught just a taste of the numbing wave, but it wore off in a moment.

She drove the van forward until it bumped against the base of the lab table. The lab technicians stared at her, heads cocked like baffled puppies.

"Whuh?" said one.

She gave the van more juice and pushed the table toward the next set of doors, which were standing open. Thick blast doors; the next lab room doubled as an emergency shelter in case of insurgent attack.

Once she'd gotten the van and the table inside, she swung the heavy doors closed and threw the magnetic bolt. Then she looked around and picked up a wrench. She smashed it repeatedly against the switch until sparks flew and the switch was dead.

She then opened the back of the van and pulled out Riker and Picard. The two men stumbled onto the floor and looked blankly at her and each other.

"Sit," she said, pushing Riker into a chair. "You have to wake up."

She slapped his face several times.

"Cut it out," he said irritably, waving her off as if she were a fly.

"No! You have to wake up!"

The concrete doors clacked against their stops. The CS were trying to get in.

She slapped him again. "What's your name?"

"William."

"William who?"

Riker looked at the doors, heard them being struck repeatedly from outside.

"Someone is at the door," he said frowning. "Shouldn't we let them in?"

"No! You need to wake up!"

He shook his head, trying to get rid of the cobwebs. "What happened?"

"They almost deleted your mind, that's what. And they're going to have another chance, if we don't do something right now."

"Why do I feel so . . ."

"I had to use a thought-numbing grenade to get you free."

"Oh . . ."

Riker looked at the inert, synthetic-skinned form on the table. He broke into a broad grin.

"Hey, I know him."

"Can you revive him?"

Riker nodded slowly.

She leaned close to his ear.

"Do it."

Riker got up and went over to the lab table. He put his hand under Data's back and felt for the switch.

Data's eyes suddenly popped open. He looked at Riker bending over him.

"Commander Riker. I am pleased to see you alive, sir."

"Ummm, likewise, I think."

"You aren't sure, sir?"

"Ummm . . . I don't know."

"Oh." The android was nonplused. He looked about him at his surroundings. The room was largely devoted to tools, spare parts, and emergency rations. Amoret was searching frantically among the tools in the cabinets.

Riker stared at her.

"Don't I know her from somewhere?"

"Sir," said Data, "she was the woman we were arrested with at the ore factory."

"Oh."

"Commander, I have no wish to offend you, but you seem a bit . . . slow. As in simple-minded, addle-pated."

"I feel a bit slow, but it's getting better."

"And that is a strange hairstyle, sir," said the android, looking at Riker's partially shaved scalp. "I trust it was not voluntary."

Amoret threw Riker a wrench.

"We'll explain later," she said to Data. "He's been through a lot."

Riker started working on the bolts holding Data down.

"You just get them started," said Amoret, "I'll back them off the rest of the way by hand."

The concrete doors boomed. Someone was using heavy equipment on them.

"It's worn off now," said Riker after a minute had passed. "Whew, and I thought Klingon tea was rough stuff. You in one piece, Data?"

"Apparently so, sir. I performed a diagnostic when you powered me up. Some mechanisms in my thoracic section have been exposed, as a preliminary stage of disassembly, but I do not seem to have lost any memory sectors."

"That's enough, both of you."

They looked over at the new interlocutor.

Picard stood a few feet away, brandishing a long piece of metal pipe.

"Number One, please get away from Mr. Data."

"Captain, sir, you're a bit confused. You can feel that, right?"

"It's wearing off. Just a stun from the weapon she threw into a detention room," he said, pointing to Amoret. "I know what's what."

The doors boomed again.

"No you don't, sir. You've been brainwashed."

"I've been saved, Will, not brainwashed. Now I order you to stop what you are doing, and give yourself up to the people outside."

Picard advanced a step.

"Keep loosening those bolts," Riker said over his shoulder to Amoret, as he walked forward to meet Picard face-to-face.

"Be clear on this, Will. I'm ready to break your bones to save you."

Picard swung the pipe and Riker spun out of the way.

"I'd even rather see you dead than suffering a lifetime with the Allpox," said Picard.

Riker feinted at Picard, then tried to grab the pipe. Picard dodged and swung again. The pipe struck Riker's shoulder blade.

A white-hot pain shot up and down Riker's body and bounced around in his head. He stumbled back. For an instant a memory seized him: that fight with his father when they were both grown, the betrayal he'd felt as his father had rained blows on him with the heavy anbo–jyutsu staff.

Riker shook off the memory. Picard came at him again, swinging the pipe at his head. Riker dodged like a boxer. He heard the pipe whistle past his ear, and had an idea.

"Captain, do you remember any of this fiction: 'To hold, as 'twere, the mirror up to nature; to show virtue her own feature, scorn her own image' . . ."

"Damn it, Will!"

Picard dropped the pipe and put his hands over his ears.

Riker reached down and threw the pipe across the room. As he came back up Picard struck him across the jaw.

Riker put his arms up to block another blow, then struck back. He caught Picard above the eye, but it wasn't enough to knock the man out. The captain had always been in prime shape. Riker knew he'd have to hit him seriously, and knew he'd have to be willing to hurt him.

"This body is not my captain—my friend Jean-Luc," he told himself. "This body was just a vehicle for someone that is no longer here."

He swung hard, connecting with Picard's chin, and the captain went out like a light.

"I didn't enjoy that at all," said Riker, looking down at the sprawled man.

Amoret finished removing the bolts from the restraints holding Data. She swung the steel restraints outward, and Data sprang onto his feet.

He pulled up his shirt. The skin on his chest was partially opened, like a ripped plastic curtain. He reached in and made some adjustments by hand to the gleaming mechanisms inside his chest, then pulled his shirt back down.

The doors boomed again.

"Do you know of an escape route?" Data asked Amoret.

"I didn't assume I'd make it even this far," said Amoret. "I thought I would come up with something as I went along. The one thing I wanted to do most was . . . here, let me show you."

She brought Data and Riker around to the van, and showed them the disk and a full rack of blanking equipment.

She then told them how she had saved Picard's original mind on the disk, and how the blanking equipment in the van could be used in reverse, to refill Picard's mind with what it had lost.

"Usually when the CS does something like that, they only put back selected parts. That's what they did to your captain last time. For that you need a lot of supplementary gear. But to just put back the whole mind, I can do that with the equipment in the van."

"Data," said Riker, "check out this equipment."

"Yes, sir. However, I have been examining it, and I believe I understand the theory behind the device. If it appears operational on closer inspection, I recommend we proceed with her plan as soon as possible, as we do not know if we will escape with Captain Picard, the disk, and the equipment. And the magnetic emulsion used on the disk is probably no more stable than a—"

"Okay, Data."

Data checked the equipment and found it satisfactory. Within a few minutes Amoret was hooking up Picard.

As they worked, the booming sounds from the concrete doors ceased.

To Riker, it suggested only that the CS were changing their mode of intended entry.

Chapter Fourteen

Troi had expected the Dissenters to enter CephCom through some preexisting opening, such as a sewer.

She now saw that she was wrong. They were going to roll a boulder off a high cavern cliff to smash the concrete basement wall from outside. Lomov and several others were already working the boulder loose.

It seemed an unlikely way to enter the belly of the whale, but Troi was even more worried about Odysseus himself.

She perceived that his Odysseus-persona had shrunk and weakened. He paced by himself along the bank of the rushing cave-river, casting dark looks at the concrete wall on the river's far bank. He was succumbing to regret and anxiety. He looked exhausted.

She approached him with the intent of a counselor: to bolster a flagging spirit. She would need his help getting into CephCom. She would have the best chance of completing her mission if he was able to complete his. He needed to be Odysseus again, with all his wiliness and resourcefulness. The mood of that character was the source of his effectiveness; without it he could do nothing.

"Are you okay?" she asked.

"No."

"Do you want to tell me about it?"

He inclined his head toward the concrete wall.

"I don't think many of us are going to leave that place alive. And it'll be my fault. This was my plan."

"I don't understand," said Troi. "I thought you were Odysseus, and this was your moment to return home. To string the bow no one else could string, show your true self, restore order in your house."

"Sounds great doesn't it," he said. "But I used to work in there. I know what's behind that wall. I have no bow, and what you're looking at is my true self."

"Are you telling me you aren't Odysseus anymore? You've gone back to being the man who arrested his own family?"

"I arrested them and sent them to their deaths," he said. "Nothing I do, no mind-game or heroic story, no pretense that I'm someone else, is going to change that. It'll be with me until the moment I die."

Troi could feel his Odysseus persona slipping away like sand through an hourglass; it was almost completely gone. She cast about for something to say. She thought of how she'd spied on him back at Alastor and seen him using props and pictures, like a method actor, and she realized he'd had to leave those props behind when the CS attacked. He had never gone back to his room before the skirmish and the flight. Now, without them, he couldn't sustain the character.

She had to help him or lose this chance to get into CephCom.

"No, it doesn't have to at all! That's not you. That was never a person at all, that was a programmed automaton. That man didn't have free will, he didn't have his own brain or his own thoughts. He was just a mass of pre-approved reactions and feelings created by the stupid thought police! You didn't even exist as a man until you became Odysseus."

"But I can't actually do what Odysseus did," he said. "I can't do all those impossibly great things he did at Troy, or in the Cyclops' cave. So in what way can I be Odysseus?"

"Who are you to say what's possible? Who gave you the authority?" asked Troi. "The arrogant people on the other side of that wall think they have that authority—and that's what makes them so foolish. That's the gap in their armor!"

Troi let him think about it for a moment. They watched the Nummo twins throw a rope across the whitewater.

"You say it's impossible," Troi went on. "Didn't you also say, last night, that I'm a seer? That I'm not like other women, that I'm not a human? That shouldn't be possible either, should it? But I'm going to prove it's true. Concentrate on a feeling, and I'm going to tell you what it is, right now."

Odysseus stared at the river.

Troi strained her perception to its limits. She picked up a feeling so complete it was nearly a visual image. He was walking under a great open sky and someone small was sitting on his shoulders, shouting or laughing with joy.

"You're going back to a pleasant memory. Being with someone you loved. Your little boy. Your son, riding on your shoulders. Am I right?"

He turned to look at her in wonder.

"Now you know I'm a seer," she said. "I really am from another world, as you said I was. I'm no more an ordinary human than Calypso or Circe. I've been to countless worlds and most everything I've seen would be called impossible by the people on the other side of that wall. And as a seer I know that you really are Odysseus, no matter what you tell yourself otherwise. You're that very same hero of Homer's stories—how and why, I can't say, but you are. You will come through this alive, and we'll meet again when it's all over, just like you said last night. I already know how this story has to go."

Odysseus ran his hand through his gray-flecked beard.

"I was right," he said. "You really are from some other world. Like Circe or Calypso."

Troi felt a change taking place within him. She had supplied the support he needed to get back into character, and he was doing it with a vengeance. He was dropping doubts that had always been with him, doubts that he could ever overcome his personal agony and become who he wanted to be.

She left him so he could prepare himself. She sat on a rock from which she could watch him.

He stood near the river and gathered all the personal strength and will he possibly could. He was Odysseus now more than ever, just in time for his peregrination to end, just in time to come home and restore order where evil now reigned.

At the river's edge he bent over, scooped up dirt with his hands, and rubbed it into his clothes. Troi was baffled for a moment, then remembered that in *The Odyssey,* when this man returned home to Ithaca, he disguised himself as a beggar.

He looked up at the cliff. Lomov gave him the "ready" signal. The other Dissenters moved away from the cliff.

There was a moment of stillness, a sort of inner deep breath taken collectively by the Dissenters, an invocation and gathering of the emotional power of their mythoi. Troi could feel them tuning like an orchestra, two dozen people of all different races and cultures ready to merge into one sustained chord.

Then Odysseus returned Lomov's signal. Lomov got directly behind the boulder and gave a great shove, pushing with his head as well as his body, and the boulder rolled off the cliff, bounding and crashing downward, gathering momentum.

It hit the concrete wall with tremendous force, shaking the ground under Troi's feet.

A great cloud of dust rose in the air. Odysseus pulled Troi toward it, and all the Dissenters followed. They swam across the river, holding on to the rope that the Nummo had strung. Then, coughing concrete dust from their lungs, they clambered up over the remnants of the boulder and the broken slabs of the wall itself, which had indeed shattered.

They were now in a square room with large water pipes on one side.

Two men, shocked into immobility, wearing blue CS service coveralls, stood at their water-control station. A television set on a stand intoned a rerun of the news report about the new CS truth drug. Cups of coffee sat steaming on top of the television.

"Hello gents," said Odysseus. "I gather you handle a lot of water here. Do you know how to swim?"

As the CS men tried to reach for a phone, Odysseus and Lomov each grabbed one, pulled them to the hole in the wall, and pitched them out. Their splashes were followed by shouts that faded as they were carried downstream.

The Nummo twins were already taking readings and pulling switches on the water-mains console.

"They were hydraulic engineers when they lived above ground," Odysseus whispered to Troi. "They designed this system. They're going to overload the water pressure and burst the pipes right above us."

Meanwhile Lomov wedged a huge piece of concrete against the one door into the room, and other Dissenters jimmied the elevator controls and forced open the elevator's hoistway.

"Rhiannon," said Odysseus, "you know what to do."

The adolescent girl almost started directly on her way; but instead, walked over to Troi and gave her a hug. Troi realized this was her good-bye. She found herself hugging back.

Then Rhiannon let go, and without looking back, climbed into the hoistway and disappeared up a ladder.

Odysseus climbed in after her and motioned Troi to follow. They began to climb the ladder. The steel rungs were slippery with black grease, and Troi had trouble maintaining footing.

Far up the shaft Troi could see Rhiannon climbing fast, fearlessly. She was already several floors above them.

Troi waited while Odysseus peered through the crack between the hoistway doors. "Wait here," he said, then parted the doors and stepped out.

The doors shut again and Troi watched through the crack. Beyond was a huge parking garage housing fleets of CS vans and armored personnel carriers. There was chaos as CS soldiers and service personnel ran in all directions. Water spouted from burst pipes along the walls. The floor was a lake.

A helmeted CS man fumbled with the door of a huge personnel carrier-truck, scrambling to get it out of the garage before the flooding got worse. Odysseus approached him with the body language of a vagrant asking for a handout.

The CS man shook his head, annoyed but obviously not surprised—there were a lot of poor on this planet.

Other CS officers watched for a moment, then,

seeing no danger from the pitiful homeless person, went back to moving vehicles.

The CS officer Odysseus was petitioning grew impatient and pushed at him. Odysseus let himself be pushed until both men were hidden from the view of the rest of the garage. Then Odysseus yanked the man's helmet off and knocked him unconscious.

Odysseus hid him under a mobile radiation cannon, took his keys, and jumped into the armored truck. He started the monstrous diesel-turbine engine, drove over to the elevator doors, and slammed a switch that opened the back of the truck.

The Dissenters climbed in. Troi sat next to Odysseus in the cab.

Odysseus drove his Trojan Horse ahead through the lapping waters. He'd gone only a few yards when a one-eye pulled up beside his window and peered in.

Odysseus floored the gas and spun the truck's wheel. The truck bounded over a barrier and crashed onto a spiral ramp. The truck's tires screeched as he careened up the ramp. In the rearview mirror Troi could see the one-eye losing the race behind them.

"Keep your heads low," he said. "Deanna, you'll be with me for a ways. I'll physically show you where the cell blocks are and where your communicators might be, if they're here at all. Then you're on your own."

Odysseus spun the wheel again and the truck veered into another parking garage. He drove among the rows of CS military vehicles for a while, and then stopped.

"First team," he said. Coyote, Gunabibi, and several other Dissenters disembarked. Each embraced Troi as they left.

"All done. This will wake him up," said Amoret. She flicked a switch on her blanking equipment. Picard's eyes opened. He looked into the faces of

196

Riker, Data, and the red-haired woman who had blanked his mind in the first place.

He put his hand up and touched the electrode-cap on his head.

"Commander Riker . . . Data . . . Strange," he said. "Just a moment ago, I was about to undergo this same operation, in my cell, alone with this woman . . . and I blinked, and the scene shifted entirely. And now my jaw feels as if it's been kicked by a horse."

"Looks good," said Amoret. "An indication that we've restored his brain to its state at the moment the original disk was made."

"Would someone please explain . . ."

"Yes, we will, Captain, but I want to try something first," said Riker. "Bear with me. Complete this, please. 'To hold, as 'twere, the mirror up to nature; to show virtue her own feature, scorn her own image . . .'"

Picard completed the line.

"'. . . and the very age and body of the time his form and pressure.'"

"Thank you, sir. Glad to have you back."

"I would like to express my approbation as well, sir," said Data. "But please excuse me for a moment." He got out of the van and could be heard pacing around the room.

"Well, I feared the worst had happened to you both," said Picard. "I saw your capture on Rampart television. But is either of you going to tell me what happened?"

"Sir . . ." said Riker with a sigh, "you were brainwashed for several hours. It would have been permanent if Amoret hadn't saved your mind on a disk. We just got finished feeding it back in."

Amoret smiled in spite of herself. "I looked at some of the things on the disk. I got to know you. That's what did it."

"What do you mean, looked at it?" asked Picard.

"Experienced it."

"And my whole mind was there? Everything? All memories?"

"Absolutely everything."

Picard thought through the implications of that "everything."

"Please don't be embarrassed," said Amoret as she removed the cap from his head. "It turned me back into a Dissenter. If it had been censored or filtered, maybe it wouldn't have worked."

Suddenly all three realized that Data, outside the van, was speaking.

"Murray Hill spicules mogul in pajamas decorated with vermilion arch supports and re-entry vehicles.

Pork-pie hat reflected in the eyes of maggots which she produced from her wallet as an alibi.

Praying mantis protocol for Piña Colada of scorn and hate, of scorn and hate, accompanied by redness and irritation.

The flying binky formed under his upper lip while the President breaded a group of marmots."

The three humans peered around the sides of the van and saw the android with his back to them. They couldn't see what he was doing, but by the movements of his shoulders he seemed to be manipulating something in his hands.

He continued to speak in the same incomprehensible vein, but took one of his hands away from his mysterious hidden task and gestured for the people behind him to get away.

They looked at each other for a moment, baffled, but then Picard and Riker herded Amoret back into the van. From inside, they heard his utterances continue for another minute. Then there was the sound of a slamming door.

Riker looked around the side of the van.

Data faced him now, but one of his hands was behind his back.

"Data," said Riker, "are you hiding something from me?"

"Yes, sir."

"May I ask why?"

"No, sir. It is vital, sir, that none of you know why, and that you do not ask me about it or even think about asking me.

"Further, it is essential that none of you watch me until I give you further notice. Stay in the van, shut the windows, and completely forget about me."

Riker drew his head back into the van and shut the back gate. He and Picard looked at each other and nodded in silent assent.

"Is he usually this strange?" asked Amoret.

"Please do what he asked," said Picard. "Why don't you tell us what you can about possible escape routes from this room?"

She began to tell all she knew about the layout of CephCom. Picard listened carefully. He had no time for actual embarrassment or squeamishness, but, still, he found he was more comfortable when he wasn't looking at her face. In spite of the gratitude he felt toward her for saving his mind, the idea of her sifting through his most private thoughts took some getting used to.

Outside the van, in a corner of the room, Data sat on a fifty-gallon drum. His attention was occupied by a small object on his lap.

"What do you mean the transmitter just went down!"

Crichton cradled his head in his hands and massaged his temples.

"That's impossible!" he said. "That's a triple fail-safe system!"

"I know, sir," said the voice on his headset. "But some teenage girl climbed way up the transmitter tower and crossed a bunch of wires, and now it's off-line. She's still up there. Do you want us to shoot her down?"

"This is all wrong," said Crichton. "The Dissenters were to be forced into the quadrangle. Ferris is already there, the one-eyes are already there . . ."

"Ferris is still there, sir, and so are the one-eyes, but as you know, all of the one-eyes on the CephCom grounds have to use the transmitter, and can't relay information or coordinate their fire until the transmitter is back up. Some of the Dissenters have entered the building. I'm getting damage reports."

"Look," said Crichton, "I want all of the Dissenters forced out of the building *now,* including the girl. Don't wait for the one-eyes, don't worry about coordinating fire, just do it. These people should be no problem—they aren't even armed! Since we don't have the one-eyes, we'll have to use cameras in the hovercraft to get our video. Make sure they get plenty of close-ups of Ferris firing at the Dissenters. And I want a hand-to-hand scene as well—Ferris one-on-one with a Dissenter, no guns. Make sure he takes his helmet off."

"What about the criminals we've trapped in the shelter behind the clean room? The three from the *Enterprise?*"

"Just leave them there with guards posted outside. They can't go anywhere from in there. We'll arrest them after we finish with the rest of the operation."

"Yes, sir."

Crichton looked up at the lenses and antennae that

pointed to the interrogation platform in his office. He rose from his chair and went into his private bathroom. There were no antennae or cameras in there.

He washed his hands compulsively, for the twentieth time this day. As always, he didn't know why he had to do it. The compulsion was irresistible and it made him feel much better to just go along with it.

At least it gave him time to think. A moment ago he had only barely suppressed the insane fictions in his mind. But he was sure that by now some antenna somewhere must have picked up a bit of them. And it could only be his value to the CS and the Council of Truth, his peculiar talent for creating video images the public wanted, that was keeping him from arrest. Who could they get to replace him?

He blamed the *Enterprise* people and the Dissenters for the fictions. The blasphemous tales had started surfacing in his head the moment the *Enterprise* had arrived, and, clearly, the *Enterprise* had come to help the Dissenters. The ship was full of the Allpox.

At the foot of the steps in front of CephCom's grand main entrance, Ferris waited. He knew the one-eyes were out of commission; still, he didn't anticipate major problems. There were several hundred CS soldiers crouched behind jeeps and personnel carriers, weapons at the ready. Ferris held his own service weapon at his side.

Two white CS hovercraft circled above, cameramen and their cameras visible through the open doors.

Ferris looked at the formations of soldiers around him. He was back in his tactical, operational element. That fiasco in Riker's cell had been entirely his fault. He'd let Riker goad him, manipulate him, but it wouldn't happen again. He was fully in control.

He heard a noise on his headset and responded.

"OpsCom, you back on-line? This is Ferris."

"We're back, Major."

"I want a situation report."

"Roger that. Uh, wow, radar is showing something big crossing the perimeter from the southwest."

"Hostile?"

"I don't know . . . it's . . . it's a Navaho Rainbow Guardian, sir! Coming at your position!"

Ferris turned reflexively.

"I don't see anything."

"Watch out, sir, he's going to deploy hozho, the Path of Beauty! Watch out!"

"What—" Suddenly Ferris realized he was being fed something blasphemous through his helmet. The headphone filters weren't working. He ripped the helmet off as though it were full of anthrax germs.

"I guess he didn't want to hear it," said Coyote, as he put down the mike. He sat in a mobile communications truck, in a nest of patch-cords he'd rigged for the disruption of military communications.

Next to him, Gunabibi's eyes were closed as she played the dijiridu into a mike she'd set up in front of it. Her circular breathing, the special technique that allows breath in through the nose while the mouth continues to expel air through the instrument, enabled her to indefinitely sustain the sounds.

"There," said Coyote as he plugged in a cord, "this will patch your mike into all intercoms and headsets. Play! Play!"

It was a song with no words; a single, deep, main note with many intertwining sub-tones and phases. Gunabibi's fertility song. It was the continuous all-note of the entire chain of life, the song of DNA itself, double-strand after double-strand entwined a trillion-trillionfold, helixing back into the dark time-well.

Coyote peered out. The communications truck was

parked on an upper level garage. Even up here there was confusion because of the flooded lower garages; vehicles were jostling and CS men were scurrying about like ants. None of them had spotted the cables leading from the truck into the communications box on the wall.

Coyote could see some of the CS men tweaking their helmets as they tried to identify the strange music playing in their ears. Their panic and confusion multiplied as he watched.

A few of them fell to the ground or covered their eyes or cried out in terror. They were having seizures in their right temporal lobes. The creative image-and-music parts of their brains had been starved and straitjacketed for so long that Gunabibi's song had triggered bursts of wild hallucinations.

Odysseus drove the armored truck on a service road that ringed the CephCom complex.

Troi could see disruption everywhere. Convoys roared past them in both directions. Troops ran across the road. Gunabibi's dijiridu hummed from the truck's CS-frequency radio.

The dijiridu-sound stopped and Coyote's voice replaced it.

"Let me tell a story the Tlingit Indians tell, about the Statue that Came to Life. A ma—"

Coyote's voice was cut off. Troi heard muffled shouting from the radio, then a silent interval, then the voice of a CS officer.

"All sectors—the transmitter is up and the one-eyes are back on line. The intruders in sector C have been caught."

Odysseus speeded up.

"We'll still make it, and we can get them free too," he said, "if we make it to that bridge."

Troi could see the high, narrow bridge, still far ahead.

She had a feeling of foreboding. Then she realized an actual shadow had descended on the truck. It was as if a black cloud were following above them.

Slowly, a huge olive drab–colored object, much larger than their truck, lowered itself into view in front of them. It was flying along with them, tracking their course.

Guns, missile-tubes, and antennae covered its surface, and a single, huge purple-tinted glass lens stared out from its nose.

"Battlefield one-eye," Odysseus said. "Keep cool. I'll deal with it."

He slammed on the brakes and the truck slewed all over the road. When it stopped the airborne behemoth stopped with it, hovering, peering into the truck's windshield, its antennae searching for thoughts.

Troi ducked below the dash, waiting to feel the pulse of radiation that would kill her. She looked up at Odysseus. He was sitting with eyes closed, in rapt concentration.

He remained like that for several seconds.

Then he opened his eyes.

"We got it. It heard my thought."

Troi peered over the dash.

The huge battlefield one-eye had backed off. It jerked about randomly in the middle of the sky, pointing at the ground, the clouds, the side of a building, as if it had lost its mind. The movements accelerated.

"Get down," said Odysseus.

They both ducked. There was a flash, followed by an explosive blast. The truck windshield shattered. Debris rained down outside. There were a dozen secondary explosions.

When they stopped, Odysseus looked over the dash, then down at Troi.

"You okay?"

Troi brushed glass off herself. "I'm fine."

There was a small bleeding cut on her arm. Odysseus stared at it for a moment, then their eyes met.

Troi wondered if the blood might make him doubt that she was from another world. But if it did, she couldn't perceive it.

Odysseus started driving again, rolling right over chunks of the exploded behemoth.

"There's a speculative equation that screws up the control programs in the battlefield one-eyes," he said as he sped on toward the bridge. "That Cyclops ran on numbers. We fed it too much of its own wine."

In front of the main entrance, Ferris waited, gun drawn, as his headset crackled with CS voices. The voices, still a bit confused from the Dissenters' escapades, still had information to impart to him. They said that one of the Dissenters was being chased toward the door.

Above, the two hovercraft circled close, their cameramen setting up shots of the doorway and of Ferris himself.

Ferris was alone in that part of the quadrangle. The rest of the men had pulled many yards back to isolate him and make the video image more forceful.

Ferris saw a running figure inside the building, strobing light and dark as it passed windows, heading toward the wide doorway. A Dissenter, the headset voices told him.

The figure burst into the open. Ferris fired at it.

The figure fell. It was an adolescent girl. She had long hair and crooked teeth. Stunned instantly unconscious, she lay at the top of the stairs, her hair flaring out like a fan on the concrete.

Ferris could hear voices on his helmet headset saying "Oh, no, she's too young," and "Crichton can't use a picture like that."

Ferris was unfazed, self-possessed, as he readied himself for the next Dissenter. Then the comm officer told him that the other Dissenters had already been captured in the building. All except three: one man alone, and one man with a woman—all were being reserved for Ferris.

Odysseus stopped the van and led Troi up a spiral stair to the bridge's upper level.

They spotted Lomov at the other end of the bridge.

"Niki!" cried Odysseus.

The hulking barge hauler was trying to pry open a door with a tire iron. The door was a metal-grate type with an electronic lock. Lomov was bending the steel of the door but the lock itself was not giving way.

Lomov turned to look at Odysseus, then, realizing there was no more time, redoubled his efforts.

Suddenly a huge assault hovercraft appeared from behind the building, coming toward Lomov. Lomov pulled and smashed at the door in desperation.

"Wait till I call for you," Odysseus told Troi, "then run across the bridge to us."

She was about to plead with him not to try and defy the hovercraft himself. But she stopped herself, because she knew he'd try anyway. She would do best by strengthening his Odysseus character, the clever persona by which he achieved all his successes. She remembered that Homer's Odysseus, resourceful as he was, sometimes needed help from beings of another order.

She pointed at the sky. The *Enterprise* was up there somewhere.

"My people are with you," she told Odysseus.

He looked at her and knew, on some level, what she meant.

He left her there and ran toward Lomov and the hovercraft at the far end of the bridge. The craft's door opened and a cameraman leaned out.

In front of Odysseus, a head and shoulders came up into view above the edge of the bridge—a CS officer climbing up from the lower level.

The officer pointed a gun at Lomov.

"Niki! Behind you!" shouted Odysseus.

Lomov turned and saw the tableau in an instant, but there was nowhere to duck. Instead he threw his body against the door, bloodying himself on the unyielding metal.

The CS officer fired.

Lomov fell. Odysseus ran toward him, and so did the officer.

But before they reached him, Lomov staggered back upright. Again he made his own body into a projectile and smashed once more against the door. This time its lock burst and it banged open. But Lomov lay unconscious on the pavement.

The CS officer stopped before he reached Lomov, and turned to face Odysseus. Holding his weapon in one hand, he pulled off his helmet with the other and cast it away.

Odysseus froze when he saw the man's face.

"Ferris," he said in astonishment.

"Powell." Ferris seemed equally surprised. "Long time no see. I've been waiting ten years for this. Now I'm going to need some payback for all the men I've lost to your Dissenters' Allpox. Yeah, I think it's time for some payback."

Ferris holstered his gun, then lunged at Odysseus. The two men fought, pounding each other, wrestling, and trying to push each other over the edge. They were closely matched but Ferris seemed to have the slight advantage in size and strength.

The hovercraft circled overhead, blowing both men's hair wildly. Its cameraman tilted and panned his camera to keep both men composed in his frame, the one garbed in sleek white uniform, the other in a street-bum's rags. There were no other CS men on the bridge, and no one-eyes, nothing else in sight to detract from the image that would be seen on millions of Rampartian television screens. Just Ferris in manly combat with the chief of the criminals.

Ferris used a karate kick on Odysseus, who lost his balance and had to hook his arm over a metal post to keep from falling off the bridge.

"Powell," said Ferris, "maybe you should have stayed with the CS after all. Your physical condition seems to have slid a bit."

"My name isn't Powell."

Odysseus leapt up, swinging fiercely at Ferris, finally connecting with a stunning blow.

Ferris stumbled back, dazed, and dropped to his knees.

Both men were now nearly right in front of Troi. She could sense something dangerous happening to Ferris. The controlled mien of the CS military officer was giving way to unfettered fury, a blood lust, a need for consummation.

In that instant Troi knew Ferris would disobey orders, whatever those orders were. She distinctly felt something snap inside him.

He thumbed a button on his weapon. She sensed his grim animal satisfaction and knew he was going to kill Odysseus instead of stun him.

"No!" shouted Troi.

He fired.

The radiation pattern hit Odysseus square in the chest. The bearded man yelled something unintelligible at the sky as red stains bloomed all over his muddy tunic. Then he fell heavily on his back.

Ferris stood over him. Troi felt Ferris get himself back under control. Ferris became once again the operational military man.

Odysseus was still alive, for the moment. Troi could sense that as well.

Fifty one-eyes suddenly rose from under the bridge, where they had hovered in hiding, and now surrounded the scene. The camera-hovercraft flew away.

A squad of helmeted CS men came up behind Troi. One put handcuffs on her.

Ferris bent over Odysseus, slapped his face. Odysseus mumbled.

Ferris was going to follow proper procedure to the letter. He unclipped a small case from his belt and removed a squeeze bottle. He squirted some of the CS-developed pharmaceutical up both of Odysseus' nostrils.

He slapped Odysseus' face repeatedly as he waited for the combination of drugs to elicit a state of absolute, involuntary truthfulness.

"Stay with me, Powell. I need information from you, the names of other insurgents."

Odysseus mumbled softly. Troi couldn't catch what he said.

"Who are your co-conspirators above ground?" asked Ferris.

Odysseus mumbled again.

"Hurry!" said Ferris. "The names of your principal helpers in the city!"

"Eumaios," said Odysseus.

"Eumaios who?" asked Ferris.

"Eumaios . . . pig farmer."

"Relay these into the computer as I give them to you," Ferris shouted to the CS men around Troi. "First one is Eumaios, a pig farmer."

Odysseus' voice seemed to gain in strength. "Euryclea—she is a nurse," he said, "and Autolycos, and Polipses . . ."

"Euryclea, who is a nurse, and Autolycos—" said Ferris, stopping as the one-eyes suddenly drew up in a tight circle around him.

"What are you doing?" he asked the machines. "Let me finish my report. Autolycos, Polipses—"

The one-eyes drew closer. Attack formation. Ferris knew it well enough. They were going to shoot him.

"Get back!" he commanded.

He could hear the one-eyes start to prime their weapons. In a soldier's reflex he reached for his own gun. He had gotten it halfway out of its holster when the combined radiation from fifty one-eye guns vectored directly through his head and killed him instantly.

There was a moment of quiet, except for the wind blowing past the high, exposed bridge.

The CS men walked over to the two prone forms. They took Troi with them.

As Troi stared at Odysseus, perceiving he was now dead, she heard snatches of conversation between the CS officers.

"Looks like Ferris tried to report fiction . . ."

"You hear any of it?"

"No. Filtered out of our headsets . . ."

"But Ferris used the truth drug on that guy. The drug's foolproof!"

"Okay, so how could he have given Ferris any fiction to report?"

210

". . . don't know . . . maybe to him it was the truth."

The CS soldiers began to pull Troi away. She got a last look at Odysseus. His eyes were open, reflecting a sky full of thunderheaded cumulus clouds—the clouds of Zeus Alastor, Zeus the Avenger.

Chapter Fifteen

"CHOPS, WE'RE OUT OF TIME," Geordi said. "The one-eyes have shut down the impulse engines. Our orbit is starting to decay. All I've got left is enough warp engine power for partial shields. The one-eyes are heading back in my direction. I think they're going to try and finish off the warp engines for good. We'll either fall like a brick, or get shot full of holes, or both."

Geordi was trying to coax more power out of the warp engines even as he talked.

"I'll have the first Cyclops-buster ready in twenty minutes," said Ensign Chops Taylor's voice, from Geordi's communicator.

"We've only got ten max."

"Can you spare Skoel for a while? . . ." She paused and Geordi could hear her make a rapid sequence of welds. ". . . I create at my best with a little help from some IDIC."

"You've got him. La Forge out."

Geordi's communicator then spoke with a much lower voice.

"Worf to La Forge."

"La Forge here. You still in sickbay?"

"Correct, sir. However, I'm feeling fine, and I'm ready to leave. What is the situation with the one-eyes?"

"The same two who were down here before are coming back to finish me off."

"Sir, I believe it is possible that I could destroy those two hand-to-hand given another chance. Only one of the two is armed, and I believe it can't read my brain waves as easily as it does a human's, though I can't be sure. Permission to intercept them, sir?"

Normally Geordi would have said no to anything entailing a risk of life and limb. But this wasn't "normally," this was a Kobayashi Maru situation.

"Are you recovered enough to function, Worf?"

"If you please, sir, I'm very eager to get going."

Yes, thought Geordi, you would be no matter what condition you were in. But there was no choice now, and no time for formalities with Dr. Crusher.

"Okay Worf, you're on."

In sickbay, Worf rose from his bed with crisp alacrity. Wentz had filled him in on the progress of the one-eyes toward Warp Engineering, as well as the status of Wesley's Cyclops-buster.

Shikibu, on the bed next to him, had heard all of it. She had been awake for several hours, and had tried unsuccessfully to convince Dr. Crusher to let her return to duty. She had considered just walking out, but rejected it. She never forced an issue—there was always a middle way, the easiest path of water down a hillside.

Now, with her superior officer awake, she saw that the way had created itself.

"Sir, may I help?"

"Yes. You can accompany Wesley when he tries his device."

"Aye, sir."

Shikibu got up from her bed and retied her ponytail.

Dr. Crusher, who had been treating a radiation case in another suite, returned to the room.

Before she could object to the autonomous departure of two of her patients, Worf spoke.

"There is no time for any more of your babying, Doctor. The ship is in critical danger. Both Shikibu and I are ready for duty, and our help is needed."

"Worf, I don't see how you expect to function. I happen to know you both have headaches that could melt an iron asteroid."

"Yes," said Worf. "It feels quite refreshing. Wouldn't you say so, Ensign?"

"Like a cup of strong coffee, sir. Let's go."

Worf and Shikibu left before the doctor could speak again.

She had wanted to wish them luck.

Worf stayed in communication with the bridge and got to the corridors outside Warp Engineering just before the one-eyes.

"They could appear at any moment," Wentz had said, though she couldn't pinpoint the spot where they would ingress into the corridors, or even if they would use the corridors at all.

Worf paced quickly, choosing a route through the corridors that would regularly circle him past Engineering. A smoking rage fulminated inside of him, a hatred for the devices infiltrating the ship, and for the people who invented them and set them in motion.

He felt the muscles in his thick neck tighten like steel cables. He growled softly, as the feeling of tautness and readiness spread through his body, a sublime combination of absolute control and feral abandon. To Worf, honest, unsublimated rage was an intoxicant bordering on ambrosia.

But now there was something different about it— his secret quest for glory called with a voice separate and distinct for destruction of the one-eyes. It spoke to him of a future triumph that would spread his name throughout the Federation and the Klingon Empire and keep it alive when he himself and his children's children were dust, and maybe long after.

Primed and ready, Worf found himself breaking into a run as he mentally rehearsed his various attack strategies. He kept his internal dialogue confined to his native Klingon tongue, reasoning that the one-eyes wouldn't be able to decipher it if they picked up his brain waves.

At a certain point Worf realized something was amiss. He hadn't heard from Wentz for at least a minute. If the one-eyes had not entered the corridor but instead taken a different route into Engineering, Wentz would have told him. And if they had entered the corridor as expected, he would have found them by now. Unless they were . . .

. . . following behind him.

He slowed to a walk. He kept his thoughts confined to the most uniquely Klingon elements of his heritage —the bleeding hands of love's touch, the trial-by-pain of his Rite of Ascension . . .

Presently he heard the hum of the infernal one-eyes behind him, closing slowly with him as he maintained a steady walk. The sound stabilized and he sensed they'd picked what they regarded as a safe distance from which to observe him. They weren't going to let him lay hands on them again, or so they thought.

Worf had already planned what he would do at this moment.

He opened his mouth and let out a magnificent yell,

a shout from the secret catacombs of his soul. It was the traditional Klingon death-howl, a signal to the inhabitants of the afterworld: beware, a Klingon warrior is coming.

And even as Worf yelled, confusing the one-eyes with this incomprehensible behavior, he brought himself to an abrupt halt, and with predatory agility reversed his momentum, turned, and caught his pursuers off-guard.

The two devices had just begun to slow down as Worf reached up with both his powerful arms, gathering the one-eyes in, pushing them tightly together.

In a split second he saw the dents he'd made on one of them in their previous meeting. This time a victor will be decided, he told himself.

He felt their antigravs kick in with all their power, dragging him forward, and he heard the whine of the armed one-eye's gun charging to blast him with radiation.

But before it could fire, Worf dug in his heels and stopped himself, then whirled with all his strength like a discus thrower—whirled once, twice, accelerating the one-eyes at the rim of his turn with all his strength and speed. Then he smashed them against the bulkhead.

One of the two devices slipped out of his hands. It was the locksmith one-eye. Out of the corner of his eye he saw it move away, slowly and tentatively, as if it were stunned. He held onto the other, whose gun had quit whining and whose antigravs were fading. He smashed it again and again into the bulkhead, hearing and feeling it come apart in his hands, the jagged edges of sheet metal and IC's cutting into his flesh. Still he felt parts of it moving, and he continued to hurl the mangled mass against the wall, until he realized it had disintegrated and he was holding only a piece of metal chassis.

He dropped it and looked down. One little solenoid relay near his boot continued to click stubbornly. He crushed it underfoot.

He looked down the corridor, and saw the other one-eye, the locksmith, floating slowly, bumping intermittently into one wall. He sprinted after it, locked his hands together and struck it right on top, crushing its antennae. It hit the deck and rebounded upward. He grabbed it and tore it apart piece by piece, savoring the moment.

When he was done, he composed himself, cleared the thick satisfaction from his throat, and touched his communicator.

"Worf to La Forge."

"La Forge here."

"I have destroyed the locksmith and its guard."

"Worf!" Geordi gave a primal triumphant yell. "Whoooooeeeeeeee!"

"Interesting, sir. Is that an attempt at a Klingon death-howl? It wants for a bit more frenzy."

"That wasn't a death-howl, that was a job-well-done-howl."

"I believe I can destroy others if you can give me their positions, sir."

"The others are closer to Wesley, and he's about to try his device on them. I'm going to send you up there anyway, Worf, but let's hope Wesley can get rid of them without any more risks on your part."

As Shikibu walked along the corridor toward her cabin, she recognized she was in too agitated a state for what lay ahead. She needed the tranquil state known in Zen archery as mushin.

Don't resist, she told herself, just let the thoughts and feelings play themselves out.

She allowed herself to think of the one-eyes themselves. That thought subsided. Other thoughts stubbornly jumped in to fill the void: Wesley touching her hair in the Ryoanji rock garden and her heart rate's corresponding jump . . . her Archery Master's "parting-with-life-verse" he composed and spoke as he died . . . the marble pattern on the inside cover of a book she once saw . . .

The thoughts became more random and sparse, until, by the time she'd reached her cabin and gotten what she needed from it, she was in the state of mushin. Ready.

The two security men flanking Wesley didn't have their phasers drawn. If Wesley's Cyclops-buster didn't work, the security men had no weapons they could safely use on the one-eyes; they could only retreat and attempt to hustle Wesley and his machine into a safe haven.

The machine was a lopsided mass of small generators and wave-guides, an awkward package Wesley held with both hands as he walked. The thing's power source was already on, and it hummed and purred, ready, like an obedient little animal, to release its energy at the prompting of Wesley's touch on its activation button.

"Two of the intruders coming your way from starboard," said Wentz over Wesley's communicator. "Shikibu will arrive at your position to provide more support, but not until after the one-eyes get to you. I don't know what's been keeping her."

Wesley saw they were not in a good spot to make a stand. One of the security men started to run back to the closest door to set up a place for retreat. It seemed awfully far away. Before he got there a one-eye came gliding, alone, around the corner from the other direction.

Wesley fumbled for the button on the Cyclops-buster. His hands were shaky and he almost dropped the machine before he triggered his shot. The Cyclops-buster built up a charge, accelerating its special subatomic particles for final release. He heard, as counterpoint, the whine of the one-eye as it prepared to fire at him.

He aimed the Cyclops-buster at the one-eye.

The one-eye and the Cyclops-buster fired at nearly the same instant. Wesley felt part of a wave-front hit him; a wave of nausea and anguish.

But he'd fired in time. The one-eye blossomed suddenly into a spherical cloud, bright and dark patches alternating around its surface, spinning and pullulating with mesmerizing complexity, and it made him think of Shiva. Suddenly the cloud expanded outward, past him, and he knew the neutrinos were passing through him and the bulkheads by the billion, but they were benign as they sought the void outside the ship.

Wesley felt feverish and uncoordinated as he reset the controls on his Cyclops-buster. He looked at the two security men; they seemed to be experiencing symptoms as well. The one next to him shook his head to try and clear it, while a second man, far down the corridor, retched and held his midsection.

Wesley realized that the Cyclops-buster had disrupted the one-eye's shot, and saved them from a lethal dose of radiation.

Yet the encounter wasn't over. Wentz had said there were two of the intruders. If they had arrived together, Wesley could have annihilated them both. But the Cyclops-buster needed thirty seconds of charging before it could fire again, and the digital counter said twenty still remained.

At that instant the other one-eye came around the far corner, many meters ahead.

The one-eye moved closer toward him. This time it would fire at closer range, to make sure of the kill.

Wesley turned to run for the open doorway, knowing already that it was much too far. The one-eye would have plenty of time to fire.

Now he saw that Shikibu had arrived and was standing near the open doorway.

In one hand she held her seven-foot-long bow. On the other hand she wore a leather glove. Under her belt were several slim tritanium arrows.

At this moment, after clearing herself of all distracting thoughts, Shikibu's mind was in perfect repose— like a mirror, or the surface of a lake on an absolutely still day.

Her breath slowed down and found an unconscious rhythm, and her posture found a balance around the centerpoint called the tanden, just below her navel.

She perceived the one-eye, sensed its motion and direction, but had no thoughts or feelings about it.

She reached, without rational hesitation or irrational fear, for an arrow from her belt.

The one-eye observed Shikibu through its lens as it moved toward Wesley. It saw the large bow she held, and the arrow. It knew what it saw was a potential weapons system, but of manual operation, requiring forethought to fire. And as it scanned her brain waves it found there was no forethought, no purpose, no thought at all. So it concentrated on knocking out the primary target, the young man with the machine that had just destroyed another one-eye.

Wesley felt as though he were trying to wake up from a dream. His legs were sluggish from the effects of the other one-eye's blast. He tried to think them into moving as he kept his eyes on the door and on Shikibu.

He saw Shikibu move through discrete postures and

motions as she grasped the arrow, nocked it on the bowstring, and raised the bow. He saw her pull the great bowstring back until it reached its maximum tension. She seemed to be in no special hurry as she took aim, sighting past the grip of the bow.

She was still far away but Wesley saw on her face, as if with magnified clarity, the peaceful expression of a contented child. Why doesn't she shoot! he screamed silently.

He heard the whine of the one-eye's gun behind him. His legs stumbled as he tried to will himself down the corridor.

Shikibu's expression didn't change as the arrow flew from the bow. It was the perfect release. She had not actively decided to let the arrow go, nor had her gloved hand lost its grip. Rather, the shot had "fallen" at the moment when all conditions were perfect, when the interaction of string, bow, hand, eye, muscle, target, and universe made release necessary. The shot happened as spontaneously as a drop of water rolls off a leaf.

The tritanium arrow flew past Wesley with a tearing sound. It smashed into the precise middle of the one-eye's lens, fracturing through the glass lens-elements, and deeper, through the microchips and wave generators. It stopped with its point protruding out of the metal back of the one-eye.

The one-eye halted and began to spin wildly on its axis like an insect in convulsions. It made pressure-hissing and metal-screeching sounds. Arcs of energy shot out randomly from its antennae.

Then abruptly it stopped and fell to the deck, dead.

The four humans stared at it, three still stunned from the effects of its partner, the fourth silent as she lowered her bow and then nocked another arrow on the string, ready if another intruder might arrive.

Wesley finally gathered enough of his wits to touch his communicator.

"Crusher to La Forge."

"La Forge here."

"Geordi, the machine works. We just destroyed a one-eye with it. Recommend that as soon as Ensign Taylor finishes assembling another, we keep the two together to work in tandem, one charging while the other fires."

"Wesley, your voice is a little slurred. You okay?"

"Yeah. . . . Could you log that Shikibu just saved the lives of myself and two other crewpersons?"

"Noted—and your contribution as well, Wes. We'll have another Cyclops-buster up there within five minutes. Hold your position until then, if you can. La Forge out."

Wesley felt his body recovering.

He went over to Shikibu to say thanks, but her expression made him freeze up.

She looked at him almost as though she didn't recognize him, as though she were seeing him for the first time. She studied his face curiously. Wesley felt awkward.

"Um . . . well anyway, thanks," he said.

He cleared his throat and returned his attention to his machine. It was charged and ready to go.

He didn't see the quiet little smile that appeared for a fleeting moment on Shikibu's face.

Geordi was losing his battle with the disabled warp engines. He couldn't get any more power out of them. The ship was already dropping, and the rate of drop was accelerating. Within a few minutes, the *Enterprise* would enter Rampart's upper atmosphere, and Geordi would have to lower the ship's shields to power it back out—in which case the Rampartian ships would blow the *Enterprise* into fragments.

Even now the hostile ships were following the *Enterprise* as it gathered speed in its fall, their weapons primed and ready to fire, with guidance systems locked onto key points along the *Enterprise*'s hull.

Geordi had several of his engineering crew working beside him, riding the mix with imperfectly repaired controls. But he needed someone with the touch delicate enough to make crucial repairs on certain equipment even while it was being operated. He knew of only one person who could do that.

"La Forge to Ensign Taylor."

"Taylor here."

"Is the other Cyclops-buster finished?"

"Finished just now, sir."

"Could you come over here?"

Within a minute she was beside Geordi, her fingers repairing and adjusting the console while he rode the mix.

He saw she needed a hand with a data chip and he reached over to help. His sleeve brushed over an exposed relay and triggered a spark. The spark arced through the air to the sensor-pads on her fingers. She shouted and fell away from the console.

"Chops!"

Geordi called someone else over to ride the mix while he bent over her.

"I can't see," she said. She was crying. He'd never seen her cry.

"I'm sorry, I'm sorry," he kept repeating. He cursed himself bitterly—it was his own fault, he should have known he'd lost too much dexterity to help her at this stage of his fatigue.

And this moment had to be worse for her than it

would have been for him had he lost his VISOR. For all the time she'd lived in darkness she'd been treated like a subhuman, an untermensch.

He helped her sit up against the bulkhead, told her to rest and that his crew could take up the slack. He went back to work riding the mix, furious with himself.

But a few minutes later she was standing next to him. She'd removed the sensor pads from her fingers.

"I don't need the hardware," she said. "I know these circuits by heart and I can fix them by touch."

He nodded his assent and continued to work, not able to bring himself to look at her. He'd robbed her of her sight.

She whistled softly as she worked, and Geordi knew it was for him. It helped.

At this moment, inside of CephCom, Picard, Riker, Data, and Amoret were about to attempt escape from the assault shelter. They had all agreed that the air vent system was the only option. Now Data had opened the air shaft and Amoret was urging them to go, as she was sure the CS would force their way into the room at any minute.

"I must first conceal something that would be visible to all of you inside the shaft," said Data. He proceeded to tear off part of a large storage box and position it inside the dark shaft. He still had not given any of the others a clue about what he had been hiding from them during the last hours.

"This is crazy!" said Amoret. "We don't have time!"

Picard put a calming hand on her shoulder.

"Please trust him."

The red-haired woman stared back at him. They held a momentary silent colloquy—she accepted his advice because she knew him with the intimacy of a wife or lover, and he saw her familiarity and had to turn away so as not to be distracted by the odd feeling. A stranger knew his innermost self.

Data lowered himself back down from the air shaft. "The concealment is complete. We may now exit."

In the next instant the blast door at the other end of the room exploded inward. CS men rushed in and arrested Picard, Riker, Data, and Amoret.

Chapter Sixteen

TROI WAITED, handcuffed and under heavy guard, outside Crichton's office.

Far down the hallway, she spotted the Dissenters as they were herded along by one-eyes and CS men. The Dissenters were turned away from her, but she could see that all those from the caves were there, plus Amoret, who, though a prisoner, was wearing a CS uniform. They disappeared around a corner.

A moment later a guard led Troi into Crichton's office.

His bald head was covered by the standard CS helmet. He had the rasters turned up very bright, burning in electronic hellfire everything that met his eyes.

He was terrified. Troi perceived that clearly.

"You're useless to me," he told Troi. "Your captain, your first officer, and your android are no longer necessary either. I've already defeated your ship. You can't touch me now."

"Then why are you telling me this?"

Crichton swiveled his chair around and pressed a button. On a monitor behind him, an image appeared:

the *Enterprise* as seen by the cameras of one of the Rampartian ships surrounding it. The *Enterprise* was plunging down toward the planet, the dull red heat of atmospheric entry already showing on its shields.

Crichton watched the image for a moment, in silence.

Troi allowed herself no panic. She had to stay focused on Crichton; figuring him out was the only way she could help the thousand people on that ship.

She strained to pick up everything she could.

His inner terror was pushing toward the surface. It was waiting to erupt. She was herself a contributor to the terror, but it was larger than any one person. It was as big as an entire alternate universe, as big as the Other-worlders, the realm of myth and imagination.

But if it was the Other-worlder phenomena, it was much worse for him than it had been for her. He had a psychotic, paranoid reaction to it. He didn't know what it was and didn't want to know.

Since she couldn't see his face, she found herself looking at his hands. Oddly, there were no scars on them; they looked as if they belonged to someone else. Long-fingered, dextrous—an artist's hands. They fidgeted compulsively.

Now he stood and spoke.

"For the high crimes specified in the Code of the Council of Truth, pursuant to and as a result of documentation gathered and on record, the detainee before me, Deanna Troi, is hereby sentenced to death, such sentence to be imposed without delay. The penalty will be bodily destruction by injection."

His voice had sped up at the end, as if the words themselves had panicked on their way out of his mouth.

He sat down and hurriedly pressed a button on his intercom.

"Send in the execution corps. I'm coming with

227

them. We'll execute all of the *Enterprise* people together, and the Dissenters afterward."

"Director Crichton, before you do anything else, listen to me," said Troi. "I know you're hiding something in your mind. Maybe your computers don't know, but I do. I've experienced the syndrome myself. I've had those mythical creatures invading my mind."

"A fabulist to the end," said Crichton. "Spin your fictions until the moment you die." He hit the button on his desk insistently.

"No, wait!" she cried. "I'm a counselor, a scientist of consciousness. It doesn't matter to me if mythical characters are considered criminal here. Nothing in the mind is criminal to me. Nothing need be judged or condemned. I don't have anyone to report you to. Please just try to tell me about it. What can you lose by trying? How do you know I can't help?"

Troi realized there had to be validity to her perceptions. The protective headgear Crichton wore was not filtering out her words—or at least not all of them. Crichton really was experiencing a recurrent mental problem, and the CS computers knew it.

Crichton seemed to pause and consider her offer. Troi sensed that for the briefest of instants he admitted to himself how wonderful it would be to just talk, to seek help without fear of judgment or stigma.

But the dominant part of him, the tyrannical, paranoid side, reasserted itself. Troi knew she'd lost her gamble.

The CS execution detail came in. The four officers surrounded Troi, and one of them hooked her handcuffs to his own wrist.

"Let's go," said Crichton.

As they left his office, they paused before a large monitor in the hallway. Ferris' stern carven-oak face stared out over the dates of his birth and death.

The image was replaced by shots of Ferris' fight with Odysseus on the bridge. The sequence ended with both men lying dead. There were no shots of the finale. The Rampartians would not see Ferris' death at the hands of his own one-eyes.

The narrator said something about the treachery of the Dissenters, and how they murdered Ferris, the defender of truth. A photomontage of scenes from Ferris' life and career followed.

Crichton ordered the group to move on. They walked Troi to an elevator and took her up several stories to the level of the bridge.

In a glassed vestibule opening onto the bridge, a dozen CS guards stood in formation around Picard, Riker, and Data. All were handcuffed. They looked up and saw Troi coming. Riker and Picard seemed beaten and exhausted. Data had no expression at all.

"Why is the android with them?" asked one of the CS officers walking with Crichton. "Isn't he going to be dismantled in the lab rather than injected?"

"Yes," said Crichton, "but I want a video image of all of the criminals together, being executed. The public should be allowed to see this."

Troi was led past the other group. The guards around her blocked her view and she was not able to make any further eye contact with her shipmates; but as she was pushed through the doors and onto the bridge, she could sense her friends being led along behind her.

It was a clear night outside, with a light wind. The great blue rho Ophiuchi nebula filled most of the sky, but a large number of background stars shone through it.

Ahead of Troi, groups of one-eyes hovered, surrounding the bridge, gathering images of the doomed group and their escorts. Banks of lights on the surrounding buildings painted the bridge with neutral white light.

Troi looked ahead and saw the cage-like security doors at the other end of the bridge. They were still broken, as Lomov had left them, but several guards were there.

She looked down, watching her own trudging footsteps. The experience of seeing Picard, Riker, and Data all condemned to death was worse than her own death sentence; it was physically devastating. The events of the last few days caught up with her all at once.

For a brief moment she blacked out and collapsed. The CS man she was cuffed to kept her from hitting the ground, and the whole group paused.

She recovered a few seconds later. When she felt able to walk again, she nodded, and the group moved on.

The room itself was stark and gray. There were four chairs in it, plain but sturdy wooden affairs, bolted to the floor. Mounted at various positions along the walls were several cameras that swiveled to track the condemned as they were led in.

Again Troi tried to look at Captain Picard, Riker, and Data, but the CS men flanking her and leading her to her chair were too close and blocked her view.

She was pushed gently down into the chair and strapped in. When the CS men stood aside she saw that her shipmates were already strapped into their chairs and blindfolded.

She craned her neck and saw a nurse standing behind them at a little table. On top of the table, four syringes waited in a glass rack.

Troi felt her heart racing. There was something she hadn't quite understood about this whole thing, something about Crichton, the Other-worlders, and imagination, but it was too late.

She heard Crichton talking with a low voice into his headset. She heard the breathing of her shipmates and the clink of the syringes rattling faintly against their rack.

Now the nurse was standing in front of her, lifting a blindfold to her head. As the black cloth blocked her vision, Troi's heart pounded so hard that she began to think the earth was throbbing.

And suddenly, the earth really *was* throbbing. The throbs felt like seismic tremors, except they were evenly spaced, like timed explosions or a great drumbeat.

The nurse, confused by the noise, dropped the blindfold and Troi could see again. The CS men looked at each other, alarmed. Troi leaned her head around one of them and caught sight of Picard. The captain was looking expectantly around the room, as if readying himself to take advantage of the situation and lead an escape.

Crichton grabbed the nurse and shook her shoulders.

"Inject them!"

The nurse reacted quickly. She grabbed a syringe off the rattling cart and moved toward Troi.

The vibration emanating from the ground reached a peak. Suddenly the roof itself caved in, crushed downward by some unseen force. Wood and plaster fell all over the place. A great hole had opened up and Troi could see the morning-twilight sky.

Something huge and flesh-colored moved in through the hole and felt around the room. Crichton, the CS men, and the nurse desperately crawled, fell, and rolled away from it.

It was a giant human hand, searching around the

room, feeling for something. Finally it grasped Crichton between two fingers and lifted him right out through the hole.

Now the owner of the hand became visible through the aperture. It was a man roughly a hundred feet tall, perfectly proportioned. He was dressed in the fashion of an eighteenth-century seafarer, with a buff-colored jerkin and knee breeches. He looked to be in his late thirties, intelligent and cultured. There were slim cords dangling from his arms and legs, as though he had been tied up but was now free.

Troi realized she had seen him before. She'd seen him in an illustration on a certain page burned by the CS in her presence—a page from Gulliver's Travels. This giant was Gulliver himself, in the flesh.

Gulliver dangled Crichton from his fingers, letting the Director of Cephalic Security swing, struggling and flailing high above the ground. The giant seemed amused by the angry little mite. Then he paused and looked around him in a wide arc at the spread of CephCom, and even wider, at the city of Verity. He grew more thoughtful.

Gulliver set Crichton down somewhere out of view, then leaned his head close over the execution room.

"Let the prisoners go," he said, and his voice was like the soughing of a giant bellows.

One of the CS men reached for his weapon.

Gulliver put his hand back into the room and flicked the CS man with his finger, sending him sprawling onto a pile of debris. Then Gulliver crushed the weapon like a small seed with his fingernail.

"Let them go!" he repeated, in the loudest human tone Troi had ever heard.

The CS men hurriedly undid the straps on the chairs. The prisoners stood. Riker put himself in front of Troi, shielding her with his body.

But when Gulliver's hand slid over and gathered up

the four from the *Enterprise,* there was nothing Riker or any of them could do to prevent it. Troi felt the flesh of the hand against her own hands. It was warm and alive. It even had the whorls and ridges of an individual handprint.

Gulliver lifted the four up near his face. He looked at them and laughed. He was delighted, as though he'd found new friends.

Picard whispered to Troi.

"Counselor, can you feel anything from his mind?"

"Yes. He's real, and alive. Very alive."

"Intriguing," Data commented.

Gulliver slowly lowered his hand and set it down in the quadrangle between the CephCom buildings. Riker quickly stepped off and helped the others to the ground.

Across the quadrangle they could see Crichton, sheltered under the overhang of the main CephCom entrance. In the shadows his eye-rasters glowed with an evil green light. He was talking into his headset and looking into the sky expectantly.

Gulliver rose to his full height. He looked off into the distance.

Troi heard the throb of hovercraft.

Within moments two white CS assault craft were flying round Gulliver, making passes at his face. Troi could hear their weapons firing. Gulliver dodged and weaved.

A phalanx of CS officers appeared on the quadrangle. They knelt in unison and began squeezing off shots at Gulliver.

Gulliver seemed to feel the sting of the radiation weapons on his face. He swatted at the soldiers and hovercraft, forcing them back.

Crichton kept speaking into his headset. Now he motioned with his arm and the CS men retreated into the complex. A truck-mounted radiation cannon drove onto the quadrangle. Crichton ran up and stood behind it. He pointed up at Gulliver, and barked some orders to the men in the gun's turret.

The gun swiveled on well-greased gimbals as it was aimed. Gulliver eyed it with surprise.

It fired a great blast of energy.

The giant swayed, and reached for the gun. It fired again. He fell to his knees with a tremendous crash.

The gun tracked him and fired a third time.

Gulliver collapsed. His body came to rest outside the CephCom complex, out of view. The earth shuddered for several seconds, and then all was still.

The hovercraft circled over the area where Gulliver had fallen. CS troops ran back onto the quadrangle. For a moment Troi thought the CS were going to rearrest her and her shipmates. But in the next moment pandemonium broke loose.

A huge crowd of beings swarmed into the quadrangle and around the CephCom buildings. They were all characters from myth, metaphor, fiction, all forms of human imagination.

The charge was led by Sekhmet the Egyptian Lioness-deity, goddess of the desert sun, terrifying Daughter of Ra. The head of an asp protruded from the hair above her eyes, and over the hissing asp was a solar disk, radiating heat and light all about the quadrangle. Sekhmet roared and bared a full set of awesome feline teeth as she charged. The characters from imagination all charged with her and as a body they attacked the CS troops.

Troi tried to grab onto Riker but lost contact with all her shipmates in the confusing melee. The air was filled with shouts and cries in many languages.

Troi saw jinns, love-goddesses, and golems cavorting among the CS, disrupting their ranks, and pulling off the soldiers' helmets, depriving them of their censoring eye and ear filters.

She saw a Chiruwi half-man from Central Africa —a man with only one visible side—befuddling a CS officer who tried to shoot him, showing first his visible side, then his invisible side.

She saw a Chinese Nung-kua-ma—a ravenous creature with the body of a giant bull and the head of a measure of rice—devour a one-eye in one gulp. A CS man, terrified at that sight, dropped his gun and put his hands up. The Nung-kua-ma ate the gun.

Fresh squads of CS soldiers swarmed into the quadrangle and formed a line, firing their weapons continuously at the invaders. Crichton pointed here and there with furious gestures and barked orders into his headset.

But the line of CS soldiers was swamped by a tide of Hopi Kachinas, beings embodying the eternal forces of nature, which had humanoid shapes that were made of cloud-terraces, living trees, thunder, and interstellar space.

The CS guns had no effect on them, and the line of CS soldiers broke up, scattered. The Kachinas pursued, laughing, thundering, singing, stripping off more CS helmets.

Proteus the shape-changer took form right in front of Troi, changing from a man to a fish to a puddle, and finally into a three-headed Cerberus dog, the guardian of the underworld. His roar, the voice of Past, Present, and Future, was deafening. A trio of de-helmeted CS soldiers backed away from him in terror.

The CS soldiers backed straight into another trio who made their stand together: Sir Gawain the Round Table knight, Uyemon the blind samurai, and Stagolee, the invincible blues-playing troubadour of African-American folktale.

"I'd say you'd best be on your way," the fearless Stagolee laughed at the soldiers, "or we'll have to whup you good."

"Yes," said Gawain, "ye must yield you as over-come men."

Gawain and Uyemon drew their swords, and Stagolee brandished his fists.

The three CS soldiers, having lost all taste for battle, bolted away.

Crichton stood on the flatbed of the mobile gun and frantically tried to rally his CS. But they seemed to be losing, their weapons ineffective, their helmets gone, confusion supreme. Some had abandoned the fight and were looking around in pure bewilderment. Some were laughing hysterically.

Troi saw several of the Dissenters walking among the myth-beings, helping them. She saw, impossibly, Caliban, even scruffier and bolder than when he had been alive; yet Troi sensed that he lived still—or lived again. She saw Rhiannon, now a beautiful grown woman in queenly dress, riding a magnificent horse. Rhiannon had become her own myth. The horse carried her about the quadrangle, leaping, galloping, taunting, neither man nor one-eye able to catch them or shoot them.

She saw Gunabibi dancing in the middle of the quadrangle. Her body was painted with thick white lines and circles. She was spreading her nature-fertility all around her. Vines grew from the concrete at her feet, spreading and multiplying like a time-lapse film, entwining guns and feet and jeeps in a green arabesque. Little bandicoot marsupials with young in their pouches were suddenly everywhere. One CS soldier found himself awash in a friendly tide of the bandicoots, and fell to the ground, not sure whether he should scream or laugh.

Troi saw a high-ranking CS officer who'd apparently defected. He was running about the quadrangle, ordering CS soldiers to destroy their own weapons, and the men were obeying. He got close to Troi for a moment and she saw he was Coyote, in disguise.

Still Crichton managed to rally his most dedicated men. A core group of them stayed round him, firing their weapons with fierce intensity at the impossible beings invading the seat of CS power. Some of the mythical characters were affected by the blasts of radiation. Some collapsed and some disappeared. Finally, the group of mythical characters began to fall back.

Then the colossal Aztec figure of Tezcatlipoca, the Mirror Man, thundered onto the quadrangle, dragging the leg that had no foot. His head reached the tops of the buildings. His mirrored surfaces reflected the scenes around him, splitting and multiplying them. His mirror-eyes flashed as he saw Crichton.

Crichton screamed orders like a man possessed. He looked wildly about him, up at the sky, where no CS air support was evident, and out beyond the buildings of CephCom, where no more ground support came.

But he still had his mobile radiation cannon, his one great gun that had done away with Gulliver. He reached into the turret and manually aimed the gun at Tezcatlipoca.

Tezcatlipoca stood his ground. He spoke at Crichton in an indecipherable booming language, but made no move to defend himself. He pointed at his own chest, a mirror-surface of smoke and darkness, where something throbbed redly: his heart.

Crichton's mask-face cracked into a bitter smile as he slammed the firing button.

A great flash erupted from the gun.

The radiation reflected off the mirrored surfaces of Tezcatlipoca's chest and returned, in equal and opposite angle, straight at Crichton.

Crichton's frozen grimace unlocked itself and he

cried out as his body dissolved. He disappeared in a cloud of vapor. A little puddle remained on top of the truck bed where he had stood.

His air strike came too late to save him.

CS jets and battlefield one-eyes filled the sky, firing their growling guns and launching their missiles and guided bombs.

The ground itself began to shake violently and the sky grew dark. A terrible wind began to blow. A female voice, the Matriarch, the voice of all living things, told Troi to lie down and absorb her protection.

And then the Matriarch and her husband, a pair otherwise known as biosphere and cosmos, Gaia and Ouranos, Awitelin Tsita and Apoyan Ta'chu, moved to re-establish natural harmony.

The CS buildings collapsed in on themselves, as earthquakes wracked the ground.

The wind reached the force of a continuous explosion and the planes were swept away like chaff.

Debris blew all over the ground, pinning Troi against a wall. Chunks of earth, wood, and plaster piled on top of her.

Suddenly the noise subsided. The wind and earthquakes had abruptly ceased. Supreme quiet.

Troi's head hadn't been covered by the debris and she had a clear view of the ruins of CephCom.

The mythical characters began to rise from the wreckage. They picked their way around, pulling wounded CS from the fallen structures.

Some of the CS quailed before the mythical characters. But some seemed to have been shocked to the point where they just accepted what they saw, and even welcomed the help. Some of the CS talked and laughed openly with members of the invading host.

Troi didn't see her crewmates in the crowd. She

tried to push some of the debris off her and found she couldn't budge it.

Then she realized that she couldn't move her body at all. She couldn't even twitch her fingers or wiggle her toes.

She thought perhaps she had received an injury after all, but then she recognized the feeling. She had experienced it during her earlier encounters with the Other-worlders, the characters from imagination. The transformation they had tried to put her through twice before was now completed. It was as though her body had changed into a different substance. The feeling of immobility was terrifying.

She struggled and strained to move her eyes, but found them locked in their sockets.

She calmed herself as best she could. At least she wasn't blind. She started examining the scene presented to her. She couldn't see her body under all the debris covering it, except for part of her hand, which was extended in a reaching gesture.

It was covered with dust except for the upper edge of her index finger. The finger was dark and smooth, with flecks of sparkling material embedded in it. The finger looked like polished stone.

At that moment Troi realized that she had become a statue.

She panicked silently, cried out mentally. But no one came near her or even seemed to notice her. With her gaze now locked irrevocably straight ahead she couldn't search for Picard, Riker and Data.

She realized that she would never be found. A statue doesn't emit life signs. The *Enterprise*'s sensors would never be able to locate her.

The sadness of the situation overwhelmed her, and she tried to weep, but couldn't. The sadness itself began to dry up. Her emotions were petrifying.

In another moment all emotions were gone. Nothing and nobody mattered to her. All that was left was a hard, dry rock of continuing awareness.

She watched a group of mythical characters pull a CS man from under an overturned jeep. Proteus turned himself into a stretcher for the injured man. Troi saw another figure, nearby, with his back turned to her.

The man turned in profile for a moment and Troi saw that it was Odysseus.

As she watched him she felt a slight pang of emotion—the most basic possible emotion—reawaken in her. It was a desire to live, a desire that he should come and help her.

He walked away from the jeep and was gone from Troi's view. But a few seconds later he came back and looked across the field of rubble, directly at her.

Troi strained to move, to make some kind of sign, but it was futile.

He noticed her anyway. He walked toward her, weaving his way around the piles of wreckage.

When he reached her he stood looking at her face for a long time.

He appeared slightly different in facial structure and dress than when she had last seen him. Yet it was unmistakably the same man. It was as if the specific aspects of the person she had known were diminished and a more universal Odysseus had emerged. This was Homer's Odysseus, the immortal, mythical Odysseus.

His myth-character was much the same as the man Troi had known—the resourcefulness, the endless fearless questing across the wide seas and the limits of the known and the unknown.

"I know you, do I not?" he said. "From some other place or time?"

He stared uncertainly at her.

"And wasn't I prophesied to meet you again? . . . Well . . . I can see you can't answer me."

He began to pull the chunks of earth and wood off her.

"If it's so, I know how to free you. I know how to reawaken the woman-trapped-as-a-statue. Pygmalion the sculptor did it once. With his touch he warmed the stone, and the stone softened into flesh."

He picked up a flat piece of wood and used it to fan the dust off her. When she was clean, a perfect, polished, poised stone image that looked as though it should have stood in a museum, he put down the plank and knelt next to her.

He touched her wrist, and squeezed it gently.

Slowly, her skin began to tingle where he touched it. It felt as a limb feels when it has slept and then been awakened by the tide of circulation.

All the cells in her hand seemed to come alive. She could feel blood moving through the veins.

His hand moved up to her shoulder and squeezed it. The shoulder became soft under his touch. The warmth spread. She could move the arm. The sensation was so divine she wanted to utter some word or sound, but still she had no voice.

He moved his hands to her face, stroked her cheek and her hair.

Now she felt her entire body re-awakening. The sensation was so intense, so electric, that she had to shut her eyes tight and couldn't breathe for a moment.

Then the transformation completed itself and she breathed and moved her limbs.

Emotions came back in a rush. She was supremely, inanely happy and sad at the same time. She let it flow.

Then she realized Odysseus wasn't touching her anymore.

She opened her eyes.

She was alone, lying on her back, staring at a night sky, a blue nebula with stars behind it.

A delicious warmth bathed her body. For a minute she just looked at the stars and enjoyed the feeling of being physically and emotionally alive. Some place inside her had been tapped and had released a secret, an inner conflict.

Then she became aware of voices around her. She moved her head and saw that she was in the middle of a circle of CS men and one-eyes. Crichton stood near her. A CS guard knelt beside her, his hand still cuffed to hers. Picard, Data, and Riker were still handcuffed as well.

She saw that she was still on the bridge, near the actual spot where Odysseus had died.

She understood that there had been no invasion by mythical characters. No Gulliver had come to rescue them, no Tezcatlipoca had destroyed Crichton. Odysseus had not come back to life. She had merely passed out for a moment, and had one last Other-worlder dream, on the way to her own execution.

She stood slowly. The CS men helped her up, and the group resumed its progress across the bridge.

Still the emotions swirled within her, rising up from deep places long forgotten, more and more intense and insistent, as if to make themselves known in her last moments so that she could die with her totality. Tears were streaming down her face.

They neared the steel door that Lomov broke. As Troi was pushed through she sensed the presence of Picard, Riker, and Data very close behind her.

Then, suddenly, she felt the unmistakable body-dissolving rush of the *Enterprise* transporter.

In the next moment she found herself standing, safe and sound, in the *Enterprise* transporter room with her shipmates.

Chapter Seventeen

THE FOUR OF THEM checked in at the bridge, and found that the ship was safe. All the one-eyes had been destroyed. The engines had been repaired enough to keep the ship in orbit around Rampart, with shields and a capability of warp four. The sensors had found a hole in the nebula and contact had been established with Starfleet.

Picard went into his ready room for a few minutes. When he emerged he said the *Enterprise* would be leaving this star system in an hour and Starfleet would be further pursuing the matter of the *Huxley*.

Worf was still busy with security mop-up and Geordi was asleep somewhere, so the four went to the conference room to debrief each other.

Troi still didn't know how the beam-up had been accomplished.

"We have the illustrious Data to thank for that," said Picard. "He, Riker, and I had been hiding in a storeroom behind a lab, along with the Dissenter named Amoret, when a one-eye gained entrance through an air shaft.

"Data caught and disabled the one-eye, and then dismantled its antenna array. He fashioned a communicator out of the parts and tuned it to a frequency that would punch through the surface jamming and give the *Enterprise* our coordinates. When all of us were in the same spot—just after your fainting spell on that bridge at CephCom—Data signaled the *Enterprise*. O'Brien was at the transporter controls. He'd stood there for two solid days waiting for any kind of signal from the planet's surface.

"Now, here was the keystone of Data's plan: He made sure Riker and I knew nothing about the one-eye he'd dismantled or about the communicator he'd made. He hid it all from us, even stuffed the dead one-eye back up the air shaft where we wouldn't see it. When we were caught, none of us humans—whose brain waves could be read—knew what Data had done. The one-eyes couldn't read his brain, so his secret was safe. All he had to do then was wait until we were all together so he could signal the *Enterprise* and have us beamed up."

"How did you disable the one-eye?" Troi asked Data.

"I will refrain from taxing you with an exhibition, Counselor, as I have noticed that humans have a peculiar reaction to it. Suffice it to say that I confused the one-eyes with my poetry. My poetry is apparently hard to classify as poetry at all, and the one-eyes momentarily stymied themselves trying to figure it out."

Troi didn't know if she should ask the next set of questions, or pursue them on her own. Why had she experienced those vivid visions of mythical characters? What were their meanings? And why had Crichton appeared to experience them as well?

Picard's communicator came to life.

"Worf to Picard."

"Picard here."

"Sir, from our new position, atmospheric conditions are allowing us to pick up video from the planet's surface."

"Thank you, Worf. Send it down here, please."

Picard swiveled the monitor on the table so all could view it.

They saw the same memorial video piece on Ferris that Troi saw outside Crichton's office—the same carven-oak face, the dates of birth and death.

Then an attractive newscaster's face appeared on the screen. She said that although the man who killed Ferris was dead, some of the criminals that participated in the attack were in custody and would be executed today.

Her words became a voice-over for shots of the Dissenters being herded into their cells by the CS.

Coyote passed close to the camera and Troi could see a gleam in his eye. He didn't seem defeated at all.

"Captain," said Troi, "I was with these people after I became separated from the away team. They protected me and got me into CephCom."

She wished she could do something for them. Maybe the captain wanted to as well. But there was no chance of helping them. The Prime Directive prohibited such meddling, and Troi had seen the wisdom of non-interference demonstrated over and over again. Any positive change on this planet would have to be made by the people themselves, not by the intrusion of a paternalistic hand.

Troi heard the conference room doors swish open. She looked up and saw two diminutive people enter. They looked like children but had the bearing of adult life-mates. She remembered them as Oleph and Una.

They came directly over to Troi.

"May we discuss a professional matter with you in front of others?" asked Una gravely.

"It seems to have involved your crewmates as well as you," added Oleph.

"Yes, please do," said Troi. "I've been wanting to talk to you, in fact. What did we do during those hours we spent together? I have the most stubborn amnesia."

"That's what we wanted to talk to you about," said Oleph. "We visited Earth not long ago, and as ethnographers we traveled all over that planet, recording fiction, myth, speculation, and all forms of creative imagination. We used our favored medium, something like your holography, except the images, sounds and so forth are played directly into the brain of the viewer. Virtual reality."

"Well, as a counselor you wanted to view our ethnographic movie. We told you that sometimes, rarely, a life-form has trouble with the medium after they experience it. They find the movie stays in their mind and plays back later, in fragmented flashbacks and dreams.

"You insisted on viewing our movie anyway. You watched the whole thing straight through, all four hours," Oleph concluded.

"And with the most enthusiasm afterward I'd ever seen," said Una. "You said you'd be doing further research, and I took it to mean that you were going to do it right away. You left our cabin, and that was the last we saw of you."

As they spoke, the memories of the meeting broke free and rose into Troi's conscious mind.

"I must have blocked it out because of some kind of shock, when the flashbacks occurred," said Troi. "A way of trying to suppress the trauma, I suppose. Was there something in your movie about a statue of a woman that comes to life?"

"More than one," said Una. "There was The Winter's Tale, Pygmalion, a Tlingit Indian story, and some others as well."

Troi could now remember seeing these in the movie, along with Sekhmet, Tezcatlipoca, and all the rest of the cast of Other-worlders.

She knew what the next question had to be. Possibly the key to it all.

"Did you ever show Crichton your ethnographic movies?"

Oleph and Una looked blankly at each other.

"Who is Crichton?" asked Una.

"The Director of Cephalic Security on Rampart."

"We've never met anyone on Rampart, have we?"

"No, my sweet."

Troi felt disappointed. It was as if she had opened a series of Chinese boxes, one within the other, but the final, smallest box, holding the kernel of the mystery, had remained stubbornly locked. While she sensed that she was closer than ever to finding the key to that last box, she knew she couldn't very well hold up the ship and the investigative machinery of Starfleet just so she alone could pursue a riddle.

Una and Oleph came closer to Troi, reached up with little pink toddler hands, and clasped her own hand.

"We just wanted to say, in case we don't see you again, Counselor, that we're sorry."

"You don't have to be," said Troi. "It seems I took the risk willingly."

A startling thought occurred to her. It came out of nowhere and had the crystalline elegance of truth.

She excused herself and hurried to her cabin to access the ship's computer.

"Why aren't they somewhere more comfortable?" asked Picard as he and Riker walked toward Engineering.

"Apparently they'd been awake since Crichton first came aboard the *Enterprise,* days ago," Riker replied. "But when everything was over, she still wanted to stand by in case her help was needed. She wouldn't leave Engineering, and Geordi wouldn't leave her."

Technicians were repairing the doors to Engineering as Picard and Riker entered. More technicians were quietly at work on the equipment inside.

Riker showed the captain over to a corner. There, Geordi sat propped against the wall, deep in slumber. His VISOR hid his eyes as always, but the lines of pain and exhaustion on his face were clear. He seemed to have aged years.

Beside him, Ensign Chops Taylor lay curled up on the floor, her head resting on her arm. Her visor was lying next to her, along with the ten burnt sensor pads that once capped her fingers. One of her hands moved and gestured as she dreamt.

Riker had never seen her without her visor. Her face was pure poetry.

"I don't believe I've met that ensign," Picard whispered.

"Her name is Chops Taylor," whispered Riker.

Geordi stirred slightly, and his hand came to rest on the ensign's shoulder, as if he were afraid someone would take her away.

Picard looked at them both for a long moment.

"Thank you for saving my ship," he said finally, in a voice too soft to wake them.

He turned and left, and Riker followed him out.

Picard took his seat on the bridge, with Riker to his right. Troi's chair was empty.

Data was at the Ops position. Wesley's Conn position was occupied by another ensign as Wesley took some much needed rest.

Worf had, of course, scorned rest as a decadent

luxury. He stood at the tactical console and surveyed the readouts.

"The Rampartian ships have backed off several thousand kilometers and are holding. Nobody on the surface has answered our hails."

"Thank you, Worf. No more communications from Starfleet?"

"None, sir."

"What about the videocasts you've intercepted? Anything new?"

"The Dissenters are in captivity and will be executed soon by the CS."

Picard stared at the deck.

"I suspect this will be a major loss for Rampart," he said.

He lapsed into silence, despondent over the prospect of another hundred years, or maybe another thousand, of schizophrenic rule on this planet.

The bridge crew waited for the order the captain would normally give next—the order to engage the engines and leave this star system behind.

Picard prepared to speak, but before he got any words out, his communicator came to life with a familiar accented voice.

"Troi to Captain Picard."

"Picard here."

"Sir, I think I've found the missing piece to the puzzle."

Chapter Eighteen

RHIANNON LAY ON the hard bed in her CephCom cell, staring at the wall.

It was night outside, and the video screen in her room had been dimmed, but she had no desire to sleep on this, her last of all nights.

Crichton had decided that the Dissenters' bodies themselves would be destroyed. Blanking wasn't enough. They were the most devilish people in history, Crichton said. She had heard the same thing on the television before it had been dimmed. She had also seen a news report that showed Odysseus fighting with a CS man on a bridge, and then both of them lying dead.

She had cried a long time about that, and for the rest of the Dissenters, and for herself. She had cried until there was nothing left but a hollow feeling.

Rain had started to fall outside. She watched the dripping shadows on the walls. Then there was a larger shadow, as if something was moving around right outside her window.

Some guard probably.

The shadow remained, amorphous, wobbling this

way and that. Something about the way it moved told her she should see what it was.

She had to stand on tiptoe on the bed.

A familiar face with large golden falcon-eyes looked back at her through the window.

"Saushulima!"

The haguya was perched on a narrow ledge outside. It couldn't hear her through the thick bulletproof glass, but seemed content just to look at her. It had to flap a wing occasionally to maintain balance.

Rhiannon put her hands on the glass, wanting very badly to touch the beast's familiar solid bulk and speak to it as she used to.

They exchanged a somber glance. Rhiannon was sure he knew this would be the last time they would see each other.

A hovercraft flew by outside, then swung around, its searchlight projecting a white disc that slid along the wet sides of the buildings.

The light swept closer and closer.

Suddenly the haguya moved its great wings and took flight, just before the searchlight hit the window.

Rhiannon stood by the window for the remainder of the night, but the haguya never returned.

As soon as the gray, drizzly dawn came, a troop of CS men led by Crichton marched down the corridors in highest alert mode. The hum of their hundred fully charged weapons filled the air. One-eyes kept pace with them, an integral part of the troop.

The troop had rolling along with them a special wave propagator; it would prevent anyone from using a transporter to escape. No chances were being taken.

One by one, the CS took the two dozen Dissenters from their cells. Rhiannon, Gunabibi, and Coyote were the last three to be inducted into the death march.

Coyote sang a song in an Indian dialect as he was hauled from his cell. The white-haired old man continued to sing as the troop pushed him forward. The push wasn't necessary; he walked proudly, with the gait of a young man.

Crichton called the group to a halt.

"What is he singing?" the director asked the officer next to him.

The officer was young Daley, survivor of the infamous cave ambush. In the absence of Ferris, Daley was now Crichton's right-hand man.

A one-eye moved in front of Coyote and began to scan his brain waves. Daley listened to his headphones to hear what the one-eye would be able to tell him about Coyote's singing.

"The one-eye doesn't know the language," he said finally. "Apparently this singing went on continuously all last night, and the one-eyes couldn't make a thing out of it."

Crichton went up to Coyote.

"Shut up, damn it!" he yelled in Coyote's face.

Coyote closed his eyes. He kept on singing.

"Use the truth serum on him," said Crichton.

Daley produced his chemical warfare kit and prepared the squeeze bottles.

Coyote opened his eyes to narrow sight-slits and stole a look at Crichton's wristwatch.

Then he stopped singing and smiled.

"The one-eye's picking something up now," said Daley, pausing as the information was relayed over his headset.

"He apparently . . . inserted some criminal material, some pages, into the outgoing mail last night. He tricked an orderly into helping him. Proper postage and everything. A lot of different envelopes going to different places."

Crichton looked at his watch.

252

"Thank you, that's exactly right," said Coyote. "They will have been delivered by now, to random addresses. Pages from the stories of Gunabibi, Lomov, Rhiannon, Odysseus, of all of us."

Daley listened to his headphones. "The one-eyes are picking up more. They say he snuck the pages into CephCom on his person. Didn't even tell the other Dissenters about it. Thought about them only in an unknown language he calls Miwok."

Crichton continued to look at his watch, as he thought through the implications.

Coyote tried to hold back, but a laugh forced its way out and grew into a guffaw.

Crichton spoke with an arctic voice.

"An exercise in futility. The one-eyes will find every single person you so cruelly exposed to the Allpox. All of them will be cleansed or blanked. All the pages will be destroyed."

"I don't know, sir," said Coyote. "Seems likely you might have a few more Dissenters on your hands before this is through."

"That may be. But the worst ones will have been executed."

Crichton spoke curt orders into his headset that would set into motion a search for the pages. Then he started the procession moving again.

He felt as though he'd just been pushed off a cliff. He'd been poised on it, teetering on it, and Coyote's trick was the final push.

The abyss had first opened when the *Enterprise* had shown up. An abyss of fiction in his mind, of insane hallucinations. The worst part of it was that he himself appeared in these hallucinations. He was a fictional character among the other fictional characters. A central character. The crazy stories were always about him.

If he had to finally lose his grip and let the fictions

253

run rampant in his mind, he was determined he should not do it here, now. He used his own abhorrence of the Allpox, of its devilry, its obscenity, to push the imaginary world back into his unconscious. God will help me, he told himself.

He led the procession up a long stair and arrived at the bridge. As they passed through the glass doors and onto the pavement of the bridge, the Dissenters stopped walking.

They had all seen the video reports and knew this was where Odysseus had died.

Crichton saw what was happening and knew he had to keep the procession moving. No time was to be wasted, no change in itinerary allowed.

But the CS guards didn't have to be told. They pulled the Dissenters forward.

The security around CephCom was unprecedented, all as Crichton had ordered. Dozens of hovercraft circled the complex, and one-eyes lined the bridge and hung in rank upon rank in the air farther back, like rows of headstones in a hovering cemetery. Above them, mammoth battlefield one-eyes flew in precise holding patterns. Sharpshooters stood at the corners of every roof. There would be no mistake this time. Nothing would happen that Crichton himself did not order.

Rhiannon watched the backs of the CS officers in front of her. Suddenly she desired a last look at the sky. She turned her head upward as she walked.

Vast gray and white clouds moved in stately unison overhead, dwarfing the complex. A small blue space had opened up between them, a minor interregnum.

Rhiannon saw a flock of circling birds, nothing more than specks at this distance, high up in the blue gap.

There were no birds on Rampart.

Rhiannon froze in her tracks, causing the CS officer behind to bump into her. Her face was still upturned, her eyes wide.

"Saushulima," she said to herself.

Now the CS men around her stopped, and looked up as well.

Crichton sensed the break in ranks behind him and turned to ascertain the problem. He followed the many gazes upward and saw the distant flock of creatures.

Now the entire troop had halted. All eyes were turned up toward the inconceivable. Neither Crichton's helmet nor those of the other CS officers were filtering out the sight. The military computers controlling the helmets had identified the airborne creatures as a real threat, which the men needed to see so they could shoot at them.

The haguya pulled into a tight arrow formation, so close they almost looked like one united creature. As they began to dive, their formation changed to three smaller arrow shapes. Their groupings were precise.

As they became more visible, and undeniably, extravagantly alien, Crichton experienced his awakening.

Time slowed down to a stop, as if to help him undergo the process.

The haguya seemed to hang in the air in the middle of their dive. The clouds were a painting, and the people around him were statues.

The other person inside Crichton now awoke from his ten-year sleep. He awoke as if he had fallen asleep only an hour ago. He was Captain Alfred Bowles.

He recognized that the fictions trying to "take over" were not fictions at all. They had all really happened. They were his experiences. His ship, a thing that had dominated his psychotic episodes, a ship he'd regarded as mythical, was in truth his ship after all. It was no science fiction. It was the U.S.S. *Huxley*.

The personality of Crichton, an artificial construct, folded itself into a corner like a piece of furniture. Bowles was now in control. He still had the memories of what he'd done as Crichton, but he knew that the Crichton persona was not his true self.

Now his sense of time came back to him. The haguya were diving at him. They grew from tiny bird shapes into large animals, living alien airships, dropping with great speed and momentum.

The stunned CS men recovered their wits enough to raise their weapons.

Their motion drew his attention away from the haguya and his own revelations.

He stared at the men for just a second. His Starfleet training took over. The most basic part of the training, how to handle contact with alien life.

"Everybody hold your fire and lower your weapons!" he barked into his headset.

Some of the soldiers obeyed, some didn't. A lot of weapons were still raised.

"Lower them, damn you, and keep them down, and move all aircraft back two kilometers. I want no hostile moves of any kind."

Now the haguya's golden falcon eyes and massive tendoned wings were clearly delineated against the clouds. They split ranks in a complex maneuver, and with mathematical precision regrouped and finished their dive at an angle, coming straight at the bridge.

With a great rush of wind, they flew directly over the Dissenters and the CS men holding them. Some of the CS men ducked in fright as leathery wings and bony talons whooshed past them.

The haguya turned in the air beyond the bridge and

256

came in for another pass, even lower this time, specifically targeting the CS men around the Dissenters. The men fell flat on the ground to avoid impact, while the Dissenters shouted exhortations to the flying aliens.

Bowles could see what the alien attack was all about. These Dissenters—who Crichton arrested—were the aliens' friends!

Some of the CS raised their weapons again.

"Put 'em down!" Bowles yelled. "Let go of the Dissenters. Step away from them."

They obeyed.

The haguya flew upward and then began to wheel about in a circle. One glided back down solo and, flapping heavily, braked itself to a landing next to the Dissenters.

Rhiannon ran up to the beast and touched its head. She whispered some words to it, then leapt nimbly to its back.

As it beat its wings and bore the girl aloft, another haguya came in for a landing and took its place. Gunabibi climbed onto its back, and she too was borne skyward.

One by one the other haguya landed and took off until all the Dissenters were riding on their backs, high up among the clouds.

Bowles didn't let the CS soldiers move a muscle or fire a shot during the entire process.

Many of them were too stunned anyway. One soldier named Lieutenant Redman was among the more affected. His training and inculcation had made him fear fiction, but this science fiction in the flesh turned out not to frighten him at all. He thought the haguya were the most beautiful creatures he'd ever seen. However, his aesthetic rapture could not help him retrieve the memories of his previous life as a

Dissenter—when he was the son of a CS officer named Powell. Those memories were gone forever.

On the bridge of the *Enterprise,* Picard, Troi, Riker, and Data watched the viewscreen. Data tabbed his panel repeatedly, choosing between several different views of the CephCom bridge, the haguya, the CS, and the man Troi had just suggested was Captain Bowles, of the U.S.S. *Huxley.*

"This is all raw feed from their one-eyes and cameras," Data told Picard. "Uncut images being fed into the CS video control room."

"I daresay the CS won't be able to do much with this," said Picard, "unless they want to expose themselves as fools and publicly admit that alien life exists right under their noses. Counselor, can you tell us anything more about these haguya, as you call them?"

"As I said, I could never feel any thoughts or emotions from them. They seemed generally helpful to the Dissenters but I couldn't verify anything beyond that."

"Captain," said Data, "I am separating a component of the audio signal from the video feed. I believe it to be the haguya. Their speech, perhaps."

The android looked at Troi. "You would not have heard it. The frequencies are twenty thousand hertz above your hearing range."

Data looked back at his console. "The sounds are definitely a form of information transfer between them. I estimate the speech to be three times as information-intensive as human language. This is a highly intelligent form of life. It is likely that the frequency of their neural impulses prevented you from sensing their minds empathically, Counselor."

Data's hands danced a pas de deux on the keyboard. "Sir, I believe that the ship's computer and I will be able to decode this language. We are already detecting a repeated string."

"Perhaps we'll call it Data's Cartouche," said Picard. "The key to your Rosetta Stone."

"The cartouche is already giving up its secrets, sir. The computer has translated it as a string of names. Odysseus, Rhiannon, Gunabibi, Coyote . . . there are two dozen of them."

Troi watched the viewscreen as the last of the Dissenters, Amoret as it happened, was borne away from CephCom by the haguya.

"There was one thing the Dissenters told me that I didn't believe at the time," Troi said. "They said the haguya understood human speech and sat around the campfire at night, listening to all the stories. Now I have a feeling that it was no exaggeration."

"It may not have been," said Data. "The patterns of their own communications resemble long stories, like the songs of whales. These haguya could be storytellers themselves."

"Mr. Data," said Picard, "have the computer record as much of the haguya-talk as you can. But let's track our man now."

Data tabbed his keypad.

On the screen, Bowles turned and headed alone into the CephCom building. He seemed to be in a hurry.

"Stay with him, Data."

Data switched between the signals of several cameras, putting the various scenes up on the viewscreen. In a view from a one-eye, looking over somebody's shoulder, a knot of huddled CS men on the bridge talked a blue streak, a torrent of excited confusion in the aftermath of the haguya's appearance. In another view, down on the quadrangle, several CS men could be seen pointing toward the sky.

"I am afraid we will not be able to pick up signals inside the buildings, sir."

"Keep at it," said Picard. Then he turned to Troi.

"Counselor, you still feel strongly that Crichton is Bowles?"

"More than ever. The CS could have brainwashed him. It could have been incomplete—Odysseus told me such things happen. The Bowles persona could have been waiting for a cue to re-emerge. And we could have been the cue. This incident with the haguya may have pushed him past the critical point. What he did just now, freeing the Dissenters and protecting the haguya, certainly didn't look like the actions of Crichton."

Picard nodded to himself.

"It fits," he said. "His disfigurement could have resulted from the destruction of the *Huxley*. That crude reconstructive surgery would have kept our computer from recognizing him."

"If we get him back," said Riker, "let's hope he still has some memories about the fate of the *Huxley* crew."

"Yes, Will, let's not forget we're looking for more than just one crewperson. Worf, what's the status of the Rampartian ships?"

"Holding at a radius of five thousand kilometers, sir."

"Advise the moment you see a more aggressive posture. In the meantime, see if you can hail Bowles. But just say that we want to talk to Director Crichton."

"Aye, sir. Trying . . ."

"And please advise Starfleet that we'll be staying here just a bit longer, on my authority."

"Aye, sir. So far we are getting no response from Rampart."

"Captain," said Troi, "they may be too confused by the appearance of the haguya to reply right now. It is also possible they will not allow us to speak to the one they know as Crichton. He could be in danger of arrest. I would guess he has been for a while."

Bowles was acutely conscious of the possibility of arrest as he hurried back to his office.

Crichton's office, actually. Bowles still had all the facts about Crichton and the CS in his memory.

He tried to appear calm as he brushed past CS officers and soldiers in the corridors. He stayed as far as he could from the one-eyes.

He knew what the procedure would be if he were caught. Crichton had ordered such procedures on others many times. The CS didn't bother re-blanking the minds that had already failed the procedure once. They got rid of them the easy way, with a lethal dose of barbiturates.

His hope was that the confusion caused by the appearance of the haguya might supersede reports of his own strange behavior—reports that would eventually be given to the Council of Truth.

The chatter on his headset confirmed his hope. The live sighting of the haguya, and the capturing of the entire incident on videotape, had stunned the entire CS organization. There was no precedent, no prior experience with alien life. The manual didn't say what should be done when confronting the impossible.

He pictured the CS video editors scrambling, impelled by the necessity of presenting something, anything, to the Council of Truth for inspection. No one would dare tell this story to the Council without tape to back them up. It was just too fictional to be believed.

Bowles suddenly realized he couldn't go back to his office. The place was filled with brain wave antennae and camera lenses, and he needed to do some dirty work.

He diverted his steps into a room that had a disk reader and terminal.

His fingers stumbled in their eagerness as he commenced a search in the disk library for the name Alfred Bowles.

There was no such person listed in the regular files, but he had Crichton's knowledge of the system and he could get anywhere, even into the Council of Truth's own files.

He broke into the Council's data base, found that a disk did exist, and retrieved it from the vault.

When he put it on the disk-reader he got a message on-screen:

This disk contains mental material from the only surviving crewman of the U.S.S. Huxley, *Captain Alfred C. Bowles. Only the material relevant to future conflicts with other hostile expeditions has been saved herein. All information on this disk has been filtered and certified as sanitary.*

"Subject's mind was blanked and replenished with filtered memories of James Crichton, CS officer killed in the line of duty on date 7/8/12."

Within a few moments Bowles was watching events from his life as a Starship captain unfold on the little monitor. He found plenty of verification that his "science fiction hallucinations" were real memories, but he noticed that there were no images of alien life on the disk.

The CS saved only the material the computer recognized as factual.

He typed a command into the computer: Search for the last images of the *Huxley*.

And there they were. He saw himself crawling around inside the ship. It had crash landed. It was burning. CS men pulled him out, only him. His face was on fire. They rolled him in the dirt to put it out. He tried to go back in, because all his crew were inside, but the CS held him back, and then the ship exploded.

His eyes shifted focus and he looked at his own reflection on the monitor. He, Bowles, had never seen that face before. It was keloid-scarred, and the features were so strange—as if his face were pressed against a clear membrane.

Bowles suddenly looked away from the screen. Had he heard someone outside the door? Suddenly aware that he hadn't listened to his headset for several minutes, he turned it back on. He heard the comm officer telling patrols to find the Director of Cephalic Security and report back, because the director was not answering his page.

There was no more time to look at the disk. He left it where it was and fled.

As he hurried toward the evidence repository he saw several CS personnel looking at him and speaking into their headsets, reporting that they saw him.

The clerk at the repository looked startled at the director's demand for one of the *Enterprise* communicators, but relinquished it without question.

Bowles then rushed to the electronic warfare room, and ordered the Electronic Warfare Officer to turn off the jamming for the *Enterprise* communicators.

The EWO, a thick-necked young man with crew-cut hair, just stared at him and listened to the voices on his headset.

"Something wrong with your hearing?" Bowles asked.

The EWO's face started to shine with sweat.

"Instructions have just been issued. Your orders are to be ignored by all personnel, sir."

"No one except the Council itself can override me, Lieutenant."

"The order came from the Council, sir, with all the proper verifications."

The EWO listened to his headset some more, then steeled himself to do his duty.

"A squad is waiting on the other side of that door to arrest you, sir. Would you please unlock it and step outside?"

"It's a fiction, Lieutenant. The Council hasn't ordered any such thing. Dissenters have been at work here. Didn't they just yesterday compromise our communications system with their blasphemies?"

The EWO hesitated.

"But sir, they say you helped the Dissenters . . ."

"You actually believe that?"

The EWO rose, a gun in his hand.

"Lieutenant," said Bowles, "I'll have you arrested for disobeying the Director of Cephalic Security. I'll have you blanked!"

The EWO cupped his hand over his headset, trying to listen.

Bowles reached over and ripped his hand away.

"Look at me. I'm Crichton. Your eyes tell the truth. Those voices are giving you fiction!"

On the bridge of the *Enterprise,* Picard sat in his command chair and waited as his crew continued to attempt contact with Crichton/Bowles.

Troi and Riker sat on either side, both evincing more anxiousness than their commanding officer.

Worf looked up from his console.

"No answers to our hails. No sign of our man in any video signal."

"Sir," said Data, "the time allotted by Starfleet for our continued reconnaissance has elapsed."

"Noted," said Picard. "Continue to scan, Worf."

"Shall I prepare to warp out of orbit, sir?" asked Wesley.

"No, Mr. Crusher," said Picard, with a slight edge to his voice. "Rest assured I will advise you when I want you to do that."

Data turned around in his chair. He wanted to see the appearance of a human doing something deliberately independent from the forces which had due authority over him. Such a thing was so typically human, so eminently useful to an android in the adolescent stage of his social development.

Picard smiled at him.

"I wish to give the counselor's hypothesis a full test," said the captain. "We won't be leaving until I'm sure we've done so."

"Sir," said Troi tentatively, "I don't want the ship to be endangered more than necessary. I could be wrong."

"You could be."

"Captain," said Worf, "the Rampartian ships are moving . . . they've now got us within the radius of their weapons."

"Increase power to the shields."

The bridge speakers vibrated roughly. It was the sound of someone clearing their throat.

Then, "Come in, *Enterprise.*"

Picard stood up.

"It's coming from the surface sir," said Worf. "From one of our own communicators."

"This is Captain Picard. To whom am I speaking?"

"To Captain Alfred Bowles. Permission to beam aboard your ship, Captain."

"Are there others with you?"

"No. There are no other survivors from the *Huxley.* I'll explain when you get me aboard. I suggest you hurry sir, before I'm arrested by my own soldiers."

"Worf—have the man beamed up. Wesley, lay in a course for Starbase Eighty-one, Warp Factor Four."

"Aye, sir. Course laid in. All systems answer ready."

"Beaming complete," said Worf.

"Engage," said Picard.

On the viewscreen, the stars and the clouds of blue nebula dust changed shape, stretching into an illusion of linearity as the ship shot away from Rampart at one hundred times the speed of light.

Chapter Nineteen

TROI SAT INTROSPECTIVELY in Picard's ready room while Picard and Riker talked about their experiences on Rampart.

Riker held open Picard's copy of the complete works of William Shakespeare.

"I was lucky to remember anything at all, given the circumstances," said Riker. "My commanding officer was brainwashed, the CS were trying to break down the door, and I hadn't read Hamlet since . . . longer than I care to mention."

"I think I see a cautionary tale here," said Picard.

Riker laughed, closed the book and put it on Picard's desk.

" 'To hold, as 'twere, a mirror up to nature' . . . Maybe if the man were alive now, in the age of non-linear spacetime, he'd make the mirror curved; his plays would be a curving mirror for a curving universe."

As the two men talked, Troi could feel how relieved they were to have gotten each other through their ordeal unscathed. But she sensed more than that: inside, they really did feel a lot like father and son.

Perhaps they could fulfill for each other those needs which the courses of their lives had left unmet.

She wondered if Picard would let down his reserve and show his feelings just a bit. Riker already had—one didn't have to be an empath to see it.

Bowles arrived at that moment and received cordial greetings. He wore a new Starfleet uniform. He seemed a bit tentative about his surroundings, but relaxed. His scarred face had a new mobility—he wasn't exactly smiling, but his mouth did have a hint of upturn.

"How are you feeling, Al?" asked Picard.

"Not bad, actually. I guess when you've been asleep for ten years, at least you're fairly well rested. There are huge areas of my memory missing, though. My childhood and teens don't exist. I have never been young. My personal life doesn't exist, either. My Starfleet training is still with me; I have the knowledge itself, but I can't remember going to Starfleet Academy. Were you and I there at the same time?"

"Yes. And, yes, I did know you."

"Oh." Bowles seemed almost afraid to ask for more information. "I guess I must have done all right. I made Captain."

"You were brilliant," said Picard. "Actually, you were torn between two pursuits, Starfleet and holography. You were a holographic artist. I expect when you get back you'll be able to visit galleries and see plenty of your work."

Bowles was stunned. He had to sit down.

"That explains so much."

He stared at his hands.

"When I was Crichton and I started having . . . 'hallucinations,' one of them was of myself making a holostatue of a talking thousand-year-old tree. Crichton had a great deal of trouble with that one. It had everything—aliens, art . . ."

268

"Why do you think you—or rather, Crichton—were chosen to become Director of Cephalic Security?" asked Picard. "Wouldn't he have been a bad risk?"

"Not at all. It didn't matter what a person had been before blanking. One became a clean slate. Crichton was given someone else's past. But he had a special aptitude for creating images the public needed, and rose through the ranks. He was the best they'd ever had in the Director job. It wasn't until your arrival that the Bowles memories started emerging."

"Sort of like pentimento," said Troi, "when a painter paints over his original work, but then years later the original shows through."

"Yes." He continued to stare at his hands. "But I guess the Rampartians were using my innate abilities all along. Or misusing them."

"Al," said Picard, "I highly recommend that you talk some of these things out with the counselor. She is the best Starfleet has to offer."

"Let me second the invitation," said Troi, "while disclaiming the flattery."

"Appreciate the offer," said Bowles. "I was just remembering that Crichton had a compulsion to wash his hands. I think he was really trying to wash off my art."

"Yes," said Troi. "The hand-washing was a clue for me. I eventually remembered that Captain Bowles had been an artist. Everything fell into place then. I saw how I'd been wrong and at the same time right all along . . . how I had first felt Crichton was secretly remembering aliens . . . then how I felt he was hallucinating fictions. In fact, he was remembering aliens —those he'd seen in Starfleet—but he mistakenly believed them to be fictions."

Bowles looked away from his hands and gazed out the porthole.

"What do you think Starfleet will do about Rampart?" he asked, directing his question to all of them.

"They'll want to know all they can about the *Huxley*," said Picard. "They'll gather any further evidence, and give the Rampartians a warning about attacking other ships. And that's probably it. We had to evolve our own way out of our age of horror, and the Rampartians will have to do likewise. If they don't, they'll be stuck on their isolated little rock forever."

"They've already discovered," said Bowles, "that alien life exists on their own planet. They saw science fiction become real. You know why the Council kept the *Huxley* incident so secret? Why they blanked it out of the minds on Rampart? They were afraid the mere idea of space voyaging would spread the scourge of science fiction on their own planet and people would imagine a universe full of alien life waiting to be discovered, and clamor for useless exploration. Now, maybe in a few generations, Rampart actually will begin exploration."

He rose.

"Anyway, thanks to you all."

"It's the counselor you should thank," said Picard. "We would have left Rampart knowing nothing about you and the fate of the *Huxley* if it weren't for her."

"Then, thank you especially, Counselor Troi."

Now he really was smiling.

"I hope I can be of further help," she said.

"One favor," said Bowles. "Don't tell me too much about my past. My childhood and teens and all that. I was in your Ten-Forward lounge earlier, talking with your alien hostess-philosopher. She said I was in an enviable position, because I get to do all that all over again. Anyway, I think I'm going to go have some more of her tea and advice."

He left and the doors swished shut behind him.

"Why don't you take the bridge for a moment, Number One," Picard said to Riker. "I need to speak with the counselor. Afterward, I have something in mind for us."

"Aye, sir."

When Riker had gone, Troi and Picard sat silently. She watched the stars outside the porthole, and Picard watched her.

"Still having regrets about your choice?"

"What choice?" she asked.

"The choice to watch Oleph and Una's movie. Take a risk in the interest of discovery."

"No. I learned something. I had an anxiety I wasn't even aware of. You remember I had been telling you lately that you were concealing too many emotions?"

"Yes. I believe we still have a meeting pending on that."

"Well . . . I was actually afraid that I was burying my own feelings and needs too much. That was my anxiety. That, being an empath among a crew of a thousand, responsible for their emotional well-being, I was neglecting my own feelings."

"You wouldn't be the first counselor to have that problem."

"Well, whether it had any basis or not, the anxiety itself was there and had to be reckoned with, and before all this happened I was projecting it onto others.

"Still, I couldn't see the cause of it all. But in those Other-worlder myth-dreams, I ran right up against it. That's why I kept seeing myself turn into a statue—it was my own fear of turning into a cold, unfeeling person. In the end, when I passed through that stone state and came out alive again, the fear worked itself through."

"The statue-woman who wakes," said Picard. "The Winter's Tale." He patted the book on his desk, and was silent for a time.

"Are you going to continue your research into the works of human imagination?" he asked finally. "The research you started after seeing Oleph and Una's movie?"

She felt herself tense up at the thought.

"On an intellectual level, I know I should continue the work. But the flesh is weak. That research was how this all began. When I started the research I released the mythical characters from the movie to run rampant inside me, and I'm not ready to face that kind of loss of control. It could happen all over again, as soon as I make my first inquiries to the computer. And neither I, nor Oleph and Una, can say how long that danger will persist."

"Counselor, I'm not suggesting you should do anything you don't want to, or anything dangerous. I just hope you'll one day continue with the research, that's all."

"I promise, I will."

She had tried to sound fearless, but failed.

He paused before speaking again, and she could see the little wheels turning.

"Deanna," he said casually, "do you remember that Big Number you once told me about?"

She had to smile at his mental agility. He had a way of coming up with something you said long ago and rubbing your nose in it.

"You're talking about the number," she said, "based on average synapse count, of possible states of one human brain—the number of possible thoughts and feelings one individual is capable of."

"Yes, I think that's it. How big did you say it was?"

"Two raised to the power of ten trillion."

"And that's considerably more than the total num-

272

ber of atoms in the entire known universe. Which, as I see it, means the exploration in here," he pointed to her head, "is as unbounded and vast as the exploration out there." He pointed out the porthole. "And bear in mind the occupation of the man who is making that claim."

"I know what you're telling me. I won't give this up."

"Good. Now, did you still want to speak to me regarding my own suppression of feelings?"

Troi laughed. Then she realized the captain really meant it.

But at this moment she didn't feel the necessity. As an empath she could tell that the captain was allowing more of his emotions into consciousness. He wasn't showing them as openly as she might want, but that was his style of command. At least the feelings were there; especially now, after the mission to Rampart. That would figure. Amoret had apparently sifted through his mind—through everything, no matter how private and emotional. And afterward she had decided to save his life. Anyone would be less stiff after that.

"No, I don't think that's necessary right now."

"Thank you. Since I now have the counselor's seal of good mental health, I think I'm ready for some recreation. Care to join Will and me for a little horseback riding?"

"No, but thanks," she said. She was grateful enough that the two top officers of the ship would carve out some time to relax together.

She followed him onto the bridge.

"Come on, Will," said Picard. "Some holographic horses need a holographic sweat. Data, you have the bridge."

The first officer rose and accompanied Picard toward the turbolift. Troi noticed that the captain had his hand on Riker's shoulder in a decidedly paternal way. They could indeed have been father and son.

It was enough to make a ship's counselor proud.

After a day off, Wesley had already caught up on his sleep.

Now he paced around his cabin, considering the present alternatives for possible diversion, some edifying, some just fun.

The one that popped into his mind was in a different category altogether. A startling idea. He decided to act on it immediately, lest he lock himself into a hesitation-loop and delay it forever.

He called Shikibu and suggested the holodeck. She answered simply, "Yes, Shikibu out."

He beat her to the holodeck entrance and programmed in the Ryoanji rock garden, with the same soft rain as before.

He let the slim young woman precede him into the holodeck. Her black hair was free, swaying, her feet silent as mist on the stones. She led him toward the wooden patio. The rain was hypnotic, pattering on the gravel, dripping from the cedars and running in rills off the ancient tile roof.

For a moment Wesley found himself worrying what he would say to her, and if he should touch her again, and why he still felt awkward. She was still a mystery to him, after all those koan and mondo he'd read trying to understand her.

As they sat under the eave, he decided to just do what she was doing, and watch the garden. He decided not to try and understand any of it and simply gave up.

Then, as he looked at the garden which so skillfully blended the works of man with the works of nature, he had a strange sensation. He, himself, was a work of nature. At the smallest level he was composed of an inconceivable number of quarks and leptons, oscillating and spinning. These particles were organized into atoms, which were structured into vastly complex molecules in frenetic interaction that, in turn, made up his trillions of cells—each cell containing a DNA polymer with two billion "bytes" of information . . .

And all of it happened spontaneously, with no volition on his part. He didn't have to tell the quarks or the DNA what to do. In fact, he wasn't even the same person from moment to moment—the cells of his body were continually dying, and new ones were growing in their places, and as he looked at his hand now he knew that it wasn't the same hand that had existed yesterday. The very quarks and leptons that comprised him were not exclusively "his"—they were descendants of the energy of the universe-creation explosion, and after they existed as Wesley they would exist in a star or planet or tree.

He was, he felt, like a wave, which travels briefly across the surface of an ocean—the waters form the wave momentarily and then transfer that wave-energy elsewhere. The wave has no permanent parts; it is only a process, inseparable from the rest of the ocean, as he, Wesley, was not a separate entity confronting the universe. Rather, he was a manifestation of the universe. He was a natural process of a nameless infinite "it."

He remembered something Shikibu had told him, when he prodded her about explaining Zen archery. She'd said the archer himself does not shoot the arrow. If the technique is right, the shot falls spontaneously. She explained it this way: When a sage bush produces a flower, the sage doesn't "know" that a bee will be attracted to it; and when the bee takes the pollen from that flower, the bee doesn't "know" that some of it will be deposited on his back, and later, miles away, pollinate another sage plant. Yet the bee does take the pollen and, thus, other sage is pollinated. Through both bee and sage, "it" dances. Just so, the archer, in proper frame of mind, does not deliberately shoot the arrow. "It" shoots the arrow.

Now, just as spontaneously as that proper arrowshot, Wesley found himself turning toward Shikibu, and kissing her, as she spontaneously did the same to him, and through them both, "it" danced.

The Dissenters had returned to the caves and tried to retrieve their books. But the cache had been found, and the books were gone.

They had then flown, on the backs of the swift haguya, high up into the mountains.

Now they were encamped for the night just below a very windy pass, an inhospitable place not likely to be visited by pragmatic Rampartians.

The Dissenter tradition of campfire bard-stories was being fulfilled. The haguya were perched on surrounding rocks, listening.

Suddenly one of the haguya, perched on the highest rock, took flight in alarm.

Coyote climbed up to the rock to look around. He saw a figure coming from far down the trail.

The Dissenters hid, and when the newcomer appeared, Coyote confronted him.

He was a CS officer, but he wore no sidearm.

"I want to join you," he said without preamble.

"Why?" asked Coyote.

One of the haguya swooped in low, almost touching the CS officer. He looked at it in awe.

"I was at CephCom when you people came. After I saw you, and those creatures . . . I had to, uh, rethink some basic assumptions. In other words, I decided everything I'd been taught was a lot of bull."

Coyote gave the man a long, penetrating stare.

"Good reason," he said finally. He looked at the

man's nametag. "Does anyone else know you're here, Lieutenant Redman?"

"Well, actually, I'm accompanied by some others who'd like to join as well. We've brought a little present."

Coyote climbed nimbly back onto the rock, to see if he could verify Redman's statement. He saw a most amazing convoy. Books, the Dissenters' books, still wrapped in their old cloth bundles, were being brought up the trail at the head of a procession of several hundred unarmed CS men and women. At the front was an old, white-haired, slightly paunchy Hispanic man. Coyote recognized him as a Dissenter-sympathizer from years back, whose name had been Montoya. He'd been arrested for trying to smuggle a book to the Dissenters.

The new arrivals had brought blank paper with them. Later that night Amoret got hold of a pad and a pencil, and went to sit alone at the top of the windy pass.

All the excitement had inspired her. She felt like writing a story.

She wanted to tell a story about Captain Picard. She would extrapolate, interpret, tell it how she felt like telling it.

For some reason—and she had no idea where this inspiration came from—the first adventure she imagined had him shipwrecked on an ocean, on some far-off planet. He would float and swim until he found a beach, and then fall asleep on it. A race of people six inches tall would find him and tie him up . . .

Chapter Twenty

As the *Enterprise* sped on its way, the staff on the bridge was complete save one—the ship's counselor.

And though the seat on the captain's left was thus empty, the seat on the right was commodiously filled by the first officer.

First Officer Riker was staring at Worf.

Riker had just remembered incidents over the last few days that suggested a clandestine activity on the part of Worf, and involving Oleph and Una. There had been hushed meetings between Worf and the two little beings. There had been the assertion by the ship's counselor that Worf was hiding something . . .

Worf stared back, obsidian-eyed, stubborn, knowing why he was the object of attention and disinclined to respond. He bent his gaze downward to his tactical console, and presented to his audience the mute prospect of his sagittal skull-bumps.

This action caused Riker's eyes to twinkle with amusement. He knew Worf well enough to assume that the Klingon's secret was harmless. And he had been through so much serious business lately that his innate lightheartedness just insisted on taking the reins.

Some of the officers presently on the bridge had already heard rumors of Worf's furtive behavior. And, as all of them knew each other well enough to sense the subtle whorls in the currents of their shared company, Worf now became the focus of several more stares, some covert, some brazen.

"Worf," said Riker, "you know, just the other day I was thinking about how many times you've told us personal things, Klingon things, and how that candor always helped us all in the end. Have you ever noticed that effect?"

"That has been the pattern in the past, sir."

"And I've been trying to imagine a circumstance when it would be better for you, and all of us, if you didn't tell us, but it's the damnedest thing—I can't come up with one. Can you?"

Worf stared at his console, and cleared his throat several times. Finally he lifted his massive head and spoke.

"As I am tired of being stared at, I shall satisfy your curiosities. Soon after Oleph and Una were brought on board, they asked me about Klingon culture and I read them some of my own poetry. They saw my writing talent and suggested I write a novel. Their advice was to keep it a secret as long as possible so as to be unencumbered by the expectations of others. I have been writing that novel and contacting Klingon publishers."

He looked around with a slightly challenging air, as if he expected someone might try to ridicule him.

"Worf," said Captain Picard, "I think I can speak for all of us when I wish you the best of fortune with your novel. I'm sure you will attack it with the thoroughness you bring to everything. And I intend to exert no encumbrance."

"Thank you, Captain. I believe the recent incidents in the rho Ophiuchi system illustrate that the warrior of the pen achieves a glory outlasting the warrior of the sword."

Worf seemed taken aback, but not entirely displeased, by his own sudden outburst of verbosity.

"I couldn't agree more, Worf," said the captain.

"So what sort of book are you writing?" asked Riker. "Are we in it?"

"Will," said the captain, "I think we should let Worf choose when he wants to say more about it."

"Thank you sir," said Worf.

"Worf," said the captain, "did you know that our own Mr. Data has been involved in literary pursuits?"

"Sir," said Data, "I would hardly call it—"

"Don't be modest, Data. Your poetry has already saved several lives, after all. Why don't you give Worf a sample."

Data looked down at his console.

"Sir, too many of my internal processors are at the moment involved in the tasks of ship's operations to allow for random word and phrase recombination."

"Not inspired at the moment, is that it, Mr. Data?"

"Perhaps you could say that, sir."

The android glanced at his console.

"I will observe, though," he went on, "that as we have just passed the point in space where Counselor Troi had her first experience with the Other-worlders, we may be said to have followed the pattern observable within the very first and very last sentences of *Finnegan's Wake* . . ."

"How so?"

"The end comes back to the beginning."

For Troi, at this moment, conditions were indeed similar to that moment when she first encountered the "Other-worlders," the characters of imagination. She sat in the same chair, in the same cabin, and looked at the computer monitor as she finished a personal log entry.

". . . So I am recommending the establishment of a special data base for counselors that would help us use fiction, myth, and all forms of speculative literature in our work. I believe there is no better way to understand the minds of those we counsel than through the mind's own deepest, most spontaneous creations . . . and no better channel of communication between races, nations, and planets, than through these "dreams of the many." And I plan to begin contributing to this data base immediately, through my own research into the imaginative literature of the worlds both inside and outside the Federation. Log entry over."

She hadn't seen fit to voice her anxiety about starting the research. It was a personal problem, having to do with the aftereffects of Oleph and Una's ethnographic film.

There was a worrisome coincidence much on her mind—a feeling that her experience with the mythical characters from that movie had somehow led her, and the *Enterprise,* to Rampart, where such imagination was forbidden. A kind of synchronicity, perhaps? A linking of her the observer to the events she observed, the way some theories of physics postulated? If so, might another attempt at research throw her and the ship into another situation beyond control? There was, at the very least, a chance, an undeniable chance, that the mythical characters would re-invade her mind.

But the captain had been right. You can't start backing away from knowledge. If you start, there's no end to it.

"Computer, please monitor my metabolic rate until further notice. If there are any radical changes or if I become unresponsive, please send someone to my cabin immediately."

"Procedure has been implemented," said the computer's gentle female voice.

"Thank you. I wish to commence with some research."

"Ready," said the computer.

It was a crucial moment. She was going to speak the title of Oleph and Una's movie. The word that had started the whole thing last time.

Troi's throat was dry. She gripped the armrests of her chair until her fingers hurt.

"Tell me about the Tukurpa," she said. "What does the word mean?"

She held her breath, and waited for the room to begin spinning, for her world to begin disintegrating.

"Working," said the computer.

After another endless moment, the computer spoke again.

"Tukurpa: a word used by several aboriginal peoples of Australia. It refers to the Eternal Ones of the Dream; the beings of myth, or the myth-world itself, the Eternal Dreamtime. It is also called the Altjiranga Mitjina. Do you wish further information?"

She let herself breathe again. Nothing terrible had happened. She was still in her chair, in her cabin, on the *Enterprise*.

Her anxiety seemed to have evaporated. In its place she felt relief and the exhilaration of embarkation.

"Yes," she replied.